WORKING GIRL
'Afflicted'
Book One
Roxy Rich

WORKING GIRL 'Afflicted' Book one.

Copyright @ 2024 Roxy Rich.

All rights reserved. No part of this publication may be reproduced, distributed, or transmitted in any form or by any means, including photocopying, recording, or other electronic or mechanical methods, without the prior written permission of the author.

Legal Disclaimer.

This is a work of fiction. Unless otherwise indicated, all the names, characters, businesses, places, events and incidents in this book are either the product of the author's imagination or used in a fictitious manner. Any resemblance to actual persons, living or dead, or actual events are purely coincidental.

WARNING.

This book entails, human trafficking, prostitution, domestic abuse, family courts. Along with scenes of date rape. Please do not read if you have a delicate constitution.

Table of Contents

WORKING GIRL 'Afflicted' Book One (WORKING GIRL SERIES Volume 1, #2)..1
CHAPTER 1: Exciting times..3
CHAPTER 2: University life..7
CHAPTER 3: Stranger Danger... 11
CHAPTER 4: Not the only one... 15
CHAPTER 5: You make me feel.. 20
CHAPTER 6: Purity and Passion... 25
CHAPTER 7: Introductions... 31
CHAPTER 8: Devastation.. 35
CHAPTER 9: The Stakeout.. 39
CHAPTER 10: Save Them.. 43
CHAPTER 11: Jolene.. 50
CHAPTER 12: First Fight... 54
CHAPTER 13: Possession... 59
CHAPTER 14: The news.. 62
CHAPTER 15: Controlling... 66
CHAPTER 16: Unlimited... 72
CHAPTER 17: Welcome Home... 77
CHAPTER 18: Sudden death... 83
CHAPTER 19: Show must go on... 88
CHAPTER 20: Bereft.. 95
CHAPTER 21: Different worlds... 101
CHAPTER 22: Adultery.. 108
CHAPTER 23: Abduction.. 112
CHAPTER 24: Truth.. 116
CHAPTER 25: Lies... 121
CHAPTER 26: The club... 127
CHAPTER 27: Systems and Bias... 132
CHAPTER 28: Family... 138
CHAPTER 29: The Business.. 142
CHAPTER 30: A brave new world...................................... 148
CHAPTER 31: Go with your gut.. 156

CHAPTER 33 : The escape..164

Dedications.

To the fans who have believed in me from the beginning and those who are about to join this wild ride.

Thank you for entrusting me with your darkest fears and brightest hopes. This tale about bravery, friendship, and the complexity of the human psyche is for you. May it plague your thoughts and energise your spirit.

Stay strong, stay curious, and never underestimate the power of an intriguing narrative.

With gratitude and an element of suspense.

Lastly, I would like to thank my proofreader, Jill Goss. Jillgoss87@gmail.com

Roxy Rich

Join the Working Girls Insider Club! Get the latest twists, secrets, and behind-the-scenes gossip delivered directly to your email. Because every heroine deserves a thrilling escape!

Email sign up roxyrichauthorpodcaster@gmail.com.

WORKING GIRL 'Afflicted' Book One
By
Roxy Rich

CHAPTER 1: Exciting times.

"I am so happy for autumn, as it heralds a momentous occasion: the commencement of your academic journey into higher learning, I never thought I would see a child of mine go to university, especially my daughter. The mere thought of this milestone evokes a profound sense of pride within me, your papa would have been so proud of you, if he had been here to witness this remarkable achievement. God bless his departed soul." Sabrina's mother tenderly pressed her lips against her daughter's cheek, a fleeting gesture of affection as she prepared to leave to go shopping." Mama, I must go, Kira is waiting for me, so we can get all the things we need for our halls of residence. I love you mama, arrivederci".

With a determined stride, Sabrina hastened towards the bus stop, her heart pounding in her chest. The relentless pursuit of the approaching bus had ignited a sense of urgency in her, compelling her to push her physical limits. As fortune would have it, the bus came to a halt just in the nick of time, allowing Sabrina to embark on its welcoming embrace. Today held a special significance for Sabrina, for she was to meet with her dear friend Kira, in the bustling high street. A palpable excitement coursed through her veins, intertwining with the anticipation danced in her eyes. Together, they would go on a shopping expedition, seeking out the essential accoutrements required for their forthcoming university journey.

In this shared pursuit, Sabrina and her friend found their spirits buoyed by the prospect of acquiring the necessary provisions. The high street, a vibrant tapestry of commerce and human connection, beckoned them with its siren song. Sabrina's enthusiasm grew, her mind brimming with possibilities and her heart alight with the promise of a fruitful day ahead. The bus, teeming with passengers, was packed to the brim, with no vacant seat for her petite frame. She found herself positioned in the heart of the aisle, her grasp firmly secured on the sturdy handrail. Her mother, in her exuberance over her daughter's acceptance to Bath University, had inadvertently caused her to be late. When

Sabrina boarded the bus, her eyes were immediately drawn to a man of extraordinary beauty. His jet-black hair cascaded down to his shoulders, forming delicate ringlets that framed his handsome, chiselled face. With his olive complexion, he exuded an air of undeniable allure. Serendipitously, he found himself seated directly across from Sabrina, his gaze fixed intently upon her. She made a valiant effort to avert her eyes, yet the task proved arduous, for he occupied a position directly within her line of sight, commanding her attention from the vantage point where she stood. Throughout the entire journey into town, his gaze remained fixed on Sabrina, his deep, intense, dark blue eyes captivating her. Under different circumstances, such unwavering attention might have unsettled her, but his undeniable attractiveness mitigated any discomfort. He made no attempt to divert his gaze, instead continuing to stare directly into her eyes. With each passing moment, Sabrina could feel an intense heat building within her, all consuming. As the bus glided into the bustling high street, its imminent halt prompted the man to rise from his seat, poised to join the awaiting passengers eager to disembark. However, the abrupt application of the brakes unleashed a cacophony of shrill sounds, jolting the passengers into a disoriented collision. During this chaotic commotion, the man found himself hurtling towards Sabrina, their destinies intertwined for a fleeting moment. In an unforeseen twist, his powerful arms instinctively caught her, providing an unshakeable anchor amidst the tumultuous sea of bodies. Their gazes locked, time stood still, their connection unyielding. Sabrina's senses were immediately attuned to his aura, a palpable strength emanating from him as he assisted her in regaining her composure. His words, delivered in a mellifluous timbre, carried a distinct Italian cadence that stirred a sense of familiarity deep inside her. With a gentle smile gracing his lips, he nodded to her, then positioned himself in the queue just behind her. His warm breath delicately brushed against the nape of her neck, a delightful shiver coursed through her entire being, leaving her with a tingling sensation that electrified every inch of her body. The moment she disembarked from the bus, her dear friend Kira materialised before her, a playful reproach dancing in her eyes. "Your late again," a hint of amusement lacing her words. Kira gestured towards her watch, as she spoke. "I am always fashionably late," Sabrina declared with an air of confidence, as their arms intertwined, and they commenced down the bustling high street. During their shopping excursion, laughter and mirth filled the air, mingling with the shared sense of camaraderie. Whilst they were in pursuit of acquiring essential items for their impending pathway to higher education, revelling in the joyous moments that unfolded as they shopped. "I'm hungry," Kira declared, her voice laced with a sense of urgency, as she gently tugged at Sabrina's arm, leading her towards the closest establishment that offered swift sustenance. "You're always hungry, I don't want fast food, can we go to a pub for lunch instead?" Sabrina's delicate features contorted as she wrinkled her nose, her voice dripping with a hint of disdain. "Only if you're paying, getting ready to attend university is costing me a small fortune," Kira uttered with a tinge of bitterness. With a hearty chuckle, Sabrina playfully ribbed her friend, before agreeing to treat her to lunch. With them both in agreement they made their way towards the cheapest establishment in the city. The two friends made a mutual decision to sit in the beer garden, basking in the resplendent rays of a scorching summer's day. Such climatic conditions were a rarity in England, compelling them to seize the opportunity and relish every moment of it. On perusing the menu with a discerning gaze, Sabrina made her way towards the bar, where she intended to place her order. There, she requested two pints of lager for her companion and herself. She stood at the bar, waiting for the pints to be poured, an inexplicable sensation overcame her. It was as if an unseen force was intently fixating on her being. Succumbing to her curiosity, she pivoted her gaze towards the pub's patrons, only to discover the very same gentleman who had gallantly prevented her from stumbling aboard the bus. Their gazes locked in a silent dance, as she collected her pints of lager and made her way towards the beer garden.

    With a graceful flourish, Sabrina placed the pints on the polished surface of the table. Settling herself into a seat, she raised her pint to her lips and took a generous sip, relishing the cool liquid. A momentary pause ensued before she spoke, her voice carrying a hint of excitement. "I forgot to tell you what happened on the bus on the way here, there was a guy, he was gorgeous, the bus abruptly braked, causing a chaotic commotion amongst the passengers. Well, I went flying, but this guy he caught me and prevented my fall. I didn't tell you earlier as I had forgotten the whole thing, until I just noticed him whilst I was at the bar." Hardly had the words escaped Sabrina's lips when, like a conjured apparition, the waiter materialised before her, bearing two frothy pints in his grasp. "These drinks," he intoned, "have been bought for you by a gentleman." Kira's mouth stretched open in a wide arc, her lips parting to form a grateful utterance directed towards the waiter. "Who is it, what does he look like. I'm going to have a look?" Kira insisted. Sabrina, her pint in hand, offered her response with a casual air. "Just look for the most attractive man in the bar, he's got that Mediterranean look, but he has most unusual deep blue eyes. Jet-black curly hair to his shoulders, tall with a muscular build, he really is quite beautiful, you won't miss him. Please don't make it obvious though."

"Deep blue eyes, but looks Mediterranean, this I have got to see." Kira said with a wink.

With a swift and calculated glance, Kira surveyed the bustling bar, cleverly disguising her true intention as a mere trip to the toilet. In a seamless display of timing, she reappeared just as their lunch was being served. Sabrina's anticipation grew palpable as she awaited the revelation that was about to unfold. With bated breath, she observed Kira taking her seat at the table. Then, with a tone of disappointment lacing her words, Kira uttered, "Regrettably, there is no trace of him. I swear there is no one in the bar that matches your description." Sabrina couldn't help but feel a tinge of disappointment, yet without dwelling on it, they both promptly delved into their midday meal.

CHAPTER 2: University life.

In the crisp autumn of September 1987, Sabrina found herself standing before the grand entrance of her student halls, a place that would become her sanctuary for the next chapter of her life. With a mix of anticipation and nerves, she awaited the arrival of Kira. The air was abuzz with the excitement of fresher week, a time of orientation and exploration, as Sabrina prepared to immerse herself in the vibrant tapestry of university life. During a flurry of activity, the friends found themselves immersed in a whirlwind of tasks.

Their days were filled with the imperative duty of procuring their student identification cards, a necessary step in their academic journey. Additionally, they were compelled to partake in the process of registration, ensuring their enrolment in the appropriate courses. To further acquaint themselves with their chosen fields of study, they dutifully attended introductory lectures for their respective modules. These few days gave them both great insight, into the demanding nature of their academic pursuits. In the realm of academia, Kira had made the conscious decision to embark on a journey of knowledge in the field of social work. Conversely, Sabrina, with a discerning eye for intellectual pursuits, had chosen to immerse herself in the intricate study of Psychology. As a result of their divergent academic paths, the inseparable friends would find themselves traversing separate corridors of learning, their shared presence in classes becoming a rarity. As they graced the halls of every social gathering hand in hand, a solemn vow passed between them, a pledge to defy the forces that sought to pull them apart, their divergent paths be damned. They reached a mutual understanding to convene on a regular basis, as frequently as their social calendars would permit. Fortune had smiled on them, for they found themselves blessed with the serendipitous circumstance of sharing the same sleeping quarters. Sabrina found solace in the fact that she would not have to share her room with a stranger. The pangs of longing for her beloved mother had already begun to assail her, despite the solemn vow she had made to return home every weekend. She missed her Mama, she missed her dinners, she missed her hugs and most of all she missed her motherly advice. This commitment did little to assuage the incessant stream of anxious thoughts that plagued her weary mind. Sabrina loved her mother dearly, she was the sole pillar of support in her world. Since her father's death, they stood united, facing the challenges that life threw their way. Her mother, a resilient figure, had endured countless hardships, often juggling three jobs, all in the pursuit of securing a brighter future for Sabrina.

In the world of academia, the advent of the second fresher's week brought forth a plethora of intellectual pursuits and the forging of social connections for the two kindred spirits. Fortuitously, they had procured an ample supply of stationary, only to be informed of the necessity to acquire certain books for their courses, books that resided on the more exorbitant end of the price spectrum. Sabrina, in her diligent pursuit of cleanliness and familial connection, faithfully embarked on the journey homeward each weekend. Seeking the warmth of her Mama and the practicality of being able to tend to her laundry. Meanwhile, Kira, embracing a more spirited and social approach to her weekends, opted to remain in the confines of the hall, engaging in jovial revelry alongside fellow students. At the mere culmination of the third week, their lives had already diverged significantly. Kira, a social butterfly, was perpetually engrossed in the company of her friends. While Sabrina, on the other hand, preferred solitude, dedicating her days to acclimating to her new surroundings and embracing a frugal lifestyle due to financial constraints.

"Listen, you've got to come out tonight, I will pay. Its Friday night. You can always go to your mams tomorrow, oh come on, please, for me." With an air of determination, Kira extended her offer to Sabrina, her countenance subtly contorting into a semblance of a spoiled child's pout. Sabrina's gaze lifted from the pages of her books, meeting the eyes of Kira, her only friend. With a nod of acquiescence, she uttered, "Alright already, I will go out with you tonight. I need a break anyway, but tomorrow I must go see my mama, okay. My dear mama is lonely, I can tell, she misses me." In a swift motion, Kira seized her, drawing her closer, and pressed her lips against Sabrina's cheek. "Eek you won't regret it," she whispered, her voice laced with a tantalising promise. Sabrina went to the pay phone in the hall, her fingers dialling her mother's number with a sense of purpose. She conveyed her decision to postpone her arrival until Saturday. Meanwhile, the two young women, their spirits buoyed by the anticipation of the evening ahead, indulged in the harmonious melodies emanating from their radio. The dulcet notes mingled with the clinking of glasses, as they savoured the rich taste of wine, only served to heighten their mirth and enhance their preparations for the forthcoming night of revelry. Kira and Sabrina found themselves in a local student haunt, renowned among students for its lively atmosphere and copious drinks at affordable prices. A large group of students, familiar to Kira, converged on them, engaging in lively conversation. They indulged in the consumption of shots, their glasses clinking together in a harmonious symphony. Encouragement flowed freely among them, each member goading the others to partake in the game of downing various shots. A young guy by the name of Michael appeared to harbour a distinct fascination for Sabrina, positioning himself in close proximity to her and engaging in conversation whenever an opportunity presented itself. Sabrina's lack of interest was palpable, for she had not pursued higher education with the intention of exuding flamboyance or indulging in overt sexuality. Her purpose in being here was to work hard and fulfil her mother's expectations.

Michael was a young man of affluence, he possessed a singular attribute that accounted for his popularity, his propensity for generously covering the costs of drinks for his companions. His golden locks, reminiscent of the sun-kissed shores, added to his charm. A regular visitor to the gym, he diligently sculpted his physique. In the limited span of their university experience, Michael had garnered a reputation among his peers as a ladies' man. His nights were spent in the lively ambiance of pubs and clubs, where he bragged to his companions about his conquests, leaving an indelible mark on the collective consciousness of those who crossed his path. He would frequently ply his conquests with an abundance of drinks, rendering them oblivious to their own actions, as he led them through the corridors of the halls to engage in sexual encounters. Sabrina harboured a certain indifference towards Michael, yet she found herself acquiescing to his offers of drinks, even Kira, was partaking in his generosity. She engaged in a logical deduction, concluding that if he displayed the willingness to cover the expenses for the entire group, it would be impolite on her part to decline his offer. Sabrina's sole concern arose from Michael's disconcerting proximity, for he persistently engaged in unwarranted physical contact and encroached upon her personal space, as though staking a claim to his territory. Sabrina, was blissfully ignorant of his notorious reputation, rendering his overtly amiable demeanour, a mere facade in her eyes.

The collective ventured forth, traversing the bustling high-street adorned with numerous inviting establishments. Their footsteps carried them from one pub to another, each imbued with its own distinct charm and libations. As their nocturnal odyssey unfolded, their destination became clear - Pulteny bridge, a picturesque landmark that beckoned them to conclude their night of merriment. With unanimous accord, they descended on the Underground club, a haven of pulsating rhythms and vibrant energy, where their revelry would find its ultimate culmination. Sabrina found herself intertwined with Kira, their arms linked in a delicate embrace, as they traversed the entire route. Throughout their journey, Sabrina, was engaged in a discreet dance, skillfully evading any encounters with Michael, whilst maintaining the utmost politeness. When they crossed the threshold of the club, Sabrina seized Kira's arm with an urgency that could not be ignored. With a determined stride, she led her companion towards the toilets. "Michael's, relentless, every time I turn around, he's there, like a space invader?" Sabrina whispered, her voice tinged with a husky timbre. "Yes, I did notice, just keep him at arm's length, unless you want a rich boyfriend and you think you could keep him interested, as he has a bad reputation as a player".

"Goodness gracious, you can't be serious! I would never entertain such a notion, he is not my type," Sabrina exclaimed, her voice filled with a jovial lilt.

CHAPTER 3: Stranger Danger.

In that moment, the two friends emerged from the lavatories, making their way back to their group. Along their path, Kira leaned in close to Sabrina, her voice a mere whisper, as she imparted her sage advice, "Be nice though. He buys everyone drinks most nights. That doesn't mean you have to sleep with him." She declared Sabrina, with a feigned gesture, mimicked the act of inserting her delicate fingers into her throat, as if to provoke the expulsion of her innermost being at the mere insinuation. The friends ventured into the busy bar, their hearts aflutter with anticipation. As they approached the counter, Micheal materialised before them. With a charming smile adorning his countenance, he inquired, "What are you drinking ladies?"

"Malibu and cokes please," Kira responded, pre-empting any potential dissent from Sabrina. With a swift motion, he retrieved his wallet from his pocket. Without hesitation, he proceeded to pay for their drinks, a gesture that exuded both chivalry and generosity. The drinks were consumed with haste by the two friends, their thirst quenched in an instant. Sabrina seized the moment and grabbed hold of Kira's arm, leading her towards the pulsating heart of the room, where the dance floor beckoned. During their rhythmic gyrations and graceful movements, Sabrina and Kira engaged in a lively conversation, their voices struggling to be heard above the cacophony emanating from the powerful speakers. With each visit to the bar, like a spectre emerging from the shadows, Michael materialised unannounced, extending his generous offer to procure their drinks. With each attempt Sabrina made to voice her dissent, Kira and Michael brushed her concerns aside, rendering her objections inconsequential. The nocturnal hours pressed on, Sabrina discovered herself succumbing to a slight unease, her senses perturbed by an ethereal shroud enveloping the club's surroundings. These circumstances left Sabrina disoriented, as if ensnared within a nebulous cloud that defied the boundaries of tangible existence. She found herself caught in a disorienting whirlwind of fleeting faces and snippets of dialogue. The realities of it all eluded her grasp, as if she were submerged in a haze of intoxication. Sabrina had always prided herself on her ability to hold her liquor. It was a strange phenomenon. Something was wrong. It left her with an unsettling sense that this experience was unlike any other. All the faces blurred into one, all the voices were in echo chambers, nothing made sense, it was a scary place to be. She needed to go home, she needed to get home as quickly as possible. She had no control over her body or her mind. The next morning, Sabrina stirred from her sleep, her mind in a haze of confusion. Blinking away the remnants, she found herself disoriented, unable to discern her surroundings. In her quest to regain her bearings, her trembling hands reached out in search of her clothes, only to abruptly halt in their motion. A surge of shock coursed through her veins, as her gaze fell on Michael's naked form, lying serenely in the bed. In a swift moment of awakening, she was struck by the realisation that an intimate encounter had transpired, despite her hazy recollection, for they were both naked. 'Oh God, no, where are my clothes? I need to get out of here now.' The urgency to locate her clothes consumed her, as she desperately needed to extricate herself from the clutches of Michael, and to disentangle herself from the intricate web of circumstances that had ensnared her.

She remained in a state of bewilderment, her mind grappling with the inexplicable events that had transpired, as she gingerly got dressed. It was then that her gaze fell upon the disconcerting evidence etched on her delicate flesh - bite marks, on her breasts and her shoulders. The mere sight of these unsightly imprints, stirred in her an overwhelming sense of revulsion, threatening to unleash the contents of her stomach. Fortunately, Michael remained undisturbed as she shut his door, ensuring not to wake him. A myriad of thoughts swirled in her mind as she traversed the labyrinth corridors, of the halls of residence. She found herself overwhelmed by a sense of violation, an urgent need to cleanse herself of his lingering scent, to erase any trace of him. She felt so dirty, so used. But the indelible marks left by his bites, would serve as a perpetual reminder of the harrowing ordeal she had endured, stubbornly defying her attempts to expunge them. A profound sense of unease gnawed at her being, as if she had been thrust into a role against her will, an unwitting pawn in a grander scheme. She Had been a virgin, and she was saving herself for marriage. But now that had been taken from her. In the recesses of her mind, she found it inconceivable that she would have willingly engaged in a sexual encounter with Michael. Her thoughts raced, a wave of nausea threatened to consume her once again. In a state of disbelief, she pondered how her own intelligence could have failed her so gravely. The absence of Kira, her trusted companion, left her questioning why she hadn't been there to save her from this unfortunate turn of events. A wave of anxiety washed over her as she contemplated the possibility that Kira, had fallen victim to the same nefarious scheme. Sabrina, with her mind racing, could only arrive at one glaringly apparent deduction. She had fallen victim to being 'date raped.' At long last, Sabrina found solace in the confines of her room, her heart pounding with a mixture of relief and trepidation. It was there, in the sanctuary of her personal space, that she quickly discerned the conspicuous absence of Kira, her bed left untouched and unoccupied. It wasn't like Kira, she had always come home. Where was she? Sabrina needed her now more than ever. Shedding her garments, she proceeded to submerge herself in the shower. Engaging in a vigorous ablutionary ritual, she scrubbed her delicate skin until it bore the tell-tale signs of a crimson hue. Tears streamed down her visage, intertwining with the cleansing droplets, as an emotional release accompanied her physical purification. The profound realisation of her violation reverberated through her being, striking her with an intensity that left her reeling. She had cherished her purity, reserving it steadfastly for the sacred bond of matrimony, it had been a commitment to honour her mother's wishes. But now, she was no longer pure, no longer a virgin. She was dirty, she was damaged goods. Now nobody would want to marry her. The unbearable circumstances in which she found herself, compelled her to seek solitude and cleanliness amidst the cascadeing waters of the shower. There she huddled, with tears streaming down her face. She had to pull herself together. The damage had been done. She couldn't turn back time. She found herself compelled to gather her shattered fragments, for she had to visit her mother today, and maintain a facade of composure. Buried within her being, she harboured an unshakeable conviction, that the state of equilibrium she once knew would forever elude her grasp. The capacity to place her faith in others, to engage in the art of social interaction, had been irrevocably extinguished. He had brought ruin upon her, seizing what was never rightfully his, and the weight of her shame was tangible, permeating every inch of her being. She must stop thinking about it, her mama always used to say, "There is no point crying over spilt milk. You just need to mop it up and get on with it child." As the hour of Sabrina's departure approached, an unsettling absence pervaded the air, for Kira had yet to make her appearance. A sense of concern began to take hold of Sabrina's heart, as she pondered the whereabouts of her friend. However, duty called, as she had made a solemn vow to her mother, that she would visit this morning. The weight of her tardiness now burdened her, urging her to hasten her steps. When she arrived at her mother's house, she plastered a smile on her face. The arduous bus journey had been a tumultuous endeavour, as she had dedicated every moment to regaining her composure. Banishing the haunting memories of the previous evening, she cast aside the shadows that threatened to engulf her thoughts. Sabrina was acutely aware that her mother's eyes should not bear witness to her current predicament. The mere thought of her mother's distress was enough to dissuade Sabrina from divulging the truth of her recent misfortune. With a resolute determination, she drew in a deep breath, summoning the strength to conceal her troubles behind a facade of unbridled cheerfulness. Sabrina crossed the threshold into the sanctuary of her familial home. "Hey, mama, I'm sorry I'm late." she declared with a radiant smile.

CHAPTER 4: Not the only one.

Her mother extended her arms, a warm invitation for an embrace, as she spoke softly, "Come here, my child." Sabrina endeavoured to regain her composure, for her mother's embrace had a disconcerting effect on her. Sabrina had never concealed anything from her beloved mother, and now, tears threatened to betray her inner turmoil. Yet, resolute in her determination, Sabrina refused to yield to their insistent pull. "Come, come, sit. I have prepared your favourite dish, Cioppino. I made the trip to Petro's fishmongers." Once seated, they said a prayer of thanks and then started to eat, savouring each spoonful of the steaming soup. Sabrina welcomed the intrusion with a grateful heart, for in her experience, family meals had always been a source of unparalleled joy and warmth. The special recipes crafted by her mother, served as a poignant reminder of the comforting embrace of home for both mother and daughter. In the world of culinary mastery, she reigned supreme, her prowess in the kitchen unmatched. With dedication, she had imparted her vast knowledge to Sabrina, ensuring that the art of cooking, in all its glorious forms was passed down from one generation to the next. "Tell me bella, how are you settling into university life? How are the lectures and the social engagements?" her Mama inquired. Sabrina, with great determination, fought against the urge to reveal her innermost emotions. "Yes, it's all good, mama. There is no need for concern, I've settled in quite well." The evening quietly passed in the warmth of Sabrina's family home, where she sought solace in the familiar confines of her childhood bedroom. In retrospect, she could not deny the burgeoning trepidation that now enveloped her being, casting a shadow over her impending return to university. The mere contemplation of the collective awareness, regarding her predicament sent shivers down her spine.

"Did everybody know?"

The thought of crossing paths with Michael in the corridors, ignited in her a fervent desire to unleash a piercing scream, at the profound sense of injustice that permeated her being.

Her mind was consumed by all that had befallen her. She could only dare to hope that Kira, would be awaiting her arrival in their shared room. A glimmer of hope emerged - an insatiable desire to unburden herself of the weighty secret that had been haunting her every waking moment. In this moment of vulnerability, she needed to confide in Kira, her sole confidante amidst a sea of acquaintances. In an ideal turn of events, Kira would admit Sabrina's fallibility, acknowledging her erroneous judgement. She would candidly confess that her decision to accompany Michael was a consequence of her being drunk, a regrettable lapse in her better judgement. Thus, she would assert that the entire situation had been an unfortunate misinterpretation, a product of miscommunication and misperception.

Deep within the recesses of her soul, Sabrina harboured an unwavering certainty that she had fallen victim to the sinister machinations of a malevolent force, succumbing to the insidious effects of a potent concoction and enduring the abhorrent violation of her body.

Throughout the course of the weekend, Sabrina's mother had persistently questioned her, expressing her observation that Sabrina appeared altered in some way. Sabrina was different, and her mama was not a fool, but she couldn't put her finger on it. All she knew was that there was a haunted look on her daughters face. It worried her, Sabrina had lost her sparkle, somehow. In response, Sabrina had confidently reassured her mother, attributing her perceived transformation to nothing more than sheer exhaustion. However, an air of peculiarity lingered, as if her mother possessed an innate understanding that something was amiss. It was early evening when Sabrina was on the bus back to the halls of residence.

The rhythmic hum of the engine provided a soothing backdrop to her thoughts as she embarked on her journey back to the halls. In certain respects, she found herself apprehensive about the prospect of returning, yet relieved to have distanced herself from her mother's ceaseless interrogations. Her mama knew something was wrong, despite Sabrina doing her upmost to hide it from her. But then it was no surprise, not really, her mama knew her better than she knew herself. Above all else, she found herself desperate to confide in Kira. She fervently beseeched the heavens, her heart yearning for the comfort and reassurance that only her dear friend could provide. Kira was like her twin sister from another mother. They knew each other inside and out. They told each other everything. As she disembarked from the bus station, her mind preoccupied and her thoughts scattered, she inadvertently collided with an unsuspecting passerby. Yet, as she raised her gaze to ascertain the identity of the individual she had bumped into, a profound astonishment overcame her. It was none other than the gentleman who had heroically come to her aid during their previous encounter, when he had caught her on the bus, and she had been the recipient of his chivalrous rescue.

"We really should stop meeting like this, Bella." With a wry smile dancing on his lips, he interjected, skillfully averting her from yet another perilous stumble. Sabrina gazed into his mesmerising deep blue eyes, her composure wavered, faltering under the weight of her emotions. With a simple yet profound gesture, he graced her with a smile, releasing her from his grasp. All that escaped her lips was a feeble "I'm sorry," followed by a whispered "Thank you," as she hurriedly continued on her way. As Sabrina drew nearer to the halls, a sense of apprehension washed over her, causing her gaze to be fixated on the floor beneath her. She instinctively averted her eyes, avoiding any potential encounters with the individuals who happened to grace her field of vision. At long last, she arrived at the entrance to her quarters, her heart pounding with anticipation. Fumbling through her bag, she frantically sought the key that would grant her access. To her astonishment, she discovered that the door stood ajar, as if beckoning her inside. When she entered the room, her eyes caught Kira emerging from the shower, wrapped in a towel that snugly enveloped her petite frame. Another towel was secured around her damp hair. Sabrina's countenance contorted with horror, as her gaze fell on Kira's shoulders, she bore the very same bite marks, that marred Sabrina's own delicate skin. In that moment, Kira's body became rigid, as if paralysed by an invisible force, before succumbing to a torrent of tears that cascaded down her cheeks. Mirroring Sabrina's actions, they clung to each other as if their lives depended on it. Among the myriad of possibilities that danced through Sabrina's mind, Sabrina had prayed that her dear friend had not become another victim of Micheals sinister intentions. They sank onto the bed in unison, their bodies finding solace in the soft embrace of the mattress. Kira, her voice tinged with vulnerability, began to unravel the events that had transpired the previous night, her words weaving a tapestry of fear and uncertainty. Sabrina squeezed her eyes shut trying to avoid her tears, as she reciprocated by recounting a similar ordeal that had befallen her on that fateful Friday evening. In a heart-wrenching display of shared anguish, the two young women wept together, their souls burdened by the unspeakable horrors they had endured. Bound by a harrowing connection, they had both fallen victim to the malevolent deeds of a single individual, their innocence shattered by the heinous acts of rape and the insidious effects of mind-altering substances. The tell-tale signs were unmistakable, for all that remained were the indelible imprints of teeth on their delicate skin. The two young friends sought refuge in each other's company, engaging in an earnest conversation that revolved around the recent series of distressing events. Contemplating the course of action to be taken, they deliberated the possibility of seeking intervention from the appropriate authorities, while entertaining the notion of devising a strategic plan to save any potential victims from falling into the same trap they had fallen foul too. A plethora of hypothetical scenarios were dissected, analysed, and contemplated with great care. Ultimately, however, a unanimous decision was reached: to maintain a discreet silence. Yet, in their collective resolve, they also pledged to extend their assistance to other young women, endeavouring to prevent them from succumbing to the same treacherous snare. During their debate, a sense of uncertainty pervaded their thoughts, leaving them perplexed as to how to proceed with their plans. Both young women, harbouring a shared desire for academic success, deciding to adopt a cautious approach, focusing solely on their studies and navigating the labyrinth corridors of university life over the course of the next three years. But were they strong enough to carry on with life as if nothing had happened? That was the question that could only be answered with time.

The weight of guilt and shame bore down on them, an insurmountable burden that threatened to consume their souls. Who, in their right mind, would believe them? The damning evidence, etched upon their flesh in the form of teeth marks, remained, a haunting reminder of the unspeakable act committed. Although they had rigorously cleansed away any trace of incrimination, the shame, the sins of another, in their quest for absolution. Sabrina, in a desperate bid to sever the ties that bound her to that fateful night, had discarded her garments in a bin in the bus station. Kira still had her garments, but remained resolute in discarding them as soon as she could, for she remained ensnared by the lingering effects of the drug. Her consciousness gradually resurfaced, only to discover that she had regained her awareness in Michael's room. The solitude and confusion that enveloped her were recent occurrences, transpiring an hour prior. Had he perhaps poured an excessive amount into her drinks, or was it the peculiarities of the substance he had administered that caused disparate reactions among individuals? Sabrina had come to her senses rather quickly after the shock of everything, whereas Kira was still slurring her words and forgetful. It had hit her hard, her mind was still foggy, and she still couldn't think straight. Neither Sabrina nor Kira had ever had drugs before. In the dark corners of their contemplation, a realisation dawned on them - the elusive truth they sought would forever elude them. Overwhelmed by an immense sense of guilt towards potential victims, they found themselves at a loss as to how to prevent such occurrences in the future. In a moment of vulnerability, they confided in one another, acknowledging their own lack of fortitude to confront Michael or to be seen in his company in any public setting. Neither of them was brave enough to confront him. Nor were they brave enough to go to the authorities. They just wanted to forget it all. Forget it and get on with their lives.

CHAPTER 5: You make me feel.

On a crisp Monday morning, the relentless hands of time seamlessly conspired against Sabrina as she found herself in a race against the clock. Having made a commitment to accompany Kira to her class, Sabrina now found herself late for her lecture. Meanwhile, Kira, still grappling with the weight of recent events, struggled to come to terms with what had befallen them. The fact that she was not alone in her torment did nothing to assuage her sadness. Finally arriving at her lecture hall, Sabrina crossed the threshold, her eyes darted around the room, searching for an inconspicuous spot to settle. She was late and she was hoping that the esteemed professor hadn't noticed. Her efforts were in vain, for her professor's keen gaze had already locked onto her presence. "Miss Morelli, I do not appreciate tardiness in my class." Sabrina heard the stern reprimand from the professor, as his voice reverberated from the imposing desk stationed at the forefront of the room. In that precise moment, Sabrina's gaze intersected with his, and a surge of astonishment coursed through her being. The individual who had been vociferously reprimanding her from afar, across the expanse of the room, was none other than the gentleman who had rescued her from two perilous falls in recent weeks. Sabrina's, cheeks flushed with a rosy hue, as she offered a sincere apology, wishing the ground would swallow her up as she settled herself into a chair. Throughout this exchange, her heart, like a captive bird, fluttered incessantly in her chest. As she removed her books from her bag, accompanied by an assortment of writing tools, an undeniable sensation coursed through her being. It was as if his penetrating gaze had become an invisible force, piercing through her soul. He could see her, truly see her. In the fleeting encounters they had shared, he had appeared undeniably captivating to her. On closer inspection, she discovered that his beauty surpassed even her most fervent imaginings. However, in this moment, an overwhelming desire consumed her, she wanted to be anywhere but here, he had spoken to her like an insolent child, reprimanding her in front of her peers. The notion of encountering him once more, especially here at a lecture, had never even grazed the periphery of her wildest imaginings. The lectures of the day swiftly transpired, their passing marked by the inexorable march of time. With the sun casting its warm embrace on the world, Kira and Sabrina, made a conscious choice to relocate their studies to the verdant expanse of the park. They slowly meandered enjoying the warmth of the day, their arms intertwined, burdened by the weight of their satchels brimming with scholarly resources, they made a conscious effort to steer clear of the crowd they had once associated with. Their footsteps carried them through the park, where they found a secluded spot, discreetly nestled just beyond the well-trodden path. It beckoned to them, promising a sanctuary of tranquillity, where they could immerse themselves in the pursuit of knowledge undisturbed. With due care, they arranged their books on the blanket, each one a treasure trove of knowledge. Accompanying these literary companions were selected drinks and delectable sustenance, ensuring a feast for both the mind and body. They immersed themselves in the written word, savouring every sentence, and losing themselves in the boundless wealth of knowledge. Hours had slipped away unnoticed, consumed by their intellectual pursuits. Both young women were engrossed in their own subject of academia. During their scholarly reverie, their thoughts were abruptly disrupted by a voice that pierced the silence. "Good evening, ladies." It resonated with Sabrina, "May I have the honour of joining your company?" In a voice adorned with the opulence of the Mediterranean, a husky timbre inquired. Simultaneously, the two young women raised their gazes, their eyes meeting the heavens. However, a slight predicament arose, for Sabrina, her vision obstructed by the radiant sun, could merely discern the outline of the gentleman before her. However, she was acutely aware of that familiar accent and voice, yet in this moment, she found herself utterly perplexed as to its origin. "I am Lorenzo Gallo," he declared, his voice resonating with a hint of confidence and self-assuredness. With a subtle gesture, Kira beckoned him, indicating for him to sit by her. As he swaggered away from the scorching embrace of the sun's rays, Sabrina found herself unable to contain her astonishment, her delicate mouth parting in awe. "It's you," she murmured, a hint of surprise lacing her words. "I didn't think lecturers were allowed to fraternize with students." With a mischievous grin adorning her countenance and a single eyebrow arched in playful intrigue, she uttered those words. Kira interjected with a thoughtful remark, her voice resonating with a hint of uncertainty. "Well doesn't that mean we are safe with him?" Sabrina interjected, her voice filled with a sense of urgency, "He is one of my professors, the very same man who valiantly rescued me from a stumble on the bus, and again at the bus station yesterday." Kira's mouth was abruptly sealed shut.

"None other than yours truly." Lorenzo uttered, "But I do arrive with gifts," he declared, his hand aloft, presenting a bottle of crimson wine and a trio of paper cups. Sabrina was acutely aware of the searing warmth emanating from him, an irresistible force that tugged at her core. Perplexed and captivated, she found herself grappling with the enigmatic allure he possessed, unable to fully comprehend its profound effect on her. As he engaged in conversation with the two women, it became evident that his attention was singularly fixated on Sabrina, sparking within her, a sense of vitality and enthusiasm. They engaged in lively conversation for well over an hour, their voices full of mirth and delight, until the last drop of wine had been savoured. At that moment, Kira, ever perceptive, detected an undeniable undercurrent of desire between the two individuals. Sensing the need for privacy, she concocted a plausible excuse and withdrew from their company. She harboured no desire to impede upon Sabrina's bliss, for it resembled a scene plucked from the pages of a romantic novel. Moreover, she found consolation in the knowledge that she could leave while the sun still graced the sky. She was happy to leave Sabrina under the watchful eyes of the learned professor. As the sun cast its golden rays on the idyllic landscape, Lorenzo and Sabrina found themselves enveloped in a serene solitude. Engrossed in each other's company, they enjoyed a heartfelt conversation about their respective lives, delving into their pasts and the boundless possibilities that lay ahead. No topic was left unexplored, as they bared their souls and shared their dreams. The depth of their shared interests and similarities was truly remarkable, bordering on the inexplicable. Lorenzo looked at his watch, prompting him to utter, "Might I have the pleasure of taking you out for dinner? Forgive my growing hunger, but it would be a travesty to squander this exquisite evening. I really would enjoy finding out more about you." A rosy hue graced Sabrina's cheeks as she received the flattering compliments. She could hardly rebuke him, he seemed kind, and attentive. His presence offered a welcome respite from the mundane company of her fellow university peers. Moreover, his chivalrous demeanour had left an indelible impression upon her. From the moment their paths converged, an ineffable allure emanated from him. An undeniable intensity coursed through their encounter, igniting a fervent flame deep in her being. In that singular instance, she became acutely aware that resistance would forever elude her, for the gravitational pull of him, was simply insurmountable. He embodied all that she had ever wished for, and the fortuitous circumstance of his Italian heritage and esteemed position as a professor of Psychology lent an air of destiny to their connection. It had been such a wonderful day, and Sabrina didn't want it to end. So, she agreed to Lorenzo's invitation to dinner. Their leisurely stride led them to the curb, where they hailed a passing taxi. With an air of sophistication, Lorenzo leaned towards the driver and requested their destination: The George Inn, nestled in the charming village of Norton St. Phillip. Half an hour later the taxi halted in front of the historic pub. Lorenzo, with an air of chivalry, manoeuvred around the vehicle to gallantly open the door for Sabrina. "We have arrived at our destination, my enchanting bella," he tenderly uttered, extending his hand to assist her exit from the car. Sabrina's gaze remained fixed on the Inn, its grandeur captivating her senses. Its sheer size commanded attention, a testament to its storied history as one of the most ancient establishments in all of Britain. The allure of this place had fascinated her for as long as she could remember. However, the absence of a driver's licence posed a formidable obstacle, rendering her aspirations seemingly unattainable, until now. The ancient Inn boasted a front exterior adorned with the timeless elegance of Tudor architecture, its charming beams and intricate details all telling a story of a bygone era. As they ventured further, the enchantment continued, for the Inn's sprawling gardens unfolded at the rear, a verdant sanctuary that beckoned visitors to immerse themselves in nature's embrace. The sun had not yet set, casting a warm glow on the surroundings. With the evening still in its infancy, they made the decision to seek the comforting ambiance of the bar. There they ordered a drink and booked a table. Eager to savour the last of the sun's rays, they ventured towards the gardens, where nature's beauty awaited. It was there, amidst the fragrant blooms and gentle whispers of the wind, that they whiled away the time, anticipating the moment when a table would become available. Lorenzo possessed a familiarity with the proprietor, affording him the luxury of securing a table without the necessity of making a prior reservation. The garden, with its breathtaking view overlooking the village green, evoked a sense of awe and wonder. Throughout the years, this verdant expanse had served as the backdrop for a myriad of events, ranging from lively fairs to dramatic battle reenactments. On occasion, the tranquil stillness of the garden would be interrupted by the spirited cheers and the rhythmic thwack of a cricket bat, as the village inhabitants indulged in their beloved sport. It had been an enchanting evening, warm and inviting. Lorenzo summoned a taxi to transport Sabrina home to her student accommodation. Having partaken in a delectable feast that delighted their palates and kindled their spirits, the chivalrous act of settling the fare befitted Lorenzo's innate sense of gallantry. The evening had proven to be an unparalleled delight for Sabrina, as their conversation flowed effortlessly, and he possessed an uncanny ability to make her feel as though she were the sole object of his affection amidst a sea of women.

CHAPTER 6: Purity and Passion.

When she reached the threshold of her room, she flung her body against the sturdy wooden door, as if using it as a shield against the imminent onslaught of inquiries that she anticipated from the inquisitive Kira. "Tell me everything, I want it all." A sly smile played on Kira's lips as she bombarded Sabrina with questions. Sabrina's countenance became suffused with a rosy hue as she uttered her words, her voice carrying a hint of fervour. "He's intense, and has a formidable intellect," she confessed, her eyes alight with admiration. "He took me to the old Inn, I've always wanted to go there for dinner, in the quaint village of Norton St. Phillip," she continued, her voice tinged with a touch of nostalgia, "It was nothing short of extraordinary. Seriously Kira, it was the most perfect night, ever. He is a true gent, and those eyes, they could see into my soul."

Kira playfully taunted. "OMG, you're in love with him aren't you?"

"It's way too soon for that Kira. But he is dreamy." Sabrina let out a disdainful scoff, her frustration palpable as she flung herself onto her bed, embracing her pillow tightly in her arms. "He's just different to anyone I have ever met before, you know?" Sabrina ventured, her voice resolute. "If I'm being honest, he's exactly what I've always wished for in a husband." Kira's gaze shifted towards Sabrina, her cherished friend whom she had adored since their early years in primary school. With a gentle smile gracing her lips, she uttered, "As long as I am the maid of honour." In a harmonious symphony of mirth, their laughter erupted simultaneously, filling the air with a joyous melody that resonated deep in their souls. That fateful night, Sabrina slept peacefully, surrendering herself to the realm of dreams. In the depths of her subconscious, she was transported to a world where Lorenzo was her Prince, the object of her affection, their destinies were interwoven. As the night unfolded, Sabrina's dreams painted vivid portraits of a future with Lorenzo, brimming with promise and possibility. The following morning dawned, and she found herself preparing for her inaugural lecture with none other than Lorenzo, whose wisdom she had the privilege of imbibing three times a week. During their preceding encounter, they had engaged in a thoughtful discourse regarding the intricate matter of circumventing the stringent regulations pertaining to interpersonal connections in the university. Sabrina, displaying an unwavering commitment to their shared cause, wholeheartedly agreed that their burgeoning relationship ought to be concealed from prying eyes. Their rendezvous were confined to the nearby environs, as if the boundaries of their affection were tethered to the geographical limits of their shared existence. In the university grounds, Sabrina assumed the guise of an ordinary student, her demeanour betraying no hint of the connection that bound them. Lorenzo's eyes, even from across the vast expanse of the lecture hall, possessed an intensity that seemed to radiate with a luminous glow, catching the light in a mesmerising manner. Unlike the customary monotonous and mundane tones adopted by his fellow lecturers, Lorenzo's discourse was a delightful departure from the norm. His endearing persona, coupled with his ability to infuse his lectures with an air of intrigue and amusement, transformed the learning experience into an enthralling journey. With his nimble wit and captivating storytelling, Lorenzo effortlessly held the entire room in his thrall. As Sabrina settled into her seat, a subtle warmth began to stir between her thighs, enveloping her senses. She found herself captivated by the melodic cadence of his voice, resonating with a husky richness that bore the unmistakable charm of an Italian accent. She remained in a state of disbelief, unable to fathom the sheer magnitude of her good fortune. He, the object of her desires, embodied every characteristic she had longed for with intensity. In the nascent stages of their relationship, she harboured no apprehensions regarding Lorenzo's preferences or any potential deal-breakers. No idiosyncrasies or peculiarities were forthcoming that she could see. He ignited a flutter within her heart, a delicate dance of desire. With determination, she set her sights on making him her own, a pursuit fuelled by an unyielding passion. He would be hers, and hers alone. Yet, a faint whisper of doubt lingered in the recesses of her mind, a subtle reminder that not all was as it seemed. Would his desire for her persist with the revelation of her non-virginal state? Not a single word of it had been broached in their conversations, for he possessed a refined sense of propriety that forbade such discussions. However, in devout Catholic Italian households, it was an unquestionable expectation that the bride would embody purity.

Sabrina still believed she was pure, she didn't lose her virginity by choice, surely that had to stand for something. A state she believed she would have been able to adhere to. Had she not experienced the harrowing ordeal, of being subjected to the abhorrent act, commonly referred to as 'date rape.' She possessed an innate understanding that should the inquiry ever come to light, she would be compelled to lie. Lest she forfeit any chance of securing a potential suitor who adhered to the principles of Catholicism and hailed from Italian lineage. It was a bitter pill to swallow but swallow she must. During the first week of their blossoming relationship, Lorenzo, ardently advocated for the privilege of seeing Sabrina not once, but twice in the span of those seven fleeting days. Their connection was an insatiable hunger, an unquenchable thirst that consumed them both. The mere thought of her, sent waves of desire coursing through his veins, everything about her, ignited a fire in him that burned with an intensity he had never known before. It was a magnetic pull, an irresistible force that drew them together, binding their souls in a dance of passion and longing. Their relationship flourished, an ever-blooming connection that defied the passage of time. Conversations flowed effortlessly between them, a ceaseless stream of words and ideas that glided across the air. Among the myriad topics that enraptured their minds, Psychology held a special place, a chosen field of study that hypnotized her intellect and fuelled their discussions. He possessed a vast reservoir of knowledge, a veritable treasure trove that she found fascinating. The convergence of their shared passion for this intellectual pursuit was a source of immense delight for her. With a distinguished academic background, he had attained the esteemed title of Master of Psychology. Presently, he was engrossed in the composition of his second opus, a book that formed a pivotal part of a series he had embarked on. They engaged in a lively conversation concerning his ancestral roots, delving into the intricacies of his family's lineage, hailing from the picturesque land of Italy. Specifically, their discourse revolved around the idyllic region of Tuscany, renowned for its stunning landscapes and agricultural prowess. It was revealed that his family, with utmost dedication and toil, cultivated the bountiful groves of olive trees, producing the finest produce. Furthermore, the mention of truffles, those elusive and highly prized delicacies, added an air of sophistication to their exchange, as they contemplated the gastronomic treasures that emanated from his family's ancestral lands. In his world of opulence, his lineage boasted great wealth, he had also one sister and four brothers. Amidst this familial tapestry, he held the position of being the eldest, a role of prominence and responsibility. He informed Sabrina it was a responsibility he didn't care to shoulder. Evidently, he had engendered a schism within the familial unit. Due to his reluctance to toil upon the agrarian expanse, a duty traditionally befitting the eldest son. His ardent passion for the pedagogical arts and the intricate workings of the human psyche, eclipsed the exigency imposed by his family. His decision had been met with respect, as his four brothers had assumed the mantle of the farm and its accompanying lands, shouldering the weighty responsibilities that accompanied such a role. The allure of the land and the art of farming held no sway over him, despite its pivotal role in the accumulation of his family's fortune. Sabrina found great pleasure in indulging in the melodious cadence of Lorenzo's voice, willingly surrendering herself to his tales and anecdotes. She would eagerly immerse herself in his narratives, losing track of time as he wove intricate tapestries of words. However, she couldn't help but notice a certain reluctance on Lorenzo's part to reciprocate her desire to share her own experiences. Despite her genuine interest in engaging him in a meaningful exchange, he remained steadfast in his determination to keep the focus solely on himself. She eloquently elucidated that her dear mother, despite the passage of a decade since her beloved father's demise, continues to don the customary attire of sombre black. Her mother, in a display of unfluctuating devotion, chose to adorn herself in the sombre hue of black until her last breath, as a profound mark of reverence for her dearly departed husband. In a candid revelation, Sabrina expounded on the circumstances of her upbringing, shedding light on the fact that she was an only child. The genesis of this solitary existence, she elucidated, can be traced back to the tumultuous events surrounding her birth, which necessitated her mother's surgical intervention in the form of a hysterectomy. It was a harrowing scene, as the doctors, with their skilled hands and furrowed brows, found themselves unable to halt the relentless flow of blood from her mother's body following childbirth. In a desperate bid to preserve her precious life, they were left with no choice but to perform a hysterectomy, a surgical procedure that would forever alter the course of her mother's existence. It forever remained her mother's most profound remorse, the inability to embrace a sizable brood. Sabrina talked about the profound bond that existed between them, emphasising the remarkable extent to which her mother had toiled, holding down three jobs, solely to provide support for her daughter's academic pursuits. Sabrina recounted the tale of her lineage, revealing that both her beloved mother and dearly departed father arrived in the United Kingdom through the benevolent act of adoption.

Their origins remained shrouded in mystery, for they possessed no knowledge of any additional family. She expressed that while her mother had harboured aspirations for her to attend university, she had afforded her the autonomy to select the vocation she desired to pursue. Furthermore, she informed Lorenzo that Kira was her sole confidante, a cherished bond that had been forged since their tender years. With Kira's arrival at her school, their relationship flourished, transcending the realm of mere friendship to that of sisterhood. Sabrina found herself mesmerized by the allure of their rendezvous, as Lorenzo orchestrated the unforgettable experiences. With each outing, he whisked her away to a new and enticing area, leaving her breathless with anticipation. To her astonishment, Lorenzo assumed the role of benefactor, shouldering the financial burden of their extravagant escapades. As the weeks unfolded, their sojourn led them to the shores of Lyme Regis, where they embarked on a voyage on a sailing vessel. It was during this maritime excursion that a serendipitous encounter with nature's most graceful creatures transpired. Dolphins, with their playful demeanour, graced the bow of the boat, their elegant acrobatics evoking a sense of wonder and awe. Lorenzo had whisked her away to the coastal town of Weston Super Mare, where they indulged in a delightful culinary journey, exploring a myriad of exquisite restaurants and charming pubs scattered along their path. In every setting they found themselves, he remained steadfast in his chivalrous ways. The simple act of holding the door open for her, became a ritual. When they partook in the fine art of dining, he would pull out her chair, a gesture that spoke volumes of his respect and admiration. Even in matters of taste, he took charge, selecting the wine that would accompany their meals, a reflection of his discerning nature. Sabrina found their excursions to be rather lavish, a departure from her usual experiences. Lorenzo's eloquent explanation of his preference for the finer things in life, coupled with his insistence that a lady should never bear the burden of expenses, assuaged Sabrina's initial feelings of guilt. They had been entwined in the delicate dance of courtship for a span of several months, yet the tender touch of his lips on hers had eluded her so far. She had tried to broach the subject, only to be met with his dismissive response. He asserted that the act of kissing her should be postponed, because she held great value in his eyes. Sabrina was ensnared by his seemingly innate ability to possess the perfect answer for any given situation. She never questioned the source of his wisdom, simply accepting it as an inherent part of his being. She found herself immersed in a profound state of infatuation, utterly obsessed by him. The fear of losing him, due to her youthful and imprudent remarks or inquiries, gripped her heart. Consequently, she chose to withhold her inner musings, preserving them in the depths of her being. She couldn't risk losing him, not now. He had become her world, her reason for living, her reason for believing that the future she had always wanted was finally within her grasp. This weekend, he found himself on the precipice of a momentous occasion - the long-awaited introduction to her mother. A family lunch had been arranged, marking the inaugural encounter between these two individuals. With certainty, Sabrina believed her beloved mother would embrace him with the same fervour that she herself did.

CHAPTER 7: Introductions.

Sunday arrived with unexpected haste, catching Sabrina off guard. Time seemed filled with possibilities. But time was not her friend. As was her customary routine, she had spent the previous evening at her mother's. A palpable sense of anticipation filled the air as Sabrina's mother busied herself in the kitchen, attending to every detail. Her prized porcelain and finest cutlery were carefully arranged, to mark the grandeur of the occasion. With dedication, she had poured her heart and soul into crafting a selection of delectable Tuscan delicacies: "Schiaacciata l'uva," "Riboliiita," and "Peposo." Each dish bore the unmistakable imprint of her mother's tender touch. Her mother's heart brimmed with excitement as she embarked on a culinary odyssey, through the enchanting realm of Tuscany. Though uncharted territory, she immersed herself in the art of gastronomy, labouring tirelessly in her kitchen to conjure a tempestuous symphony of flavours. Sabrina's mother had eagerly expressed her anticipation for the moment she would meet the man who had captured her daughter's heart. The fact that he was from Italy, like herself, only added to her delight. The sheer intensity of her excitement was tangible in the air. Sabrina tenderly pressed her lips against her mother's cheek, with both affection and gratitude. Her voice, soft and sincere, carried a hint of gentle reproach as she spoke, "Dearest mama, you need not have gone through all this trouble for me. "With a graceful gesture, her mother nonchalantly brushed aside her concerns. "Oh, my dear child, such trivialities are of no consequence. If this gentleman brings you joy, then I must leave a favourable impression upon him." Sabrina diligently immersed herself in the task of washing the pots, her mind wandered to a conversation she had recently engaged in. Reflecting on the words exchanged, she recalled uttering, "He does, mama. He makes me really happy." A resounding rap echoed through the stillness, reverberating against the walls of the home. The expected interruption disrupted the tranquillity that had settled on the dwelling, stirring a sense of curiosity. A momentary pause ensued, as if time itself held its breath, before the door yielded to the gentle push, "I will get it mama," Sabrina declared, her outstretched hand poised to grasp the doorknob. "Ah, Lorenzo," Sabrina exclaimed with a playful giggle, "Mama has been concocting a veritable feast in our kitchen. I dare say she has voraciously devoured the entirety of a Tuscany cookbook." Lorenzo sauntered across the threshold, he presented himself bearing two exquisite bottles of wine, one a luscious red and the other a delicate white. Accompanying this tasteful selection, he carried a box of delectable chocolates, enticingly wrapped, and a bouquet of flowers so resplendent that Sabrina found herself momentarily fixated on them. "They are beautiful Lorenzo, my mama will love them, how did you know they were her favourite flowers?" Sabrina asked. Lorenzo's senses were immediately inundated with tantalising aromas emanating from the kitchen, he answered. " I do my homework." It was then that Sabrina glared at him just for a minute. But she quickly brushed away any odd feelings she had emanating within her and put them to one side. Why would he go to so much trouble? The little voice persisted in her head. As he entered the kitchen, his eyes fixated on the dining room, which lay adjacent to the culinary haven, connected by a grand archway that beckoned him further. Lorenzo's lips gently brushing against each of Sabrina's mother's cheeks as he expressed his gratitude with a heartfelt "Grazie mille."

"Grande uomo, (Big man)" Sabrina's mother playfully quipped.

"Mama please speak English to our guest." Sabrina's, brow furrowed, as she addressed her mother.

"But he is Italian, no?" Mama inquired with genuine sincerity.

"Yes, mama," she replied, her voice tinged with a hint of deference. "But he prefers English to be spoken." Sabrina's mother, ever the epitome of restraint, chose to keep her thoughts concealed from her daughter. Why did he make her feel uncomfortable? In her own home. A seed of uncertainty had taken root within her, casting a shadow of doubt on the man who had surreptitiously captured her daughter's heart. A persistent sensation lingered in her, whispering that it was not in his purview to impose such demands in someone else's home. It left her with a feeling of unease. She pushed aside her thoughts, determined not to tarnish her daughter's happiness. But something was wrong with this man, something was very wrong, of that she was certain. The culmination of the feast proved to be a resounding triumph, as every individual present found themselves satiated, their appetites appeased. Moreover, the convivial atmosphere that pervaded the gathering ensured that the collective experience was nothing short of delightful, leaving an indelible mark on the memories of all those in attendance. Sabrina's mother, with a valiant effort, endeavoured to conceal any trace of her apprehension. However, as the words of Lorenzo reached her ears, an undeniable sense of doom began to settle in her. As she sat at the table, her keen senses detected the faint rustling of red flags fluttering in the air. A discerning observer, she couldn't help but perceive the unmistakable aura of narcissism emanating from him. His overt displays of dominance and control were impossible to ignore, casting a shadow over the otherwise pleasant gathering.

She found herself puzzled by Lorenzo's demeanour. Surely a man with such qualifications as an esteemed position of a university lecturer, had to be good enough for her daughter. But something was untoward, she didn't like him, one bit. He made the hairs on the back of her neck stand on end, it was a strange sensation. Even more unfortunate was the fact that she had made a solemn vow to refrain from meddling in her daughter's affairs, leaving her with no recourse but to beseech the heavens, hoping against hope that her interpretation of his conduct towards her beloved offspring was somehow defective. All she could do was pray, pray she was wrong. Her daughter was besotted with him. But Sabrina's mama wasn't so easily impressed. It confused the hell out of her, on paper he was everything she had dreamed of for her only child. But his mannerisms, his dominant ways and his behaviour as a whole was leaning towards a sociopathic nature. She found herself discontented with the current situation, a sentiment that extended far beyond mere dissatisfaction. There lingered within her a profound unease, there was something off about him, yet she struggled to articulate the precise nature of her misgivings. Perhaps it was due to her recent proclivity for fatigue, a weariness that seemed to settle on her with increasing frequency. Perhaps, this was the root cause. For surely, one would assume that a professor of academia, a purveyor of knowledge and wisdom, would possess the qualities necessary to be deemed a suitable husband for her precious daughter. Undoubtedly, his capacity to impart knowledge would be curtailed if his character were found wanting. Maybe she was just having a bad day, she was always so tired lately. Maybe her instincts were doing her daughter an injustice. After the meal, Sabrina guided Lorenzo towards the door, bidding him farewell with a gentle smile. Her voice was full of warmth and love, as she assured him, that she would see him in the morning at his lecture. With a courteous nod, Lorenzo pivoted on his heel, his gaze fixed ahead as he made his journey down the street. "So, mama, I am most curious to know your thoughts on Lorenzo." Sabrina's mother responded with conviction, "Given that he is a professor at your university, he must be a good man. But in all honesty, I harbour a few concerns. He's breaking the university rules. Furthermore, I cannot help but perceive a significant age disparity between the two of you."

"But, mama, he is everything I have ever hoped for and more, and let's not forget that papa himself was twelve years your senior." Sabrina was bewildered by her mama's unfathomable position, for it contradicted her own state of blissful contentment. Sabrina was somewhat confused, she would have thought her mama would be over the moon, since when did age matter? Sabrina pushed away her concerns not wanting to pry further. She knew her mama was holding something back, but she was so happy at the moment, she wasn't sure she wanted to hear any negative thoughts her mama had on Lorenzo.

CHAPTER 8: Devastation.

That evening, Sabrina wearily made her way back to her student quarters. The weight of the day's endeavours clung to her like a heavy cloak, she needed some breathing space, and time to think. With a gentle turn of the key, the door swung open, revealing a scene that horrified her. There, sprawled on the floor in a dishevelled heap, lay Kira, her once vibrant personality now reduced to a pitiful state of incoherence. The pungent stench of vomit permeated the air. Sabrina's heart sank, her concern mounting as she knelt down, beside her best friend. With a sense of urgency, Sabrina hastened her actions, manoeuvring Kira into the recovery position. A wave of distress washed over her as she uttered, "Oh dear God, Kira, what have you done?" Sabrina's anguished cry pierced the air, as tears streamed down her face, her friend Kira surrounded by a sea of pills. The sight before her was shocking, as the remnants of Kira's sickness clung to her once lustrous red curls. Sabrina's own voice betrayed her, as her scream remained trapped in her throat, unable to escape. With a sense of imperativeness, Sabrina guided Kira to the nearest bathroom, gently holding her hair away from her face. Kira's murmurs, devoid of coherence, only added to Sabrina's stress as she pleaded fervently, filled with desperation and longing. "Come on Kira, wake up, you need to throw these tablets up." Sabrina begged, as she wiped Kira's face with a cold wet cloth, in a desperate attempt to bring her friend round to the land of the living. Then Sabrina got Kira's two fingers and rammed them down her throat to make her sick. As the two young ladies huddled together, Kira found herself compelled to convulse, her stomach forcefully expelling its contents into the toilet bowl. "That's it Kira, that's it. You must try to throw up every pill."

"I can't do this alone, he raped me, and your hardly ever here". Kira murmured softly, her voice barely audible. "You are never here, and I need you. I'm not as strong as you are." Kira's voice gradually faded away. "I'm so sorry Kira, I thought you were dealing with it all." Sabrina, stroked Kira's back, and endeavoured to shield her fiery red curls from the forceful expulsion of vomit that was surging forth. In that poignant moment, Kira released one final, convulsive exhalation into the ceramic toilet bowl, her strength waning as she slumped wearily against the cool unforgiving wall of the lavatory. Sabrina passed a few bits of tissue, to Kira, so she could wipe away the remnants of the vomit. Her gaze, heavy with emotion, fixated on her dear friend, her voice trembling with vulnerability as she uttered, "You weren't really going to leave me, were you? I would be lost without you Kira." Kira gradually regained consciousness, her senses sharpening as she uttered with genuine sincerity, "I get flashbacks when I'm asleep, it's like it happens over and over again. I can feel everything, even his breath, I can feel him tearing into me, I can hear his words as he's raping me, it's like I'm frozen in time. I can't fight back." In the aftermath, the young women held each other tight, their heart wrenching sobs, a poignant testament to the shared burden borne by survivors. After enduring several hours on the frigid floor, they resolved to seek comfort in the intimacy of a shared bed. Clinging to each other they succumbed to the gentle embrace of sleep. The following morning, Sabrina woke up at dawn. She attended to the task at hand, methodically tidying up the remnants of the previous night's events, ensuring the room was cleaned of any evidence of vomit. She had prepared a sweet cup of tea for Kira and placed it on her nightstand. With grace and poise, she knelt by the bedside, her eyes fixed on the pages of her scholarly books on the intricate workings of the human mind. Patiently, she awaited the moment when Kira would stir from her sleep, eager to ensure her friend was alright after her overdose. Sabrina was consumed by an overpowering wave of guilt, for she had allowed herself to become so consumed by Lorenzo, that she had inadvertently neglected Kira, leaving her to grapple with her own thoughts and emotions. The situation had spiralled beyond what Sabrina had ever anticipated. Deep in her heart, she knew that Kira had been a steadfast presence in her life, particularly during the tumultuous period following her father's passing. An overwhelming sense of guilt now consumed her, as she believed she had failed to reciprocate her support. Sabrina couldn't help but lament her inability to be there for her dearest friend in her time of need. She felt so guilty, she should have been there for Kira. But instead, she had been selfish, and only thinking about her needs, her wants. She should have known Kira was struggling. In that decisive moment, she resolved to disclose to Lorenzo the necessity of limiting their rendezvous, to a mere biweekly occurrence. Amidst the demands of her scholarly pursuits, with Kira needing her, and the obligatory visits to her beloved mother, the temporal landscape for nurturing the relationship with Lorenzo had become exceedingly scarce. Consequently, it seemed prudent, for the time being, to relegate their bond to a less prominent position, metaphorically speaking, like a simmering pot placed on the back burner of a stove. Lorenzo would have to wait. Daylight infiltrated the confines of their room, as Kira, stirred from her sleep. With bleary eyes, she mustered the strength to sit up and indulge in a much-needed stretch. As she did, her efforts were met with a sharp pang of pain, as a muscle in her tummy protested vehemently. The strain from the relentless retching of the previous night had taken its toll, leaving her in a state of discomfort. However, a sense of relief and shame washed over her as she contemplated her unsuccessful endeavour to terminate her own existence. 'What was she thinking? Thank God Sabrina had come home when she did.' Her heart swelled with gratitude, at discovering Sabrina, faithfully stationed by her side, waiting for Kira to stir. As the steam gently wafted from the mug, Sabrina extended her arm, offering the mug of hot, sweet tea to her friend. "Thank you, I'm so sorry about last night." Kira uttered the words sheepishly.

"No need to say sorry, I should have been there for you. How do you fancy having the day off? We can go into the city and spend the day together, grab some lunch, go shopping."

"I would love that." Kira answered.

"I think you need a shower first though, your hairs still full of puke." Sabrina retorted.

"I'm not sure my stomach can handle much food, but I will give it a go." Sabrina extended her arm gracefully, bridging the distance between her and Kira, a tender smile graced her lips as she enveped Kira in a warm embrace, their bodies coming together in a moment of shared affection. "Well, I think you had best get a shower first or your poor hair will end up in dreadlocks." Sabrina exclaimed to Kira just as she cast her gaze on her reflection in the mirror, only to recoil in dismay. "OMG, Its covered in puke."

"Well, I did find you lying face down in it." Sabrina pointed out, smirking to lighten the mood. Kira's countenance betrayed a hint of shame as she stepped into the bathroom. Once they were both dressed and ready for their day out, they started their journey towards the bustling heart of the city. Bath was a cherished haven, it thrived with bustling stalls and an abundance of shops. Some time away from the university and some retail therapy would be just the thing that Kira needed.

CHAPTER 9: The Stakeout.

They strolled through the resplendent Royal gardens, a sanctuary where they often would spend hours studying. It was a serene oasis amidst the busy city, they couldn't help but take delight in the sight of numerous tourists scattered about, indulging in leisurely picnics. Through the gardens, their path led them towards the majestic Lions gate. Adorned with pillars boasting exquisite sculptures of regal lions, these magnificent creatures appeared to be engaged in a playful pursuit of a gilded orb, as if assuming their role as vigilant sentinels, dutifully safeguarding the entrance. As the two ventured deeper into the heart of the town, they found themselves standing in the grand square, adorned with the majestic Victoria's column. Undeterred by the throngs of people milling about, they pressed on, their curiosity leading them towards the vibrant shopping district that lay just beyond. Venturing towards Stall Street, the inseparable friends navigated the labyrinth array of arcades, shops, and walkways. Bath, with its renowned beauty, possessed an inherent ability to take one's breath away. Its stunning heritage and vibrant culture imbued the city with a lively spirit that was simply captivating. The profound affection that the two friends harboured for their beloved hometown was undeniable. It was what they needed, to lift their spirits. Following a brief indulgence in the therapeutic act of retail, the two young women found themselves needing a drink, ultimately settling on a series of public houses to satiate their thirst. Their first destination, aptly named the 'Hat', served as the backdrop for their initial foray into their liberations. Kira's body stiffened, her breath caught in her throat, as her eyes fell on Michael. He was standing at the other side of the bar. He was engaged in his customary antics, at the bar ordering drinks for his group, all the while surreptitiously administering a mysterious white substance into a single glass. "Sabrina, Michael's here. He's just poured some white substance in one of the drinks he has ordered." Kira's countenance turned pallid, her complexion drained of colour, as the realisation of his actions dawned on her. "He's at it again, drugging some poor unsuspecting women. Kira's dismay led to a heightened whisper.

"Let's watch him and see if we can stop him this time." Sabrina's delicate lips caressed the rim of her glass as she lifted it to her mouth, her thoughts a whirlwind. With a subtle tilt of her head, she savoured the liquid's tantalising touch on her tongue. "Ah," she exhaled softly, her voice a melodic whisper, "I needed that." As the two young women lowered themselves into their seats, their eyes remained fixed on the collective assembly that accompanied Michael. Much to their astonishment, it was not solely Michael who was involved in the nefarious act. Rather, a quartet of other men within their midst were observed in this reprehensible behaviour, all sneakily introducing a mysterious white substance into the beverages of the women sat with them. The sheer magnitude of their astonishment was palpable, for it appeared that Michael had indeed administered the GHB to the rest of the group. Countless women found themselves in the very same predicament, their circumstances mirroring one another with an eerie resemblance. Kira found herself utterly dumbfounded, her mind grappling with the realisation that Michael's actions were not isolated, but rather part of a larger network of individuals perpetrating harm against women. Sabrina was aghast, her core shaken to its foundations. 'Oh My God," she exclaimed, her voice tinged with a mix of disbelief and horror, "they are all at it, all of his four close friends are spiking drinks so they can rape the unconscious women later. What on earth have we stumbled onto?"

"What are we going to do about it Sabrina? If it was just Michael, I'm not so sure I would intervene, but now we know all his friends are doing the same thing, we need to do something. We can't just sit here and be complicit." Kira's face contorted as she searched Sabrina's face for any emotional tell-tale signs. Kira pondered, her mind drifting through the vast expanse of possibilities. Deep in thought, she contemplated the intricacies of the situation as Sabrina uttered her words with utmost sincerity. "We must watch them closely. We must do something. Now we know the entire group engages in this behaviour. We can't just allow it to happen. We must save those girls." Kira contemplated the distressing question of how many women had fallen victim to their heinous acts. With caution, she suggested that it would be wise to remain inconspicuous for the time being, as they had not yet been detected. The plan was to discreetly trail their every move, observing their actions from a safe distance. Sabrina's voice resonated with a resolute finality as her words hung in the air, leaving no room for doubt or debate. Kira sank into her seat, her weary frame seeking some shelter in the worn upholstery. With a heavy sigh, she raised the frothy pint to her lips, its coolness a balm against the unexpected turn of events that had unfolded before her. This was a shocking revelation. It was hard to swallow. 'How many more had there been? How many girls on the campus had found themselves drugged and raped? How many times have they managed to get away with this?' Kira found herself in a state of profound astonishment and sorrow. The tendrils of anger began to coil within Sabrina, she sensed an intense shift in her demeanour. Normally known for her composed and tranquil nature, this moment marked a pivotal juncture in her existence. In a brazen display of audacity, these men have deluded themselves into believing that they possess the impunity to perpetrate such acts without consequence. In her consciousness, a resolute conviction took hold: they, the wretched beings that plagued her existence, were nothing short of malevolent demons. She wanted justice and she was going to make damn sure she got it, not just for herself and Kira, but for all the other victims. Their existence posed an imminent threat that could not be ignored nor tolerated.

In that instant, she decided to go on a relentless mission to halt their nefarious deeds, regardless of the sacrifices that lay in her path. The very moment she acknowledged this, the collective of individuals under her and Kira's observation, finished their drinks and commenced their departure from the establishment. Sensing an opportunity, Sabrina instructed Kira to drink up, enabling them to discreetly trail the group, maintaining a safe and inconspicuous distance. "They won't get away with this, lets follow them." As the alcohol coursed through their veins, the two friends left the 'Hat' pub. It was then that Kira glared at the gathering, watching their every move whilst she seethed inwardly. They had to ensure their covert stakeout, remained undetected. Both women found themselves teetering on the precipice of anxiety, their hearts pounding with trepidation. Despite their shared fear, they remained resolute in their conviction, that this nefarious group must be stopped at all costs. A plan had yet to be conceived, their discussions so far, were devoid of any concrete strategies or decisive actions to be taken. Their countenances betrayed an unmistakable tremor. They were scared, they had no idea how they were going to stop them. But they were adamant in their intentions. Sabrina and Kira found themselves idling around the bend, just a stone's throw away from the opposite pub, while most of the group opted to settle at al fresco tables. "Shall we take our seats, there?" Sabrina asked, gesturing towards a quaint pub across the way. Its outdoor tables, arranged in the bustling square, beckoned invitingly. It gave Sabrina and Kira a clear view of the group they were watching. The bustling thoroughfare that stretched before them was none other than the main Highstreet, its grandeur accentuated by its predominantly pedestrianised nature. Kira positioned herself at the table, her gaze fixed on the group seated across from her. Meanwhile, Sabrina, with an air of purpose, made her way towards the bar, leaving Kira to her own thoughts. Kira observed the antics of the assembled group with rapt attention, her body leaning forward on the precipice of her seat.

CHAPTER 10: Save Them.

Among the group, there were six youthful women, Kira wondered how many of them had been drugged already. She was studying them closely. She was concerned for them all. The presence of two women who were her classmates, heightened the precariousness of the situation. The passage of time seemed to stretch indefinitely as she wondered where Sabrina had got to. Surely, Sabrina ought to have returned with their drinks by now. Just as her gaze shifted towards the inner recesses of the establishment, Sabrina materialised, bringing an end to the suspense. Looking rather pleased with herself, Sabrina placed the beverages on the polished surface of the table. Settling herself into a comfortable position, she cast a sidelong glance at Kira, who regarded her with a curious expression. Sensing the inquiry hanging in the air, Kira ventured to ask, "You're looking pleased with yourself, what have you been up too?"

'Wait and see.' Sabrina answered with a knowing smile.

"There are two girls there, that I have lectures with. I'm worried about them. You see the one with the ripped jeans and the other with the pink flamingo top, I know them." Kira exclaimed with a heightened tone. "Please don't worry Kira, just sit back and enjoy the show." Sabrina's voice carried a soothing tone, as she spoke with an air of reassurance.

"You're up to something, I know that look." Kira retorted with a sly grin, her voice dripping with confidence. "Damn straight." With a gentle touch, Sabrina offered Kira her reassurance. Seated side by side, their anticipation palpable, they awaited the unfolding events with breaths held in suspense. Sabrina kept looking at her wristwatch. 'Where were they?'

Time stretched endlessly before her, as twenty interminable minutes had elapsed, since she had mustered the courage to leave an anonymous tip for the police. Her concern grew with each passing moment, for the last thing she needed was for the police to be too late, to collar the group. In her heart, she fervently prayed for the sight of the police apprehending those men, believing that it would serve as a balm for Kira's wounded soul. Sabrina, with a candid assessment of the situation, recognised the undeniable necessity for all parties to receive their due retribution. These men were scumbags, they were in dire need of a valuable lesson and a dispensation of justice. During their tranquil indulgence in refreshing pints of beer, a sudden turn of events abruptly shattered the ambiance. The once serene establishment, where Michael and his companions were, was instantaneously inundated by a swarm of police officers. Chaos ensued, as drinks were carelessly jostled off tables, in the commotion. The police, with unwavering determination, proceeded to meticulously search every patron in the confines of the pub. Michael found himself abruptly restrained, his wrists encased in cold, unforgiving handcuffs. The oppressive weight of authority bore down upon him, as two others from his group were subjected to the same fate. The relentless scrutiny of the officers had exposed their illicit possession of drugs, leading to the apprehension of three of his group. In a disheartening turn of events, even a few familiar faces from the local pub had fallen prey to the clutches of the law, their freedom abruptly curtailed. Kira remained seated, her gaze fixed on the unfolding spectacle, a surge of elation coursing through her being. Sabrina, with a demeanour of utmost discretion, concealed her thoughts while adorning her countenance with an air of triumph. "See, I told you, I'd sorted it." Sabrina, with a mischievous glimmer in her eye, directed her words towards Kira, accompanied by a playful wink, "I'm gutted that some of the other faces in the pub got arrested too." With unwavering determination, Sabrina pressed forward. "But at least those bastards got nicked, I do think we should maybe join the other women for a few drinks and make sure they get home safely though, don't you?" Kira's face transformed into a vivid tableau, a portrait of unbridled elation as she leapt with exuberance, her gaze fixed on the unfolding events transpiring at the adjacent pub. "Watching them be arrested is sweet retribution. You're right of course, we need to go over and make sure the girls get home safely." Kira lowered her sunglasses, delicately positioning them over the bridge of her nose, with a triumphant sparkle in her eyes, as she gazed at Sabrina. It appeared that the remaining individual, who had managed to evade the clutches of the authorities, was presently taking his leave, further solidifying the notion that the friends should join the other women. Sabrina and Kira weren't sure if the remaining friend would still try his luck. So, with that in mind, their decision was made. Sabrina, with a mix of emotions, found peace in the current course of events. She knew that Kira wouldn't grass Michael and company up to the authorities. But, faced with the gravity of the situation, Sabrina was compelled to act. With six young women in the group, the uncertainty of how many had fallen victim to such a heinous crime, weighed heavily on her. A sense of duty enveloped Sabrina, propelling her forward. Witnessing her dear friend teeter on the precipice of despair, she resolved to ensure that the perpetrators would not escape justice once more. Sabrina wanted to prevent further harm being caused by the group of young men. Sadly, concealed in the recesses of her mind, a faint whisper persisted, casting doubt on the likelihood of Michael and his accomplices facing the just consequences of imprisonment.

"Drink up, we need to go and let the girls know what's happened to them." Sabrina demanded urgently. Kira consumed her beverage in a single, fluid motion, her actions imbued with a sense of nonchalance. "Are we going to tell them what happened to us?" her countenance contorting into a grimace. "We shall tell them that it happened to a friend of mine, someone in my lectures. That way they won't find out who it was". With a gentle smile, Sabrina offered her reassurance to Kira. They gathered their shopping bags. A nonchalant air surrounded them as they strolled towards the cluster of young women, perched on the seats outside the neighbouring pub. As they approached Kira asked, "Moira, may we join you?" Moira had lustrous golden blonde curls cascading down to her shoulders, and she was dressed in a pair of rugged denim jeans. With an air of excitement, she exclaimed, "Yes of course, come join us, you're not going to believe what's just happened." With a hearty laugh, she regaled the assembled company. "The pub was raided by the police and all the lads that were with us were arrested, can you imagine? The police found drugs on them." Sabrina's countenance brightened with one of her captivating smiles, as she declared, "I will just go get some drinks from the bar, then you can tell us all about it." With a sense of urgency, Sabrina hastened her steps quick and purposeful. She knew that time was of the essence. She wasn't sure how long it would take for the drugs to take effect, she needed to hurry. The group appeared blissfully unaware of the perilous circumstances from which they had recently managed to escape unscathed. Sabrina rehearsed the forthcoming conversations in her mind as she stood poised at the bar, her utmost desire being to avoid any inadvertent missteps. This was a customary practice for her whenever she found herself in the position of engaging in weighty discussions.

It was precisely this inclination that had led her to pursue the field of Psychology, recognising the profound influence, that language wielded over the reactions and responses of others. Reluctant to instil fear in their hearts, she found herself confronted with an undeniable truth: both she and Kira were now bound by duty, to ensure the safe return of every one of these young girls to the sanctuary of their halls. Uncertainty clouded her mind as she pondered the elusive timeframe in which the drugs would manifest their effects. Her contemplation led her to a logical deduction, the reaction to such substances would vary among individuals, contingent upon their unique physical attributes, including weight and metabolic rate. Her enthusiasm waned, at the prospect of having to babysit these girls, for today was meant to be solely dedicated to Kira. Sabrina still held onto a glimmer of hope, that the unfolding events of this day would bring solace to Kira's tormented spirit. Yet, perplexing her was the inexplicable ease with which she had embraced the situation. She too had been a victim. But she had managed to deal with it, she had locked it away in her mind. She didn't want to dwell on it or feel like a victim, and the only way she could deal with it was to pretend it never happened. It was for the best. She had to be strong for Kira. Putting the memories of that night behind her, she could move on with her life. She knew that many others had fallen foul to this evil scheme, that it was a worldwide problem. And that meant that there would be many more women falling foul to this scenario in the future too. She took some comfort from the fact that she wasn't alone, it wasn't an isolated incident.

Sabrina settled herself in the vacant chair beside Kira, her ears attuned to the melodic voices of Moira and her friend, Amanda. Whose incessant interjections bore an air of exaggeration, as if she had already had way too much to drink. In that moment, a profound realisation washed over Kira and Sabrina, enveloping them in a shroud of apprehension. Amanda was succumbing to the insidious effects of the GHB, her faculties gradually slipping away.

As their gazes met, an unspoken understanding passed between them, laden with concern and a shared determination to intervene.

Moira uttered, her voice tinged with concern, "Amanda your wasted."

"I'm soccerd." Amanda's response, though given promptly, lacked coherence, and failed to convey a clear meaning. "I will go get her some coffee and water. I won't be long." Sabrina and Kira exchanged a subtle yet meaningful glance, their unspoken understanding like an invisible aura between them. As Kira made her way towards the bar, Sabrina seized the opportune moment to unburden herself, revealing the tragic narrative, that had plagued her thoughts. With a heavy heart, she confided in the group, recounting the harrowing ordeal that had befallen her dear friend. "My friend found herself in Michaels bed one morning. She was covered in bites, and she couldn't for the life of her remember how she had ended up there. The crazy thing was, she didn't even like Michael that way. She was a mess for a while. Then she started getting flashbacks. It was then she realised she had to have been roofied. I believe Amanda has been spiked too, I think you all have. Myself and Kira will make sure you get back to the university safely. It's in your best interests to go back to the safety of your halls." Moira's countenance contorted into a visage of sheer horror, while the remaining girls faces seemed to drain of colour, except for Amanda, she was too far gone. Amanda was struggling to sit in her seat properly and she found herself slithering to the cold cobbled floor. "Kira and I saw what was happening, so we thought it best to come over to you guys so we could help out. We will take you all home safely, just to be sure."

Sabrina hated to be the bearer of bad news. "Michael may be rich, but he's a snake. Watch who you choose to spend time with, in future." Sabrina's departing words to the group, left an eerie silence. 'Now I've said it, there's no taking it back,' Sabrina thought to herself. Just then Kira returned, bearing a tray with a steaming cup of coffee and a crystal-clear glass of water. Eager to assist Amanda in her current state of inebriation, Kira extended her aid, but she found herself met with resistance as Amanda's faculties had been thoroughly compromised.? "I'm going to take her back to her room, is anyone coming? I'm assuming that Sabrina has adequately apprised you of the recent developments, the sensible thing to do would be to go back to your dormitories." The collective consensus was reached among the group, they decided to leave with Amanda and Kira. While Moira, in a contrasting decision, opted to remain at the pub, alongside Sabrina. Moira, a woman of discerning wit, resolved to delve into the perplexing situation. She astutely recognised that the only path to uncovering the truth, lay in remaining behind and engaging in a candid conversation with Sabrina. The persuasive power of Sabrina's words alone, proved insufficient to sway her steadfast resolve. Driven by her determination to uncover the sordid details, she remained steadfast, unwilling to leave until Sabrina told her the truth. Sabrina's story didn't ring true to her ears. As the young ladies rose from their seats, a compassionate member of their group extended a helping hand to Kira, assisting her in supporting Amanda's unsteady form. With Amanda's delicate frame nestled between the two women, she emitted a series of unintelligible murmurs, lost in a haze of confusion. Together, they guided her towards the closest street where a taxi could be hailed, their collective determination propelling them forward.

"I'm not so sure I believe your story, please tell me the truth, you're hiding something." Moira aimed her inquisitiveness at Sabrina, her eyebrow arching inquisitively.

In a moment of candid vulnerability, Sabrina admitted, "I'm going to be honest with you, but you must keep it to yourself. It was me, it happened to me. And it happened to Kira. Promise me you won't say anything. Not even to Kira, as I promised her, I wouldn't say who it had happened too. But you kind of caught me off guard. It happened a while ago. It wasn't until today that we realised that his whole group of friends were in on it." A solitary tear descended down Sabrina's cheek, as she spoke. "Kira's in a fragile state of mind, it was only last night, that I found her face down in her own vomit after taking a load of pills." Moira's senses were overcome with a profound sense of sadness, rendering her incapable of accepting the reality, that her own ears had just conveyed to her. "Was it you guys that called the police?" Moira questioned. Sabrina, with a candid demeanour, openly confessed. "Today was meant to revolve around Kira, we were supposed to be enjoying a day out. Take our mind of things, you know. But then we saw Michael and his mates, and we had to watch them. Then to our horror we realised his friends were spiking your drinks too. That's when I decided to call the police. Moira, promise me something, that you shall not breathe a word of this to another living soul. Both Kira and I have agreed that it is in our best interest to steer clear of any inquiries, we just want to forget it."

Moira's eyes expanded in astonishment as she uttered, "Why didn't you go to the police and press charges? There's two of you so it would have made it easier."

"We had showered and got rid of our clothes, we just wanted to erase everything to do with it, Kira wouldn't have even told me if it wasn't for the fact that I caught her coming out the shower with the same bite marks I had endured. It's the shame of it all and the disgust with ourselves." Sabrina uttered softly, her voice fading into the air.

"Given that you rescued my friends from the same fate, I promise to maintain absolute silence on the matter. However, I still think you should have gone to the police with this."

"We just want to get on with our lives. Don't you think we thought about it, about everything. Let's be honest here, Michael's father holds a position of considerable influence in the British Courts. It is highly likely that he would find a way to evade any potential consequences."

CHAPTER 11: Jolene.

Sabrina, with a heavy heart and a mind burdened, had at long last found a semblance of peace, in unburdening her thoughts to another soul, other than Kira. Moira was training to be a social worker too. One of the factors that had dissuaded Sabrina from pursuing a social worker degree at university, was Sabrina's neighbour. Despite Kira's persistent pleas, imploring Sabrina to enrol in the same course as her, Sabrina remained steadfast in her decision. After all, they had always been inseparable, engaging in every endeavour together. Last summer, Sabrina's mother's next-door neighbour looked after an adolescent on behalf of a close family friend. Jolene, was a young girl who at fifteen years of age, had forged a deep connection with Sabrina during that summer. In a moment of vulnerability, Jolene had confided in Sabrina, sharing the intricate details of her life and the harrowing events that had unfolded. Two revelations lingered in Sabrina's consciousness, etching themselves indelibly on her mind. Jolene recounted the betrayal she and her sister had experienced at the hands of their social worker. This supposed guardian, entrusted with their welfare, had egregiously failed them, perpetrating unspeakable acts upon their defenceless forms, while they lay unconscious. The sheer audacity of such a heinous transgression left Sabrina aghast, her faith in the system shattered. Moreover, Jolene's story shed light on a disconcerting reality, a system that inadvertently facilitated these repugnant predators in positions of authority.

The fabric of society allowed their existence, enabling their vile deeds to go unchecked and unchallenged. Michael would be no different. Predators were enabled and hidden if they had money and power. Michael, a young man with ambition, found himself inexorably drawn to the path his father had paved before him. The noble profession of a solicitor, with its intricate web of legal knowledge and power. It was as if the very essence of his father's legacy coursed through his veins, compelling him to follow in those hallowed footsteps. If Sabrina had learned anything from Jolene it was that money and power allowed predators free reign.

In the wake of Sabrina's burgeoning friendship with Jolene, Sabrina experienced a profound shift in her academic aspirations, prompting a complete reversal in her chosen field of study at the university. This unforeseen change in Sabrina's direction, ignited a furious reaction from Kira. Kira thought they would always be together, so she was sad and resentful when Sabrina wouldn't even explain her reasons for the career change. Nevertheless, Sabrina had solemnly sworn a vow of secrecy to Jolene, pledging to withhold any knowledge pertaining to her enigmatic persona or the intricacies of her existence. Sabrina remained true to her word even with the arrival of the man with the distinctive dreadlocks, who sought out Jolene. With remarkable composure, Sabrina deflected his advances, fully aware of the perilous nature of Jolene's stepfather. She knew it was him, he was missing digits from his hands and his face laid bare the scars of torture. He scared the hell out of her , but she refused to show it. Even the hairs on the back of her neck stood on end. It was as if someone had walked over her grave. Jolene's stepfather was creepy as hell. He was evil personified. Jolene had vanished after that visit. Sabrina, had dutifully relayed the news of Otis's fateful visit to her neighbour, sealing Jolene's fate. Sabrina was deeply wounded by the situation. She didn't even get to say goodbye. She understood why Jolene had to disappear after her stepfathers visit. But it still hurt her. Sabrina was the one that had been the instigator in Jolene having to be moved on once more. A young girl on the run from her own stepfather, how could life be so cruel. Her affection for Jolene, a truly admirable young woman, only intensified the ache in her heart. Sabrina was horrified to hear about Jolene's sad life. Worse still she hated the fact that she had been unable provide the assistance that Jolene so desperately needed. That is why Sabrina changed her career path from social work to the study of Psychology, for she yearned to unravel the intricate workings of the human mind, particularly in relation to individuals such as Otis, seeking to comprehend the underlying factors that shaped their behaviour.

Sabrina wanted to know why, his ilk and men like him were bullies. She wanted to know where their empathy was, if they had any. She couldn't fathom, how they could look at themselves in the mirror and not hate their own reflection. Bullies, rapists and murderers were all the same, they were soulless, devoid of humanity and Sabrina needed to know why.

"Are you okay?" Moira whispered, her voice piercing through the fortress of Sabrina's introspection. Sabrina's gaze penetrated the depths of Moira's eyes, her voice resonating with an unmistakable sincerity as she spoke, "I was lost in my own thoughts, thinking about a friend of mine. She was failed by the system. I should have been attending the same lectures as you and Kira. But my friend opened my eyes." Moira possessed a deep-seated aversion to inquiring further of Sabrina's thoughts, as her ambitions were firmly grounded in a steadfast longing to bring about constructive transformation in the domain of societal matters. Moira was sure that whatever Sabrina knew, it wasn't her place to ask, and she was pretty certain that she didn't want to know, the whys and the wherefores. Driven by a virtuous mission of protecting the well-being of the young, Moira found herself inexorably drawn to the vocation of a social worker. "There are good and bad in all walks of life, but I want to be the one that changes lives for the better."

With a resounding fervour, Sabrina exclaimed, "Amen to that," her voice reverberating through the air, as it carried with conviction. With an air of elegance, Sabrina adorned her countenance with a smile, a carefully crafted facade that concealed her true emotions. 'If only the system could be changed for the better.' Moira was naive, but Sabrina didn't want to burst her bubble. With utmost precision, she elevated her drink, bringing it closer to Moira's, the gentle collision of their glasses producing a melodic resonance that lingered in the air.

"I'm starving, I will go fetch us a menu." Moira insisted, with a low guttural growl emanating from her stomach. Sabrina interrupted, "Moira, do you not think it's best for you to go home too? just encase your drinks were spiked." Sabrina's voice resonated with curiosity and anticipation as she inquired. "No." Moira retorted, with a subtle defiance, "I carry these with me." Moira skillfully procured a pot from her bag. A question, of curiosity tinged with anticipation, hung in the atmosphere, waiting to be answered, "What is it?" Sabrina asked.

"It's a drug testing kit, you simply place the strip in your drink."

"Moira, why didn't you tell the others you had these?" Sabrina asked impatiently.

"I did, but they said I was being paranoid, my mum insists I use them, she buys them from the USA when she goes there on business. Now I don't look so paranoid, huh?"

In the precise instant that Moira put the pot back in her bag, Kira appeared.

"They're all back in their rooms, safe and sound. Amanda will have a bad head in the morning that's for sure, and Kim was getting more incoherent, in the taxi on the way back. They've all had a lucky escape, I dread to think what would have happened, if we hadn't seen you guys." The trio of women, indulged in bowls of fries, before embarking on a leisurely exploration of the local boutiques, their footsteps echoing through the quaint streets. Engrossed in their animated conversations, they eventually found respite in the serene embrace of the Royal Crescent Gardens, where they whiled away the remaining hours of the day. Sabrina couldn't tell Kira the truth, that Moira had become privy to their status, as unsuspecting pawns in Michael's malevolent plot. Moira true to her word, maintained a composed silence. Displaying a discerning awareness that Kira, in her fragile state, would struggle to confront the revelation, that another individual had become privy to the heinous act of violation inflicted on her. As they made their way back to their quarters, Sabrina's path unexpectedly intersected with Lorenzo's. Sensing the need for privacy, Kira swiftly seized Moira's arm, as they continued their stride towards their student halls.

CHAPTER 12: First Fight.

As Lorenzo's hands delved through his curly hair, a subtle air of menace and disarray enveloped him. "Sabrina, where have you been? I've been worried about you, you weren't in class. I searched everywhere for you. You weren't in the grounds, you weren't in the food halls." Sabrina gingerly retreated from Lorenzo, her heart fluttering with unease. This unfamiliar side of him had unveiled itself, leaving her uncertain and disconcerted. Doubts began to creep into her mind, casting a shadow over her previous fondness for him. There was an undeniable air of derangement about him, evident in the restless fidgeting that consumed his every movement. His usual calm demeanour was conspicuously absent, replaced instead by an uncharacteristic restlessness.

"Kira's, been poorly. She has been having a bad time of it lately. I needed to be there for her. She needed me. We went into town, to take her mind off things." Sabrina found herself in a state of exasperation, a feeling she was unaccustomed to. Never before had she been compelled to justify her actions or thoughts to another individual. In a most unexpected turn of events, the man who had captured her heart, was now causing her to experience emotions akin to those of a petulant child. "I was worried about you. I missed you. Please, don't do this to me ever again." Sabrina's gaze met his, and in that moment, she acquiesced. "I'm sorry, Lorenzo, I didn't think. I have never had to worry about someone else before, except for my mama". Sabrina's countenance betrayed a hint of confusion, her eyes reflecting a sense of disorientation. Lorenzo, struck by the realisation that he had erred, regretted ever exposing this vulnerable facet of his being to her. In an attempt to rectify his misstep, he extended his arms and uttered with heartfelt sincerity, "I'm sorry I was just concerned, for you. I love you." Sabrina's delicate lips formed a perfect rounded "O" shape. "Lorenzo, did you just say that you love me?" Lorenzo's restless feet performed a rhythmic dance, in a desperate attempt to cast off the weight of his anger. His gaze, now fixated on Sabrina's large brown doe eyes, revealed a vulnerability that belied his words. With a voice tinged with sincerity, he confessed, "Yes,

I did. I love you." Sabrina's feet appeared to be ensnared by an invisible force, rendering her motionless. The fervent desire to rush into Lorenzo's embrace consumed her, but the constraints of their current location, the grounds of the campus, shackled her actions. The mere thought of their relationship being exposed to prying eyes halted her desires, for such a revelation would undoubtedly spell the demise of Lorenzo's career. It was an emotional standoff, both parties found themselves trapped in a web of unspoken sentiments. Sabrina, her countenance frozen in a state of disbelief, stood motionless, grappling with the weight of her unexpressed emotions. A profound silence emerged between them, punctuated only by the sound of her deep inhalation, as if summoning the courage to articulate her innermost thoughts. Finally, breaking the stillness, Sabrina uttered with measured breath, "Lorenzo, I love you too. But Kira needs me right now. My friend needs me. I haven't been there for her recently." Lorenzo's fingers glided through his tousled locks, a subtle manifestation of his inner turmoil gradually seeping into his external being. "But I need you, do you not understand?"

"Yes, I get it, but Kira's like a sister to me, I can't let her down again, I won't, not even for you." Sabrina took a deep breath as she ventured, "I can only see you twice a week Lorenzo, between my studies and Kira, I can't manage any more time with you, for now. I trust you understand and respect my decision. If you really do love me, please, say you will wait for me." Lorenzo, with an air of nonchalance, swiftly pivoted on his heels and departed from the pathway. Sabrina wanted to unleash a piercing cry, a desperate plea for him to stay, though she understood the futility of such an outburst. Lorenzo, consumed by a torrent of anger, retreated with purposeful strides. He recognised the imperative need to distance himself from the recent encounter, for his simmering rage threatened to breach the surface. The prospect of instigating a public spectacle or worse yet, permanently alienating Sabrina, loomed as his greatest apprehension. He couldn't risk it. She would have to keep for another day. How dare she, how dare she rebuke him. He didn't want to share her, not with anyone. Not even Kira.

Sabrina meandered languidly along the path that led her back to the modest quarters. The weight of her sorrow compelled her to conceal the evidence of her tears. Kira, who was already burdened by an overwhelming sense of responsibility, would blame herself. A torrent of thoughts inundated

Sabrina's consciousness, a tempestuous maelstrom that threatened to engulf her fragile composure. She fought valiantly to stifle the cascading tears that traced a melancholic path down her beautiful features. Lorenzo, in stark contrast, possessed the maturity of a grown man, far surpassing the youthfulness of his counterparts. It was intriguing to note that, despite his earlier display of devotion to Sabrina, he had also acted like a toddler having a tantrum. It was a somewhat disturbing revelation. A gentle whisper echoed in Sabrina's mind, reminding her of his heartfelt declaration of love. Sabrina found herself pondering the intricate unfolding of events. Why did life always have to be so complicated? This day, which should have been one of happiness, had instead held a disconcerting air of unease. The man she loved, the one who professed his love in return, had left her in a disquieting sense of misalignment. The dissonance echoed within her, leaving her perplexed and somewhat devastated. Sabrina brushed away the lingering traces of her tears. Inhaling deeply, she cast her gaze upon the reflective surface of the glass door, that served as the threshold to her halls of her residence. With a graceful motion, she delicately threaded her slender fingers through the cascading waves of her lustrous ebony hair. Gently, she brushed away the remnants of her tears, as if to erase any trace of vulnerability from her countenance. "You will do," she mused, her thoughts echoing through the corridors of her mind, as she grasped the ornate door handle and pushed open the weighty door. With measured steps, she embarked on a solitary journey towards the sanctuary of her room. Peeking around the corner, she discovered Kira deeply immersed in her scholarly pursuits, her attention captivated by the pages of her books. A wave of relief washed over her as she found her dear friend engrossed in the pursuit of knowledge once again. It was a glimmer of hope, a sign that Kira was recovering from the harrowing experience she had endured.

"Hello you. Come and tell me what was up with Lorenzo, as he appeared somewhat flustered." Kira implored, her gaze lifting from her diligent studying.

"He was just worried because I had missed his lecture.". Sabrina harboured an aversion towards the act of deceiving her friend, after all, one hidden truth was enough for today. "We had an argument about it." Sabrina astonished herself with her honesty. "You had an argument about me, you mean? I was the reason you skipped classes today." Kira insisted.

"Kira it's not your fault. Lorenzo was acting strange. I have never seen him like that before. He is supposed to be a grown man, but today," Sabrina stammered, "Well today, he was like a spoilt child." Kira still harboured a deep-seated fear that her actions had caused the argument. But Sabrina was determined to shield her friend from shouldering any additional guilt or self-loathing.

"Well at least he cares. I wish someone cared about me that way. Must be a great feeling."

"I worry about you. Kira, you will always have me." Sabrina declared emphatically. "I've told Lorenzo that I can only see him twice a week. I've been neglecting our friendship, and I'm truly sorry. But I'm here for you now, I will be from now on." Sabrina stated solemnly.

"You didn't have to do that. I promise, I'm fine, the fact that they were nearly all arrested is a huge healing tool." Kira's gaze ascended to meet Sabrina's, her countenance adorned with the radiance of her most effulgent smile. But in an instant, her visage transformed, a melancholic veil descending upon it. "You've been crying, what's up?" Kira observed, her voice tinged with concern. Sabrina averted her gaze, her voice full of disapproval as she simply said, "Lorenzo, he was like a crazy man, he acted way out of character, I didn't like it."

"I'll tell you what we need, let's go out to dinner, just me and you, my treat. We need a girly night, just the two of us. Then you can tell me everything." Kira implored. Sabrina's head bobbed in agreement, her eyes reflecting a shared understanding. In a swift motion, Kira gathered her belongings, seizing Sabrina's arm with a firm grip. Together, they retraced their steps, venturing back into the bustling heart of the town. As the friends crossed the threshold of Raphael's wine bar, they were met with warm greetings from the attentive staff. This charming establishment, with its familial ownership, had captured their hearts after just one prior visit, solidifying its place as a favourite destination in their repertoire. It was a well-deserved indulgence, that both young women deserved. With an ambiance that exuded warmth and informality, the establishment proved to be an idyllic sanctuary for the pair, affording them the opportunity to sequester themselves from the prying eyes of their peers and engage in intimate conversation. Sabrina was enamoured by the delightful array of wine selections, with their rich flavours and aromas. In that moment, she was transported back to the sun-kissed vineyards of her beloved Italy, a place that held a special corner of her heart. She had never been there, but she had sought out pictures of Italy, in various magazines, it was a peculiar juxtaposition, for the establishment primarily catered to the discerning palates of those seeking British contemporary cuisine. Even though the culinary offerings hailed from a different land, the wine menu served as a nostalgic reminder of her roots, evoking a sense of familiarity and comfort. As the friends settled into their seats, Kira leaned in with an air of curiosity and inquired, "So what happened with you and Lorenzo earlier?" Sabrina proceeded to divulge the entirety of her altercation with him. With Kira attentively lending an ear, albeit accompanied by a constant display of disapproval etched on her freckled features. "Wow, he sounds a bit possessive, don't you think?" Sabrina raised the wine glass to her lips, allowing the rich, velvety essence of the red wine to caress her palate. As she savoured the intoxicating flavours, her mind grappled with the arduous task of justifying Lorenzo's actions. Beneath the facade of conviction, a flicker of doubt danced in Sabrina's heart, acknowledging the undeniable truth that resonated with Kira's words. The remainder of the evening was devoted to indulging in delectable cuisine and savouring the aromatic wines, as the duo endeavoured to reconcile the perplexities of the world, and to make sense of the myriad of experiences they had encountered.

CHAPTER 13: Possession.

Several days had elapsed since Sabrina's last encounter with Lorenzo. While they had crossed paths during lectures, their private interactions had been conspicuously absent. Her heart fluttered with butterflies, her mind clouded by uncertainty as she wondered how he would act around her after their argument. They had arranged to meet up in the enchanting Royal Botanical gardens, where nature's splendour would serve as the backdrop for their encounter. From there, they would go out for dinner. With a heart full of trepidation, Sabrina ventured towards the gardens, her breath held in anticipation. Her fervent hope was that Lorenzo, the man who had captured her heart, would once again embody the man she had fallen in love with. Hope, mingled with her longing, though there was a gnawing worry, born from the memory of his recent inexplicable behaviour towards her. She found herself in a dilemma. Consumed by her love for him, she was not oblivious to his reciprocation of love. Compelled to summon her inner strength, she knew she had to make him understand. He needed to see her side of things, but how? Without losing his affections? She didn't want another argument. Kira was her best friend, she had known her all her life, they were like sisters, and they had always promised each other that no man would ever come between them. She found herself compelled to convey her perspective to him, to ensure that he comprehended the depth of her convictions. During her contemplation, Lorenzo pulled his car up to her. Parked near the gardens, he opened the door for her, while gesturing for her to proceed inside. As they settled into the car, he took the wheel and guided her towards their destination - the George Inn, a cherished locale that held a special significance in their shared history. The same place they had their first date, a memory etched deeply in their hearts.

Meanwhile during the voyage, he engaged in casual conversation with her, discussing the events of his life in her absence and inquiring about her own activities. However, he deliberately avoided delving into the matter of their prior encounter. It was as if the events that transpired had been erased from existence, leaving no trace of their occurrence. Sabrina exhaled a sigh of relief, her heart grateful to have evaded yet another confrontation with him. Deep down, she yearned for the restoration of their harmonious connection, longing for the days when their bond remained unblemished. In truth, to all appearances, that semblance of normalcy had indeed been preserved. Lorenzo, in his perennial display of gentlemanly conduct, exuded an air of calmness and affection. This was the man she knew and loved, all past grievances now forgotten. As the anticipation of Easter break loomed near, and the gentle embrace of spring enveloped the surroundings, Sabrina and Lorenzo found themselves drawn towards the rear of the pub, where the beer garden was situated. Eagerly awaiting a table, they embarked on this delightful interlude, seeking solace amidst the burgeoning season. Sabrina was totally dismayed to find a table had been specially laid out for them.

On the table sat a bucket full of ice, elegantly displaying a bottle of Champagne alongside two delicate glasses. Adjacent to this enticing sight, a water jug accompanied by two tumblers awaited. The table, marked as "reserved," boasted a magnificent bouquet of crimson roses, artfully arranged in a vase. Lorenzo gently clasped Sabrina's delicate hand, guiding her with utmost care, down the stone steps that led to the well-manicured garden. A talented musician materialised from the shadows, skillfully coaxing ethereal melodies from his violin. Sabrina, overcome with a mixture of surprise and anticipation, found herself trembling ever so slightly as she accepted Lorenzo's extended hand. The unexpected turn of events had caught her off guard. As Lorenzo gallantly seated her at the beautifully adorned table, the proprietor of the quaint pub emerged. With a flourish, he uncorked the effervescent elixir, expertly pouring a generous measure into each awaiting glass. In a sudden turn of events, Lorenzo swiftly descended to one knee, leaving Sabrina utterly bewildered. With an air of contrition, he implored her forgiveness, his voice laced with a mixture of remorse and hope. And then, as if unveiling a hidden treasure, he produced a diminutive leather jewellery box from the recesses of his pocket, its shape perfectly square. He then gingerly opened the box, revealing its contents to Sabrina's curious gaze.

"Sabrina," he pleaded, his voice tainted with desperation, "I cannot live a life without you. Will you do me the honour of becoming my wife, my bella?"

Sabrina felt faint, a wave of disbelief washing over her. "Yes, yes, I will marry you," her voice erupted in a crescendo of exhilaration. As Lorenzo slid the engagement ring onto Sabrina's slender finger, a dazzling spectacle unfolded before her eyes. It was, a magnificent gem of extraordinary proportions, it caught the sunlight with an ethereal brilliance. Its sheer size, an impressive three carats, left Sabrina captivated, unable to tear her gaze away from its mesmerising shimmer, undeniably exquisite, boasting three magnificent diamonds encased on a thick band of 18 carat gold. Overwhelmed with emotion, she found herself in a state of disbelief, exclaiming, "I can't believe I'm going to become Mrs. Gallo." Lorenzo interjected with an air of certainty, his voice carrying a hint of pride. "Naturally, we shall hold the wedding at my family's estate," he declared, his words laced with a touch of expectation.

"I trust you won't object, for it is a cherished tradition." Lorenzo concluded with a subtle gleam dancing in his deep blue steely eyes. Sabrina's voice filled with uncertainty, "but how shall I ever manage to arrange it all?" Lorenzo's hands reached across the table, gently clasping hers in a tender embrace. With a reassuring smile, he spoke in a soothing tone, "You need not worry, we have our own wedding planner, she will arrange every detail for you. All you will have to do is pick a dress. How does the month of August sound to you?" Sabrina was so overwhelmed with a surge of pure happiness, a sensation so profound that it compelled a solitary tear to gracefully cascade down her beautiful face, as she agreed with Lorenzo. "August it is then."

CHAPTER 14: The news.

The following day, Sabrina spent her day with Kira, engaging in the dual pursuits of scholarly endeavours and retail therapy. Kira's countenance transformed into a tableau of astonishment as her gaze fell on the magnificent gemstone gracing her friends ring finger. The sight before her elicited a surge of bewilderment. "Oh, my God! What the hell is that giant sized rock on your finger? Did Lorenzo propose or something? I mean, I am happy for you. I really am Sabrina. But I am worried that it's been a whirlwind romance, and everything is happening too quickly, especially after the way Lorenzo behaved the other day." Kira's voice was full of concern.

"Last night, at The George Inn Garden, he proposed. Oh Kira, I wish you could have been there. He had a musician playing the violin, there was a table reserved for us, with champagne. There was a huge arrangement of flowers, and he had specially reserved the whole garden just for us. He apologised to me for his behaviour, telling me that he just couldn't bear to live without me, the next thing I know he is down on one knee asking me to marry him. It was the most beautiful night of my life. Please be happy for me Kira."

Sabrina, with a subtle inclination of her head, indicated at the direction of her bedside cabinet, where the red and white roses bouquet, now sat in a bucket that was previously used as their wastepaper bin. She arched her eyebrow, a mischievous smile playing at the corners of her lips, as she said, "besides you're my maid of honour, so that now means you will be joining us in Italy, at his family estate for our wedding in August. Or do you not want to be my maid of honour now?" Kira charged at her friend and squeezed her tightly whilst screeching, "eeek, Italy, all's forgiven, I can't believe it. Congratulations, I am so happy for you. Maybe I can bag myself an Italian Stallion." Kira jokingly quipped.

"Kira, I need a favour. Would you come with me to my mama's this weekend, to lend me your support? Mama doesn't know I'm getting married in August, and I'm not sure how she is going to take it." Kira's countenance betrayed her emotions, yet she agreed, nonetheless. Sabrina's mother had always thought of Kira as family, and given Kira's current lack of social commitments, this arrangement proved to be a most fortunate turn of events.

"I'm lonely when you're not here weekends, so yes I would love to go with you."

Sabrina's heart was heavy with sorrow, for how could she have been so blind to her friends' plight? She should have known that Kira was feeling isolated. Why hadn't she realised sooner? She toyed with the idea of extending a more permanent invitation to Kira, why not ask Kira to go with her to mama's every weekend, a gesture that she resolved to uphold for the duration of the academic term. She perpetually found herself plagued by the disheartening notion that she was consistently failing her best friend. She had been do distracted lately.

"Kira, why on earth didn't you say something to me, you are always welcome at my mama's you know that. From now on we will both go to mama's every weekend till the end of term, okay? Mama loves having you there. I never even knew you felt like this, I thought you wanted to stay here and study. I wish I'd have known, my mamas house is always open to you, your part of the family." Kira's countenance bore a tinge of shame as she mustered the courage to speak, her words flowing forth with a simplicity that belied the weight they carried. "I feel like such a burden, I do not want to burden you, or your mama," she confessed. Sabrina looked at her beloved friend, her heart brimming with affection, as she implored her to cease her self-deprecating thoughts. With utmost sincerity, Sabrina assured Kira that she was never a burden, and that she would forever be her best friend, her sister from another mother. That their bond would never be broken. "That's settled then, no more lonely weekends for you, and as for me, I have always loved your company, so it's an added bonus. Plus, it will give mama someone else to make a fuss off, other than me." Sabrina said whilst laughing. When the two friends stepped through the porch of Sabrina's mama's house, Sabrina exclaimed excitedly, "Hey, mama, look who I have bought to see you." In the heart of the home, Sabrina's mother diligently occupied herself in the culinary sanctuary known as the kitchen. With consistent dedication, she undertook the task of nourishing her loved ones, as she had done countless times before. "Kira, Kira. Let me have a good look at you. Your so skinny, you need some meat on your bones. Take a seat, and I shall arrange a feast for both you and Sabrina." Mama, with a tender embrace and a thorough appraisal, spoke to Kira. "Sabrina," she declared with a firm tone, "from now on you must bring Kira home with you, the poor child is withering away." With a shared amusement, the two friends exchanged a light-hearted chuckle, while Sabrina, in a display of subtle understanding, gave Kira a playful wink. "Please, join us mama, I have an announcement to make." With a gesture of courtesy Sabrina deftly pulled out the chair, inviting her mama to take a seat. Sabrina extracted a bottle of exquisite red wine from her bag. With a purposeful stride, she made her way towards the cabinet, where an assortment of wine glasses awaited her attention. Meanwhile, Kira found herself engaged in a lively conversation with Sabrina's beloved mother, their voices mingling harmoniously in the background. As Sabrina delicately placed the glasses on the table's surface, her mama's inquisitive gaze met her own. Curiosity got the better of her, so she posed the question, "What's this about? What are we celebrating?" Sabrina positioned a delicate glass of crimson wine before each of her companions, with an air of elegance. Urging them to raise their glasses and utter the customary toast, "Cin cin". With a profound inhalation, Sabrina proudly exhibited her engagement ring to her mother. "Lorenzo has asked me to marry him, mama, and I said yes. We are to be married in August on his family's estate in Tuscany." Just as Sabrina stopped speaking, her mama choked on her wine, which proceeded in her coughing and spluttering into a handkerchief she had managed to pull out of her apron. "Mama, are you alright?" Sabrina inquired with concern. Mama waved her hand in the air as if to ward of some evil, and eventually managed to calm the coughing fit down and said "Si, I'm alright child, the wine just went down the wrong hole, that is all. I am happy for you, my bella, but what about university?"

"Mama, the wedding has been scheduled for the month of August, ensuring my timely return in preparation for the forthcoming winter term." In an effort to diffuse the tension that hung in the air, Kira valiantly endeavoured to infuse the conversation with a touch of levity, deftly steering it towards a different topic altogether. "I have never been to Tuscany, or Italy for that matter. Can you tell me what it's like there?"

Kira's heart fluttered with anticipation, a surge of excitement coursing through her veins. Mama responded with unfeigned candour, "Regrettably, we have never been able to afford to go to Tuscany, or Italy for that matter. Tuscany stands as one of the more exorbitant regions within Italy. The region is teeming with opulent family vineyards and sprawling farming estates, only the wealthy live there to my knowledge." Sabrina was so grateful to Kira for changing the subject, to express her appreciation she blew Kira a tender kiss. As the delectable assortment of dishes graced the table, they indulged in their flavoursome offerings, engaging in a lively conversation about the intricate art of wedding dress selection, and the enchanting choice of the wedding venue. The collective consensus was reached, as they unanimously agreed to embark on a joint venture to explore the local bridal boutiques, in pursuit of the elusive and exquisite gown that would encapsulate Sabrina's dreams. A sense of excitement permeated the air, captivating the collective spirit of all those present. Yet, amidst this fervour, a discerning observer would have noticed a subtle reservation emanating from Sabrina's mama. She harboured a deep reluctance to mar the radiant joy that enveloped her daughter's spirit, even though an undercurrent of concern coursed through her veins. In her contemplative state, she found herself ruminating over the rapid pace at which events were unfolding. 'It was too quick, too soon. Why were the youngsters of today always in such a hurry?' The notion of relinquishing control to unfamiliar hands, in orchestrating the intricate details of her daughters impending nuptials, did not sit well with her discerning sensibilities. She remained plagued by an unsettling intuition, that Lorenzo's demeanour would eventually veer towards possessiveness. The prospect of confiding these apprehensions to her sole progeny was not possible. Her daughter was so happy. She would have to keep her thoughts and feelings to herself. Sabrina's mama harboured a secret, she knew Lorenzo was not good enough for her daughter. He was all bravado and airs and graces. But underneath that dark gallant exterior, Sabrina's mama had seen through the charade. Underneath he was a monster, of that she was certain. Whilst her daughters happiness seemed to seep into the walls of their family home, Sabrina's mama had to hide her heartache. He would bring her daughter to wreck and ruin. Over the years she had met men like him before. They were arrogant, possessive and evil. Of course, she hoped she had misjudged the situation. She hoped she was wrong. She dared not think about what the future would hold for her only daughter, thus resolving to remain steadfastly present, ready to pick up the pieces when it all went wrong. What should have been one of the best days of her life was marred by feelings she couldn't shake.

CHAPTER 15: Controlling.

As the sun rose on the following day, a palpable sense of excitement permeated the household. The three women, brimming with enthusiasm, eagerly prepared themselves for the much-anticipated endeavour of wedding dress shopping. Their spirits lifted by a delicious breakfast feast expertly prepared by Sabrina's mother, they went about cleaning up the leftovers. Suddenly, without warning, a resounding knock reverberated through the air, jolting the tranquil atmosphere of the household. "I'll get it mama." Sabrina hastened towards the door. She fervently hoped that the visitor on the other side would be someone she could effortlessly dismiss. She found herself averse to the notion of displaying rudeness, towards the followers of Jehovah. Kira had always taken the micky out of her for being too polite to them. But in Sabrina's eyes they were still Christians, so she was always courteous to them. But today she didn't have the time to listen to their beliefs. Nevertheless, when faced with a door-to-door salesman, she would promptly dismiss them without a second thought. She hoped that it was the latter option, for the day that lay before them promised to be filled with a flurry of activities and obligations. As the door swung open, a wave of surprise washed over her delicate features. Standing before her, impeccably dressed from head to toe, was a private chauffeur, exuding an air of sophistication and professionalism. "Good day, madam. I am here to collect Miss Morrelli and company." Sabrina found herself quite taken aback, for there, just beyond the chauffeur, was an elegant white limousine. "Madam, I have been entrusted by Mr Gallo to accompany you and your entourage on a delightful excursion to a collection of selected boutiques, each one handpicked for the purpose of finding your perfect wedding gown." Kira approached the door with a mixture of trepidation and curiosity, her eyes widening in sheer wonderment as they fell on the imposing figure clad in a resplendent uniform. "How did he know?" Kira inquired.

"We spoke about it on the night we got engaged, but I didn't know he had planned this." Sabrina, with a calm and composed demeanour, responded.

"Can you give us some time, we are still clearing up after breakfast." Sabrina uttered her words with a simplicity that belied the weight of her request, directing her statement towards the driver with a calm and unwavering tone. "Yes, madam," he replied with a deferential nod, "I shall wait for you outside." As the trio of women departed the family home, they were met with the warm presence of the Chauffer, who dutifully extended his hand to open the door for them. With poise and finesse, they entered the awaiting limousine, there a lavish interior awaited their arrival. A well-stocked bar, complete with a chilled bottle of champagne nestled amidst the ice bucket, beckoned their attention. The plush leather chairs provided a luxurious seating arrangement, while a state-of-the-art interior commanded their attention. The chauffeur graciously uncorked the champagne, its effervescence filling the air as he deftly poured each of them a glass. Meanwhile, he proceeded to elucidate the intricacies of the vehicle's features, ensuring they were well-versed in its modern conveniences. As the women settled into their seats, Sabrina, with an air of curiosity, directed her question to the driver, "What's the destination?"

"Harrods," the chauffeur responded with utmost simplicity. The women exchanged bewildered glances, their countenances reflecting utter astonishment. "Harrods, in London?" Kira found herself deeply impressed, for she had long been aware of Lorenzo's affluence, yet the extent of his wealth now before her, was truly staggering. With a desire to preserve the sanctity of the moment, she looked into Sabrina's eyes and uttered, "Lucky girl." Sabrina's laughter reverberated through the confines of the interior. Her mother, captivated by the infectious joy, couldn't help but join in the merriment. Yet, amidst the shared laughter, a peculiar truth lingered: neither of them truly comprehended the source of Sabrina's amusement. Sabrina found herself succumbing to fits of uncontrollable laughter, her emotions spiralling into a state of hysteria. She was unsure why, she was laughing so hard. She just knew she was trying to hide her discomfort with humour. The overwhelming nature of the situation had surpassed her desires, as she had never intended for such grandeur. The weight of it all became too burdensome for Sabrina's fragile spirit, and her laughter abruptly transformed into tears, cascading down her cheeks. "This is too much. My intention was simply to find a dress locally. I never knew that Lorenzo came from this kind of money. Now, I find myself utterly inundated by the sheer magnitude of it all. Its intimidating and overwhelming." Sabrina's mother gently clasped her hand, her eyes full of love and tender affection. "My dear daughter," she whispered, her voice laced with unwavering devotion, "there is no limit to what I would do for you. Lorenzo understands this truth. Nothing is too good for my daughter. You will never have to worry financially, never have to worry about paying bills or putting food on the table. Enjoy it, you're in love. I know you wanted something less formal, but I also understand that Lorenzo can't have you turning up to the wedding in a Highstreet bought wedding dress. He only wants the best for you my child, as do I. Indulge in this, for I am confident that Lorenzo has meticulously arranged every detail on your behalf. For what other reason would all of this be for?" With a graceful flourish, she gestured, her arms undulating in a sweeping motion that encompassed the entire space around her. The arduous journey to the city of London, spanned nearly three hours, due to the ceaseless congestion that plagued the metropolis from start to finish. As the grand façade of Harrods loomed before them, the chauffeur conveyed his intention to patiently await their return, while presenting Sabrina with his elegantly embossed calling card. "Kindly summon me when you have finished, as Mr. Gallo has diligently attended to all matters at hand. It is worth noting that you possess an unlimited account with Harrods, ensuring a seamless shopping experience. Furthermore, the staff will gift each of you, overnight bags subsequent to your dress selection. Then I will drive you all to a luxury hotel and spa, for an overnight retreat. Please do not hesitate to contact me at your convenience, madam. Mr. Gallo has arranged it all."

"Oh, my goodness," Kira exclaimed with a high-pitched screech,

"He has thought of everything." Mama, with her usual assertiveness, interjected.

Sabrina's tears had long since dissipated, replaced now by a resolute determination as she found solace in the presence of her current companions. With newfound resolve, she eagerly anticipated the indulgence and lavish treatment that awaited her. Although, a lingering discomfort persisted. A little voice in her head whispered to her, 'this isn't real, it can't be.'

The opulent lifestyle now being afforded to her, was a world she had yet to become accustomed to. The chauffeur confidently escorted them to the grand entrance of Harrods, where a group of impeccably groomed and elegantly attired staff, eagerly awaited their arrival. With utmost courtesy, three members of the staff stepped forward, introducing themselves to the three women. In the regal confines of this bustling workplace, a triumvirate of key players emerged: the visionary design team, the diligent assistant, and the astute manager of the department. "Everyone here in attendance, stand ready to fulfil your every desire. Do not hesitate to ask us for any request that may arise. Our purpose is to fulfil your wedding wishes, to procure for you the impeccable gown that will bring your dreams to life. This is my entourage, may I present to you my loyal attendants. Elizabeth, shall be at your beck and call, ensuring that your thirst and hunger are quenched with utmost care. Marco, our in house designer stands ready to help you select the most exquisite shoes and accessories, to harmonise flawlessly with the elegant array of dresses." The manager graciously beckoned them to accompany him towards the exclusive lift, reserved solely for esteemed clientele.

"Dresses, you say?" Kira inquired with an air of palpable excitement.

"Indeed, Miss Harlow, each and every one of you shall be attended to with utmost care and consideration. From the esteemed mother of the bride to the maid of honour, and, of course, the radiant bride herself, no detail shall be overlooked." Kira emitted a deliberate, measured whistle. Sabrina's delicate frame quivered with anticipation, her nerves betraying her composure. Sensing her daughter's unease, her mama gently linked her arm with Sabrina's, offering both physical and emotional support. Leaning in close, she tenderly whispered into her daughter's ear, her voice a soothing balm amidst the whirlwind of emotions. "See, this is all for you, so just enjoy it, you will be one of them soon." As Sabrina and her companions were escorted into the bridal boutique, they found themselves mesmerised by the overwhelming opulence and exquisite elegance that permeated every corner of the establishment. They were escorted to a seating area adorned with opulent velvet cream seating, exuding an air of luxurious comfort. Nestled between the chairs, a regal marble table commanded attention, its elegance adding a touch of sophistication to the surroundings. As they settled into their seats, Elizabeth graciously extended a delicate flute filled with effervescent liquid, a vintage treasure from the year 1973. The golden elixir within was none other than the Krug Vintage Brut, a French Champagne renowned for its exquisite craftsmanship and timeless allure. Sabrina surprised herself slightly as she told Kira and her mother about the history of the Champaigne they were now sipping. Lorenzo had taught her everything she knew about wines and champagnes. The champagne they were currently indulging in, was of an exceptionally high calibre, boasting an exorbitant price tag. Lorenzo had meticulously considered every possible detail. This Champaigne was one of her favourites. The staff members were all busy, moving quickly and purposefully. Soon, more staff joined their ranks, carrying racks covered with magnificent designer clothing. These sartorial jewels were intended solely for the bride's mother and maid of honour.

"These dresses have been selected by the discerning eye of Mr. Gallo, who has also taken great care in curating an exquisite array of hats, shoes, and accessories." Elizabeth uttered with simplicity. Each item thoughtfully displayed to captivate the discerning observer.

"Allow me to assume the role of your personal shopper, I shall be assisting you in the selection process. Should you require any guidance or support, I am readily available to fulfil this purpose. Shall we start with colour options?" Elizabeth's lips curved into a gentle smile as she inclined her head towards Sabrina. "Rest assured, Miss Morrelli," she murmured, her voice laced with warmth, "Marko and the department manager shall imminently join you, then they will escort you to the bridal suite." Just then, Marko entered the room, commanding attention, while the manager followed closely in his wake, Marko was like a tempestuous force of nature. He possessed a towering stature, his figure slender and graceful, while his demeanour exuded an unmistakable air of elegance. His mannerisms, with their flamboyant flair, revealed a vibrant spirit that resonated with an undeniable sense of authenticity. "Please accompany me, Miss Morrelli, your exquisite beauty surely warrants a dress befitting its splendour. Martina and Jaclynn shall attend to your every need, ensuring that you are adorned in the most exquisite garments. They shall assist you in fastening every button and securing each delicate pin, leaving no detail overlooked. Shall we make our way to the Bridal Suite, where we can engage in a delightful conversation regarding the exquisite gown that you envision adorning your radiant self?" Sabrina's gaze shifted between her dear friend and her beloved mama, a glimmer of excitement dancing in her eyes. Eager to partake in the forthcoming spectacle, she trailed behind the esteemed designer, exuding an air of anticipation. "Ready for the fashion show?" Sabrina declared, her voice carrying a note of joviality. With purposeful strides, she trailed behind the esteemed designer and his entourage, their collective presence exuding an air of sophistication and purpose. As the designer stepped into the room, his discerning eyes swept across every detail, meticulously examining the arrangement of chocolates and the carefully crafted bouquet of flowers. His gaze then shifted towards the water jug, with delicate crystal goblets, and the champagne chilling in the ice bucket. With a satisfied nod, he clapped his hands, prompting the female staff members accompanying him, to pour drinks for Sabrina. With care, they delicately unwrapped the chocolates, presenting them to her with an air of elegance. Meanwhile, one of the ladies momentarily vanished, only to reappear swiftly, bearing a silver platter adorned with an assortment of canapés. The platter was accompanied by gleaming silver cutlery and a porcelain plate, embellished with beautifully embroidered napkins, adding a touch of refinement. "Very well, let us commence, do you possess any inkling as to the sort of wedding dress, that might suit your fancy?" Marko's eyes sparkled with curiosity as he posed his question. Sabrina cleared her throat, her voice poised and elegant as she uttered, "Something Satin, something that exudes class and simplicity, if you please."

"Indeed, my dear lady, your wish shall be my command." With a flourish, Marko gracefully executed a bow, that was nothing short of theatrical, his movements imbued with a touch of grandeur. And just as swiftly as he had made his entrance, he departed the opulent suite, leaving behind an air of intrigue and mystique.

CHAPTER 16: Unlimited.

Sabrina scarcely had the opportunity to savour the last bite of her canapé, before a resounding knock reverberated through the door of the bridal suite. "Come in," she uttered, her voice barely escaping her lips before a procession of staff members filed into the room. Each member carefully affixed a breathtaking wedding gown to the awaiting hangers adorning the walls. Without a moment's pause, boxes containing veils and tiaras were promptly ushered in, accompanied by an abundance of designer shoes, arranged in countless boxes. Sabrina's eyes were wide with surprise as she observed the scene before her. A whirlwind of emotions consumed her, leaving her torn between tears of joy and laughter. Her innermost feelings danced chaotically, as if engaged in a spirited waltz. Never before had she dared to imagine that such a fate could befall her, this wasn't her life. It was someone else's surely. Sabrina had never been around people with money, it was only now that she came to the realisation, that this made her feel truly inadequate. The staff exuded an exceptional amiability, their collective efforts dedicated to attending to her every desire, while also endeavouring to assist her in navigating the overpowering surge of emotions that had seized her being. Marko returned, filling the room with a renewed sense of energy. As he caught sight of Sabrina's delicate countenance, he instinctively gravitated towards her, settling himself beside her with a gentle grace. Taking her hands into his own, he offered a steadfast source of comfort and encouragement. "You possess a captivating beauty, that beckons us to indulge in lavishing you with adoration and affection. I have grown accustomed to navigating the treacherous waters, of interacting with individuals of a spoiled and detestable nature, individuals who truly do not warrant an ounce of my precious time. However, you my dear, you are an exception to this rule, for you have a unique quality that sets you apart. Therefore, allow us to spoil you and shower you with the attention you deserve." Marko whispered in hushed tones. As Sabrina's delicate countenance was betrayed by a solitary tear, a manifestation of her innermost emotions,

Marko, ever the gallant gentleman, extended to her a handkerchief, embellished with intricate embroidery. "I'm sorry." Sabrina whispered, her voice tinged with a hint of perplexity, "I don't know what has gotten into me." Sabrina declared.

"You, the radiant bride, must never apologise. Being overwhelmed, is a mere state of being that engulfs the human spirit, consumes the mind. I'm here for you, I assure you, we shall assume the mantle of responsibility and attend to every detail on your behalf."

Sabrina's heart swelled with relief on hearing Marko's words. A glimmer of hope danced in her eyes as she mustered the courage to make her request. "Might it be possible, Marko," she implored, her voice laced with a gentle plea, "for both mama and Kira to join me?"

"But of course my dear, it is your day after all, we shall spare no effort in fulfilling your every desire." Marko assuaged her apprehension, with a radiant smile that showcased his immaculate pearly whites, imparting an air of youthfulness that belied his true age. In a fleeting span of time, Sabrina's mother and Kira graced the threshold of the room. Mama, her heart overflowing with an abundance of affection, swiftly and eagerly cuddled her daughter. In the midst of the ordered chaos, the assiduous staff followed closely, their steps measured, as they eloquently carried trays with an assortment of invigorating beverages. A further platter, brimming with irresistible canapes, accompanied their diligent procession.

"Mama, It's too much. I never expected anything like this." Sabrina's voice was teetering on the edge of despair. In the heart of the room, Kira spun with an effortless grace, her eyes shimmering with a fervent sense of expectation, as she stared at the splendid assortment of shoe boxes that lay before her. "Sabrina, have you had chance to check out the shoes yet? Come and look at them, they are to die for." Kira was trying to keep the mood light for Sabrina. She knew Sabrina was struggling with all the opulence and the attention, so she wanted to help lift her spirits. Sabrina and her mother ascended from their seats, their eyes locked in a shared intensity on the exquisite collection of dresses and shoes that lay before them. The assemblage of exquisite garments, each one exuding its own distinct allure were breathtaking. "I'm not sure which to try on first, they are all so beautiful. Mama, will you pick one for me please? Kira you can pick the shoes."

Marko interjected, "Ladies, you have the whole day here, Mr. Gallo has paid for a private setting all day. So, you can try every single dress on, take your time." With maternal dedication, Sabrina's mother embarked on an exploration of the dresses that hung in the Bridal suite. Her discerning eyes, eager to unearth the one garment that would perfectly complement her daughter's ethereal beauty. After much contemplation and thoughtful deliberation, she ultimately arrived at a decision, choosing an elegant satin gown that exuded an air of elegance and sophistication. With unwavering certainty, she believed that this particular garment would enhance Sabrina's natural beauty, matching her with an unparalleled grace and charm. The attire in question showcased an off-the-shoulder arrangement, characterised by a captivating crossover bodice embellished with intricate pleats. The dress had a captivating v-neckline that exuded an undeniable allure, infusing an air of sophistication into the ensemble. Simultaneously, a generously proportioned waist band artfully emphasised the wearer's figure, enhancing its natural beauty. The true masterpiece, however, lay in the flared crepe skirt, a marvel that radiated an air of refined elegance and effortless finesse with each and every step. In the design, one could discern the embodiment of Sabrina's yearning for a harmonious blend of simplicity, style, and elegance. "The shoes, don't forget the shoes." Kira's eyes sparkled with excitement as she exclaimed, her voice filled with a sense of wonder. Within the confines of the box resided an exquisite pair of high heels, their allure emanating from the intricate Rhinestones that decorated every sinuous contour. The remainder of the shoe, fashioned from a translucent material, possessed a quality reminiscent of delicate glasswork. "I would imagine these on Cinderella, when she went to the ball." Kira stated excitedly. Kira and Sabrina's mother retreated to the adjacent room, their hearts brimming with anticipation for Sabrina's imminent arrival. Adorned in a resplendent wedding gown lovingly chosen by her doting mother, Sabrina's entrance was poised to be nothing short of spectacular. The diligent staff members were meticulously adding the finishing details to her exquisite lace veil, adorned with a regal tiara. Meanwhile, they skillfully adjusted the dress, expertly pinning it in all the right places to tailor it to Sabrina's alluringly petite and curvaceous figure. Sabrina was led by the staff, their footsteps echoing softly through the lavish hallway, as if whispering secrets of anticipation. The path led her to the grand runway, where she stood poised, a reflection of elegance and grace, before a mirror that held the promise of a transformative unveiling. Sabrina's breath hung suspended in the air, her chest constricted. As She gracefully entered the room, her visage commanded the attention of both her mother and Kira. In a synchrony of astonishment, their mouths parted, while Kira instinctively covered hers with her delicate hand. Sabrina, with an air of royalty, exuded an aura reminiscent of the iconic Jackie Onassis, evoking a timeless elegance that captivated all who beheld her. A cascade of joyful tears descended from the countenance of her mama, her emotions manifesting in a display of vulnerability. In a tender gesture, a handkerchief was proffered to her. Sabrina's appearance was nothing short of exquisite. A hushed stillness enveloped the room, as all present were rendered speechless by the celestial sight that unfolded before their eyes. The mirror, acting as a conduit of truth, unveiled the astounding beauty of Sabrina, leaving those in the vicinity in a state of awe and wonder. Sabrina stood motionless, her body quivering with a mixture of trepidation and curiosity, as she beamed at the figure, reflected in the looking glass. In the recesses of her mind, she entertained the notion that she must surely be dreaming. Maybe if she pinched herself, she would wake up. Then the walls of this fantasy would come crashing down around her. But did she really want it to end? This dress was stunning, she looked like a princess in a fairytale. Surely nothing else existed to rival its magnificence. Her mother's impeccable taste had undoubtedly shone through in her selection. The staff, particularly the charming Marco, would undoubtedly encourage her to explore other options. Sabrina resolved to indulge him, if only to satisfy his persuasive nature. Nevertheless, there was an undeniable allure to this particular gown; it was as though, it had been crafted exclusively for her. Sabrina stood resolute, her delicate frame trembling as tears of unadulterated joy cascaded down her high cheekbones. With a steadfast conviction, Sabrina declared, "This is the one, I just know it is." The remainder of the day enveloped the trio in a hazy embrace, as if time itself had been suspended. Marko, the epitome of grace and charm, bestowed on each of the women an equal measure of his undivided attention, treating them as though they were royalty. Each of the women graced the runway, the women exuded an air of confidence and elegance, draped in intricately crafted ensembles by renowned designers. In this moment, they felt an unparalleled sense of empowerment, as if they were standing on top of the world. It resembled a grand spectacle of fashion. Yet, no matter how many dresses Sabrina tried on, nothing compared to the first one. None could rival its allure, especially when paired with the glass-heeled court shoes and the delicate veil that had been gently placed upon her head by Marko's attentive staff. Everything unfolded flawlessly, every detail falling into place with precision. It was a moment of pure perfection, a harmonious symphony of sights, sounds, and emotions. The staff attended to their every need, with utmost care and diligence. Once they had decided on their outfits, Marko summoned the chauffeur to transport them to their luxurious spa retreat hotel. It had been a most exquisite experience. Sabrina found herself in a state of disbelief, compelled to pinch herself repeatedly, in order to confirm the authenticity of her current reality. Kira had selected a satin lilac bridesmaid dress, its contours gracefully accentuating her every curve. Meanwhile, her mother had opted for an exquisite ensemble, a dress suit with lilac and cream hues. The ensemble was complete with a matching jacket, hat, and shoes, all harmoniously complementing her elegant appearance. Numerous bottles of expensive champagne had been consumed, leaving a lingering sense of indulgence in the air. The luxury hotel, where Lorenzo had secured their accommodations, awaited their arrival, for an evening of refined dining at the renowned Michelin-starred restaurant. Subsequently, they were ushered into a realm of tranquillity and rejuvenation, as the spa evening unfolded before them, revealing its myriad of offerings. The die had been cast, and the verdict had been delivered: the wedding's chromatic palette would consist of delicate lilacs, creamy hues, and pristine whites. Lorenzo, in his infinite benevolence, had kindly presented Sabrina with six curated colour schemes, offering her the opportunity to select the one that resonated most with her vision. Taking the initiative, he promptly contacted the hotel to engage in a conversation with Sabrina regarding the chosen colour scheme, ensuring that he could relay the information to the family wedding planner. Sabrina found herself unable to cease expressing her gratitude towards him, for the splendid series of events he had orchestrated. In response, Lorenzo simply uttered, "Only the best for my Bella." He adored her with a fervent passion, his heart ablaze with an ardent desire to unite their souls in matrimony. He couldn't wait until she solely belonged to him.

CHAPTER 17: Welcome Home.

The following months slipped through Sabrina's grasp, leaving her in a state of disbelief as she found herself seated aboard an aircraft en route to the enchanting region of Tuscany, accompanied by her dear companion, Kira. Their destination was none other than Amerigo Vespucci Airport, nestled in the historic city of Florence. Sabrina and Kira embarked on the flight, precisely one week prior to the wedding. They wanted to oversee the final amendments. They intended on seeing to every intricate detail and making necessary adjustments to ensure the flawless execution of the forthcoming ceremony. Lorenzo had chosen to remain in the United Kingdom. His reason, he eloquently articulated, was the pressing need to assess a stack of papers awaiting his discerning eye. A formidable workload beckoned him to reclaim lost ground, as he endeavoured to bridge the gap between his aspirations and reality. In the interim, Sabrina's mother, averse to the notion of air travel, would embark on her journey a day prior to the momentous occasion of her daughter's nuptials. Sabrina and Kira, their hearts aflutter with a mix of anticipation and trepidation, found themselves on the cusp of an encounter that held great significance in their lives. The impending meeting with Sabrina's prospective in-laws stirred a whirlwind of emotions in them. Lorenzo's family had arranged transportation for the two women, sparing no expense to ensure their comfort and convenience. As they embarked on their journey, all that remained for the women was to navigate the customs process and keep a keen eye out for their designated chauffeur. On their arrival at the Airport, they would be transported to the grounds of the family's esteemed estate in the captivating Chianti Rufina area of the region. This renowned locale, adorned with sprawling vineyards and steeped in centuries-old customs, exuded an air of opulence and heritage. Amidst the undulating hills and spectacular vistas, lay a veritable treasure trove of cultural heritage, waiting to be discovered. Kira and Sabrina found themselves momentarily stunned, their breath caught in their throats, as they beheld the breathtaking expanse of the landscape before them. Its sheer beauty enveloped their senses, leaving them in a state of wonder. As the vehicle approached the grandiose residence in the heart of Tuscany, the countenances of the two companions became transfixed on the expansive windows. The sheer magnitude and beauty of the estate commanded their undivided attention, as it stood proudly on top of multiple tiers of an exquisitely manicured private garden. The entire edifice was enveloped in the charm of rustic cobbles and adorned with verandas, while an infinity pool graced the premises, offering an uninterrupted view of the sprawling vineyards. "This is a historic chateaux, si'". The chauffer proudly murmured.

The sight before the friends was nothing short of awe-inspiring, a verdant display of beauty that transcended time. The chateaux, with its storied history, had undergone numerous restorations over the years, yet each time it was revived to its former state of grandeur. It had been passed down through the generations, the family had kept it as it once was, in all of its glory. The cobbles, with their enchanting rustic hue, exuded an undeniable charm. Each stone, weathered by time, whispered tales of bygone eras. And amidst this picturesque setting, the chateaux stood tall, emanating an air of mystery that was simply impossible to ignore. Immersed in a rich tapestry of bygone eras, the resplendent edifice stood proudly in the undulating landscapes, its regal presence accentuated by the endless expanse of vineyards that stretched as far as the eye could see. As the chauffeur approached the majestic entrance of the chateau, a gathering of individuals stood on the marble steps. Among them were distinguished staff members in their impeccable uniforms, while others were adorned in exquisite attire. Every member of Lorenzo's family eagerly awaited the arrival of the two women. Sabrina's apprehension was palpable, evident to Kira who had an uncanny ability to perceive her unease. "They will adore you, just like Lorenzo and I do. No need to fret."

The chauffeur stepped out of the car, courteously opening the door for the two friends to emerge into the radiant sunshine. With utmost care, he retrieved their suitcases from the trunk and dutifully trailed behind them. The older woman began speaking, her arms outstretched as if welcoming a beloved family member. "Ah, Sabrina, I presume? Lorenzo was absolutely correct in his assessment of your beauty. Allow me the pleasure of introducing you to the rest of the family." With a warm smile, she introduced her sons to Sabrina and Kira.

"These are my boys - Petro, Anton, Leonardo, and Giovanni," she said. Lorenzo's mother spoke with a regal air, as each man respectfully nodded and kissed both Sabrina's hands and Kira's. "This is my one and only daughter, Antionette. And, naturally, I am Lorenzo's mother. However, you may address me as Mama Sofia." Mama Sofia proceeded to introduce her staff. "This is Maria, our maid," she said, as Sabrina and Maria exchanged nods. "And Martina is our head of house," she continued, with Sabrina and Kira acknowledging the staff. "Lastly, we have Dante, our butler," she added, assuming that they had already met Luca, their chauffeur. As the two friends stepped into the reception hallway, Kira couldn't help but let out a soft whistle. The sheer beauty of the place left both friends in awe. The grand entrance of the hallway was beautifully designed. A magnificent chandelier gracefully hung from above, casting a mesmerising glow throughout the expansive space. The opulent furnishings, adorned with delicate gold accents, added a touch of elegance. The floor tiles, crafted from exquisite Italian white marble, exuded a sense of luxury. The curtains, meticulously arranged, perfectly complemented the large windows, offering a landscape view of the surrounding countryside.

"I am sure you both could use some rest after your lengthy journey. Dinner will be served at 7pm. Dante, would you kindly escort the young ladies to their rooms, while Maria prepares a tray of tea for them?" Maria nodded and promptly vanished to carry out Mama Sofia's request. "You have interconnecting rooms for now, as I anticipated your desire to be in close proximity until the wedding. We can go over the wedding details during dinner tonight. In the meantime, feel free to settle in, and make yourselves comfortable. Our family wedding planner will be joining us later, along with some local families. In your rooms, you'll discover a variety of dresses to choose from for this evening's event. Lorenzo graciously provided me with your sizes, ensuring that all the dresses will be a perfect fit for both of you. Maria will inform you which rail is designated for Kira, and which one is for you, Sabrina. We are delighted to welcome new guests to the châteaux, and we are eagerly looking forward to having you become part of our family." Sabrina and Kira were led by Dante up the grand staircase to their rooms. Kira was eager to talk to Sabrina about everything, but she had a strong intuition that their conversation should be held in private. As they ascended the stairs, Sabrina couldn't help but notice the sparkle of excitement in Kira's eyes. With a raised eyebrow and a mischievous grin, Kira and Sabrina revelled in the ostentatious display that surrounded them. The walls were adorned with family portraits, elegantly framed in gold gilded frames. The hallway was graced with beautiful bouquets of flowers, adding a touch of natural beauty. Dante swung open the door to Sabrina's guest room, leaving both Sabrina and Kira breathless. The room boasted an enormous four-poster bed adorned with intricately carved cherubs and luxurious Egyptian cotton curtains. A magnificent chaise longue occupied one corner, while bouquets of flowers with elegant white and cream linens filled the space. The room was further enhanced by opulent gold gilded furniture, and a rail stood nearby, showcasing a collection of designer evening dresses. Dante gracefully moved to one side of the room, gently opening the interconnecting doors for Kira. "Welcome to your room Miss Kira. Feel free to make yourself at home. Maria will bring your tray of tea soon." Dante silently exited the room, leaving the two friends to their own devices.

"I'm absolutely gob smacked by this place. It feels like I've stepped into a scene from a blockbuster movie." Kira exclaimed with enthusiasm. Sabrina glanced at her friend and nodded in agreement. "After experiencing a day at Harrods, the sheer extravagance of all this has taken me by surprise. It's quite overwhelming. Lorenzo never disclosed the true extent of his family's wealth to me. It surpasses anything I could have ever imagined. I can't wait for mama to see it all." With that, the two friends embraced each other tightly, and then Kira suggested, "Shall we?" As they exchanged glances, they hurriedly made their way to the luxurious four poster bed, collapsing onto the immaculate white and gold sheets. They revelled in the comfort that was typically reserved for the wealthy. After a while, the maid gently tapped on their door and entered, carrying an impressive tray full of delicate finger sandwiches, and an assortment of dainty desserts, accompanied by freshly baked scones and a beautifully crafted porcelain tea set. "May I have the pleasure of pouring the tea for you, Miss Sabrina?"

"We'll be able to handle it, Maria. Thank you, this is absolutely fantastic.' Sabrina responded. Maria departed, leaving the two friends to enjoy their tea.

"I'm absolutely starving," Kira exclaimed as she grabbed a sandwich and quickly devoured it. "Yes, I am too," Sabrina replied, whilst pouring the tea.

"Are you feeling anxious about meeting everyone tonight? I can't remember how the cutlery works for dinner, do you start on the outside and work your way inwards?" Kira asked. Sabrina chuckled as she responded "Yes, that's it. And don't forget to place your serviette on your lap." Kira and Sabrina shared a joyful laugh together.

"I never even considered that. It's quite daunting, isn't it?" Kira appeared to be grappling with the excessive luxury and grandeur. "Don't worry, you'll be just fine. Just be yourself." Sabrina confidently reassured her friend. "Shall we check out the dresses on the rails next? I'm so eager to try them on. It will feel like a mini fashion show," Kira giggled.

"It's actually me who should be feeling nervous, not you. After all, I'm the one marrying into what seems like, Italian royalty. Even though Lorenzo says he wants to stay in the UK. It still feels strange to me. All this wealth, all this." Sabrina's word drifted off as she took in her surroundings. "Do you think we can put on our airs and graces till the wedding?" Kira questioned with a little hesitancy. Sabrina gazed at her friend with utmost sincerity as she tried to calm Kira's nerves.

"We're in this together, and that's all that matters. We've got this. Together, we'll face the world head-on." Sabrina was trying to convince Kira, as much as she was herself.

"I assure you that I will conduct myself in a manner that is exemplary." Kira chuckled uneasily as she spoke. "It's just for a week, but once we're back home, everything will return to normal, I promise." Sabrina embraced her friend tightly before eagerly pulling her towards the exquisite display of designer evening dresses. "Shall we indulge in a fashion show?" she suggested with excitement. The two friends exchanged a knowing smile as they reached a mutual understanding. That evening unfolded flawlessly, despite the underlying nerves of the two friends, who managed to conceal their anxiety. They indulged in a remarkable seven-course meal, each dish a masterpiece of culinary artistry. Luna Ferrari, the wedding planner, surpassed all expectations. Her warm demeanour and effortless charm made Sabrina feel like a cherished member of the family. Yearning to ensure their satisfaction, she even proposed organising a special treat for both Sabrina and Kira the next day. She was eager to give them a grand tour of the estate, a perfect opportunity to engage in a conversation with Sabrina about her upcoming wedding. Of course, the main reason for the tour was to seek Sabrina's valuable input. After all, tomorrow they would be embarking on the important task of selecting wines, cheeses, and indulging in the delectable experience of tasting wedding cakes. The atmosphere had an electrifying energy. Sabrina was beginning to settle into her surroundings. Mama Sofia had made frequent visits to see the girls earlier that day, going above and beyond to ensure they felt comfortable and at ease. The local gentry embraced Kira and Sabrina warmly, but Antionette appeared less than thrilled. She barely interacted with the two friends, and whenever Sabrina glanced her way, Antionette seemed to be scrutinising her every action. Sabrina made a valiant effort to conceal her anxiety, under the watchful gaze of the other guests during dinner. She even questioned her own suspicions. Was she being paranoid? Why was Antionette so cold towards her? Pushing her concerns away, she decided to set them aside for the time being. Once they returned to their suites, she would ask Kira about her thoughts regarding the situation. Did Kira notice Antionette's demeanour too? The week flew by in a whirlwind of wedding preparations and a packed schedule of evening events. Each night was packed with lively dances and culinary masterpieces. Sabrina and Kira were unable to catch their breath. Lorenzo had come days earlier than they were aware, but Sabrina was only alerted of his presence the evening before. Sabrina longed to catch a glimpse of Lorenzo, but Mama Sofia adamantly refused, insisting that it was bad luck for the bride and groom to lay eyes on each other before the wedding. Kira found herself slightly perplexed by the rule, but Sabrina quickly reassured her,

explaining that they were in Mama Sofia's house and therefore needed to follow the rules. Be that as it may, Lorenzo had dispatched a message to Sabrina through Dante.

It merely stated:

'I adore you, my bella. I cannot wait till tomorrow. I cannot wait to call you, my wife. Then you shall be mine always and forever, until death separates us. Love, Lorenzo.'

CHAPTER 18: Sudden death.

As Sabrina read the letter from Lorenzo, a single tear traced a path down her delicate cheek. Kira, always keenly perceptive, approached her friend with open arms, ready to embrace her. "It won't be much longer now. Tomorrow, you'll officially become Mrs. Sabrina Gallo. Have you received any news from your mother yet? Isn't she expected to arrive today at some point?" Sabrina brushed away her tear, her complexion appearing slightly pallid.

"Mama is expected to arrive at 8.30pm. I hope her flight goes smoothly, she is nervous about the flight. It's one of the many reasons we have never been to Italy. She promised me that she would gather the courage to take the flight for my wedding. It would have been great if she had joined us earlier, but she couldn't get the time off work."

"Sabrina and Kira, could we have a moment to speak with you in the reception room?" The clock struck 9pm, and the dining room fell into a satisfied silence as patrons savoured the last bites of their desserts. Mama Sofia's face was filled with worry. Sabrina and Kira gracefully excused themselves from the dining room, finding solace in the elegant reception room where Mama Sofia and the eldest brother Petro were poised, awaiting their arrival.

"Sabrina, our chauffeur has been waiting for your mother's arrival at the airport, but she did not show up. He is contacting the airline and the information desk there. If he doesn't have any success, I will personally contact the airport to inquire, and provide you with an update." Mama Sofia spoke with unwavering resolve. Sabrina appeared pale and drained. "But I don't understand, my mama, wouldn't miss my wedding for the world. It doesn't make sense."

Feeling the tension in the room rise, Kira interjected, suggesting that perhaps Mama, had missed her flight, and would need to catch a later one. Sabrina sensed a sombre aura enveloping her, unable to pinpoint the cause, yet plagued by a foreboding sense that something bad had happened. "I assure you, Sabrina, we will make every effort to locate your mother. Don't fret. It's the eve of your wedding, I am sure it's just some sort of mix up." Sabrina mustered a faint smile in response to Mama Sofia's kind words, yet an overwhelming sense of anguish consumed her, as if she had been struck with a forceful blow to her core. "Dante, would you kindly escort the young ladies to their respective rooms?" Accompanied by Dante, Kira and Sabrina, ascended the spiralling staircase to their luxurious suites. "Kira, I can't shake this unsettling feeling. It's as if the impending doom of the world is looming over me.'

"Now, don't be silly. I'm confident that your mother simply missed her flight. I'm certain Mama Sofia will uncover the truth in due time. Try not to worry."

Even though Kira expressed it as a statement, Sabrina's intuition had always been on the money, and she too began to feel a sense of concern. She made every effort to conceal it from her friend, as she was determined not to cause Sabrina any more distress.

"I can't help it, it's just a feeling, you know?" Sabrina stated meekly. A sudden, thunderous rap echoed through the room, and with a flourish, Lorenzo stepped inside.

"Lorenzo, I was under the impression that we were not permitted to meet until our wedding." Sabrina said, with a hint of surprise. Lorenzo approached Sabrina and enveloped her in a tight, comforting hug. "My mother insisted that I should be by your side, your mama, never made it onto the flight. My mother is currently on the phone, inquiring about the status of her flight reservation. My mother suggested that we deviate from the usual customs as we work through this chaotic situation. She mentioned that my presence was required, and here I am, no need to fret or overthink. I have complete confidence that everything will turn out just fine." Lorenzo's shoulders were suddenly overcome with a flood of tears.

"But mama, Lorenzo, she didn't catch the flight," Sabrina blurted out through her tears.

"I know somethings wrong, I just know it." Lorenzo's gaze met Kira's, and in return, Kira's eyes locked onto Lorenzo's. They both had a bad feeling. The room was filled with an overwhelming silence, broken only by Sabrina's uncontrollable sobs. Just as the silence hung heavy in the air, a sudden knock at the door shattered the stillness. Mama Sofia appeared, her expression grave, as she made her way towards Sabrina and Lorenzo, who sat there in anticipation.

"Unfortunately, I have to deliver some disappointing news. Your mother has not made another flight reservation. Shall I contact the local authorities in England, my dear? I am sure there is no cause for alarm." Kira couldn't bear witnessing her friend's heartbreak, so she politely excused herself and stepped out onto the veranda, to immerse herself in the beauty of the landscape and its surroundings. Her chest constricted, suffocating her with the weight of impending panic. Memories of the past assault, resurfaced, triggering a familiar sense of dread. With her eyes tightly closed, she sent a silent prayer for her dear friends beloved mother. There was a sinking feeling in the pit of her stomach, a nagging sense that something terrible had occurred. Sabrina's intuition had always been spot-on in the past. Then Mama Sofia emerged to join Kira. "Perhaps it would be best to give Lorenzo and Sabrina some space for now. I could use your assistance in communicating with the authorities in England." Kira silently nodded in agreement, gently wiping away a single tear. As the two women departed from the suite, the atmosphere was heavy with the sound of Sabrina's heart-wrenching sobs. Kira's complexion turned increasingly ashen, as she conversed with the British Authorities over the phone. After hanging up the phone, she turned to Mama Sofia and relayed the message, "They're going to do a welfare check. We have to wait by the phone." Mama Sofia embraced Kira gently before suggesting, "Perhaps we shouldn't fret. Should we consider informing Sabrina?"

"Yes, I believe she would prefer to wait by the telephone." Kira stated simply.

"Dante, would you kindly escort Sabrina downstairs. Maria, would you be so kind as to procure some chairs for us to sit on, along with a refreshing pot of tea, if you please?" Mama Sofia exuded a soothing aura with her words, yet deep down, she shared the same inner turmoil as Sabrina and Kira. "Women are quite knowledgeable about these matters, my dear. We seem to have an intuition that evades our male counterparts. I hope I am wrong Kira, I really do. But we must prepare ourselves." At that moment, tears welled up in Kira's eyes as she struggled to stay strong for her friend. Sabrina's mother had always treated her like family, and the overwhelming heaviness in her chest was impossible to disregard. As Sabrina descended the stairs, supported by Lorenzo, her heart sank even further. Overwhelmed with emotion, Kira found herself unable to hold back her own tears. They sat huddled together, tears streaming down their faces, anxiously awaiting the call from the authorities. Lorenzo served them comforting cups of tea. They were all at a loss for words, so they quietly sat together as the friends sobbed. The phone's piercing ring reverberated through the reception area, capturing Kira's attention before she gracefully handed the phone to Sabrina. On hearing the words on the other end of the receiver, a piercing scream sent shockwaves through the air as Sabrina collapsed to the floor. Kira shakily took the phone receiver from her friend's grasp and continued to attentively listen to the caller's words, tears streaming down her face as she held the receiver close. After gently setting down the receiver, Kira felt faint. Lorenzo found himself on the floor, doing everything he could, to console Sabrina. Mama Sofia cradled Kira tenderly in her arms. Sabrina's' mother was discovered in the hallway of their family home, her suitcase beside her. She was found lifeless on the cold floor, completely alone. The authorities speculated that she had passed away due to a heart attack, but that was the only information Kira managed to grasp before their words faded away. The room was overcome with an overwhelming sense of sadness as Sabrina and Kira's cries of anguish echoed through the air. Lorenzo and Mama Sofia exchanged a wordless glance, they all felt so useless. Kira and Sabrina found themselves gently guided to bed, where they were offered Valium to aid their slumber. Gratefully accepting, they nestled together on the luxurious four-poster bed in Sabrina's room, still fully clothed. Lorenzo, ever attentive, tenderly draped a faux fur blanket over them before silently departing, softly closing the door behind him. As soon as he stepped outside, Mama Sofia was eagerly awaiting him. She beckoned him to follow her to her bedroom, speaking in a soft and secretive manner. "The girls are understandably quite distressed, what on earth are we going to do? All the preparations for tomorrow have been taken care of. We are expecting relatives from all over Italy. Is it possible to convince Sabrina to proceed with the wedding? I understand that she's going through a tough time, I can't seem to find any alternative solutions. I sympathise with her, I really do. But this wedding has cost a small fortune. And the cost to our relatives, there is immense pressure for it to be a truly remarkable event, befitting our status and grand estate. How would it look if we were to cancel it now?" Lorenzo hadn't considered the possibility of the wedding being called off. It just dawned on him, that Sabrina might not be emotionally ready to proceed with the wedding while she was still grieving. "I'll have a conversation with her, tomorrow morning before the beauticians and hairdressers arrive. I believe Sabrina will proceed with the wedding, though we will have to postpone our honeymoon, at least for the time being." Lorenzo assured his mother. "Alright, that's settled then. I believe in you son. I'm confident you can persuade her."

"Mama, I assure you, Sabrina would never even consider cancelling at this point. She fully understands and appreciates the immense amount of work and effort, that has gone into all of this." It's truly unfortunate that there will be no one by her side, except for Kira." After their secretive talks, Mama and Lorenzo made their way downstairs to the smoking lounge, seeking privacy and a strong drink.

CHAPTER 19: Show must go on.

In the early hours of the wedding day, Maria gently tapped on the door of the bedroom suite before gracefully entering. She elegantly arranged a tray of breakfast delicacies on the table and proceeded to unveil the beauty of the room by drawing back the curtains. With a sense of weariness, both Kira and Sabrina slowly stretched and roused from their slumber. The room was filled with the warm glow of sunlight, offering a stunning view of the expansive Tuscany countryside that seemed to stretch right into the room. Sabrina mustered a feeble smile as Maria greeted her and Kira, informing them that the team would arrive in an hour. and that Master Lorenzo would join them shortly. Kira had to ask, "Are you considering cancelling the wedding?" Sabrina wearily rubbed her eyes and strained to see through the bright sunlight. "I can't call off the wedding," she declared. "Lorenzo's family have gone to so much trouble. The wedding will proceed as planned, although I will request Lorenzo cancels our honeymoon." Sabrina gazed at her friend, her eyes welling up with tears once more. "Mama would want me to continue." she whispered. Kira approached her friend with a gentle touch, resting both hands on her shoulders. "If you're certain." Sabrina nodded, gently wiping her tears away. "It's what Mama would have wanted," she whispered.

Maria interjected, "Mama Sophia, has placed a medicine pot on the tray, she said the pill will provide you with some relief, to help you navigate through the day."

"Thank you, Maria, I will need all the help I can get." Sabrina answered sadly.

Kira and Sabrina changed out of their evening dresses and retreated to their ensuites for a much-needed shower. They sought solace in the water, hoping to make sense of the events that had unfolded the night before. Sabrina relished the soothing and energising embrace of the hot shower. The last of her tears fell, as the powerful sedative engulfed her sadness. Simultaneously, they emerged in matching white fluffy dressing gowns, adorned with embroidered labels that read, "Bride to be" and "Maid of Honour" on the back. As they settled in to enjoy their tea, a gentle rapping on the door interrupted their thoughts. With a sense of anticipation, Lorenzo made his entrance into the room. His expression radiated a mix of optimism and worry. He gingerly approached Sabrina and humbly knelt before her, as he spoke. "If you wish to postpone the wedding, I will completely understand." Sabrina gazed deeply into his eyes, a single tear tracing a path down her cheek. She resolutely shook her head. "Lorenzo, I believe it is only fitting to proceed with the wedding. Mama would have wanted it, and your family has put in tremendous effort to make this happen. It must go ahead." She said as she maintained her smile, though it appeared fragile. Lorenzo gently cradled her face in his hands before tenderly kissing her lips.

"We will make your mama proud today, I promise you." Sabrina let out a heavy sigh, her heart aching with a mix of pride and sorrow. Putting aside her grief for her mama, she had to embrace the facade of joy, and carry on with the charade. It was crucial to ensure that Lorenzo's family was spared any inconvenience or embarrassment. She had already made the choice to consume the pill from the medicine cup, knowing that it would provide her with some much needed relief to make it through the challenges of the day. She had a deep aversion to taking medicine or drugs, but deep down she understood that she couldn't get through the day without something to alleviate her sorrow. Kira and Sabrina sat sipping their tea, engrossed in conversation. Kira didn't hold back, expressing her emotions openly to her friend. "You are so brave. I wouldn't have the courage or the strength. I would find it difficult to proceed with everything, after what has happened."

As the words escaped her lips, a wave of regret washed over Kira. It seemed that she had a knack for putting her foot in it, why did she always say the wrong thing at the wrong time? "I'm here for you. Today will be incredible, and I'll be by your side every step of the way. We' will get through this together, just like we always do." Kira said, in an effort to make up for her previous careless words. Just as Sabrina was about to speak to her dear friend, an unexpected knock at the door disrupted the room. The wedding staff entered and quickly filled the space. The furniture was carefully arranged, with makeup lights strategically placed to create the perfect ambiance for the bride-to-be. Every detail was thoughtfully considered, to ensure she would feel pampered and look absolutely stunning on her special day. With a shared glance, Sabrina proposed to Kira, "Shall we proceed?" Kira nodded in agreement. The friends were escorted to their seats and the beauticians immediately began their work. Sabrina stood before the full-length mirror, inhaling deeply as she scrutinised her reflection with a discerning gaze. "You look absolutely stunning Miss Sabrina," the wedding planner interjected, interrupting Sabrina's thoughts and applauding as if Sabrina were her own masterpiece. Sabrina couldn't help but shed a tear as she whispered, "If only Mama could see me now, she would have loved this." Luna Ferrari, the wedding planner delicately wiped away the single tear and softly said, "She sees you, you are truly a sight to behold." At that moment, Kira entered the room, gracefully donning her elegant bridesmaid gown. The two friends locked eyes, with a sense of awe and wonder, as if beholding each other's beauty for the first time. Kira's jaw dropped in astonishment as she uttered, "Sabrina, you look absolutely flawless." Sabrina glanced at her friend and replied, "You look stunning too." With a graceful gesture, the wedding planner instructed the staff to present each of the women with a flute of champagne. Gratefully, the friends accepted the beverages. Then with a flourish of her hands, Luna exited the room, leading the entire staff in her wake. "Are you ready Sabrina?" Kira inquired.

"As ready as I will ever be." Sabrina's eyes held a hint of sorrow, a stark contrast to the warmth of her smile as she responded to her friend. Kira approached the door and notified Dante that they were ready to proceed. The music began to play. An exquisite orchestra had been meticulously curated, with every piece of music carefully arranged by Lorenzo and Sabrina. They both shared a deep admiration for a particular artist. As Sabrina gracefully descended the stairs and made her way through the red carpets, the enchanting melodies of the Carpenters' love songs drifted through the air. The reception hall led her to a magnificent veranda, overlooking the sprawling gardens. A picturesque walkway of trees awaited her, ready to accompany her down the aisle. Kira let Sabrina take the lead, following closely behind. The audience were already settled into their seats, and as Sabrina approached the garden, the orchestra began playing 'Close to You' - a cherished favourite of Sabrina's. All eyes were drawn to the bride as she gracefully made her way down the aisle. Sabrina could sense the warmth spreading across her chest, as every gaze remained fixed on her. She wasn't fond of being the centre of attention, but the pill Mama Sofia had given her earlier, had softened the blow. It not only made her feel brave, but also emotionally detached.

Sabrina fixated on Lorenzo as he stood in the archway at the end of the ruby carpet. She longed to be by his side, as the world around them faded into insignificance, leaving only the two of them. Lorenzo gazed at his stunning bride, filled with a sense of pride and an overwhelming love in his eyes. In that moment, the world had drifted away, leaving only the two of them in their own little universe. As the couple exchanged their vows and sealed their commitment with a tender kiss, a thunderous applause erupted from their delighted guests. Lorenzo leaned in close to Sabrina, his voice barely above a whisper. "I have a surprise in store for you," he murmured, a mischievous glint in his eyes. "It'll be an intimate gathering, just for us and our loved ones. I assure you, you will absolutely adore it." Sabrina barely registered his words, her only desire was to escape from prying eyes. However, they still had the entire reception party and wedding breakfast to endure. The wedding breakfast was a grand and lavish event, attended by more than two-hundred guests. The tables exuded elegance, adorned with flickering candles and vibrant bouquets of flowers. Each round table in the ballroom boasted a sparkling crystal centrepiece. The melodic tunes of a live band filled the air as the guests indulged in their meal. At the top table, Lorenzo, Kira, and Sabrina sat alongside Lorenzo's mother. There was an empty seat where Sabrina's mama should have been seated. Luna, the wedding planner, had asked about removing the setting, but Sabrina firmly declined. She expressed that her mother would be present in spirit, and she wanted her to always hold a special place in her heart and be by her side. Mama Sofia couldn't help but be impressed by Sabrina's composure. Despite the recent loss she had experienced, Sabrina quietly proceeded with the wedding, not wanting to inconvenience anyone. She gracefully endured the ceremony and the scrutiny of others, showing no outward signs of her grief. Without a doubt, Sabrina would be an invaluable addition to the family. Despite her humble origins, she exuded grace, beauty, and elegance that masked her impoverished upbringing. On the other hand, Mama Sofia, viewed Kira differently. She was lacking refinement, ordinary, and overly sentimental. Her Boy Lorenzo had made an excellent choice. Sabrina found herself seated at the table, captivated by Lorenzo's eloquent speech. Kira, being the sole representative of the bride's side, also delivered a heartfelt address. Despite Luna's efforts to dissuade them, the couple went ahead with their seating plans. Sabrina was adamant, that her mama's setting, stayed in place. Not only were guests curious about the empty seat, but later in the day, she learned that Mama Sofia had managed to quell the local gossips, by explaining that Sabrina's mother had fallen ill on the morning of the wedding. A sense of relief surged through Sabrina, knowing that Mama Sofia, held a favourable opinion of her made all the difference to her. If Mama Sofia liked Sabrina, why the hell didn't Antionette? Even today on her wedding day, Antionette had gone out of her way to make Sabrina feel uncomfortable. Last night when Sabrina had collapsed to the floor, Antionette showed no emotions towards her grief, not an ounce of sympathy. Kira expressed her annoyance at the situation. She was determined to find out why Antionette was always so distant and cold. But Sabrina urged her to let it go, to avoid any unnecessary confrontation. Kira reluctantly agreed, taking into consideration Sabrina's fragile state. Regardless, she was resolute in her quest to uncover the truth. What could have caused Antionette to express such strong disapproval towards the two friends? Kira had an insatiable curiosity that often got her into trouble, but she always had to know the truth. Whereas Sabrina tried to avoid confrontations at all costs. The rest of the day unfolded seamlessly, Sabrina maintained her composure amidst the whirlwind of emotions. Between grieving for her Mama and the tranquillizing effects of the Valium, Sabrina felt as though she was observing her own existence from a distance. As the last of the guests departed, Lorenzo gently grasped Sabrina's hand and led her on a leisurely stroll through the enchanting vineyard. Standing at an opening, the entire family was gathered, including Kira. A majestic olive tree stood proudly in a spacious container, while Lorenzo presented Sabrina with a golden plaque adorned with the name and significant dates of Sabrina's beloved Mama. Sabrina's tears flowed freely as she exclaimed, "Lorenzo, this is absolutely marvellous! I cannot thank you enough," she whispered, whilst her gaze was totally fixated on the plaque.

"Your Mama will always have a place here. We invite you to dig the first hole for the tree and the plaque, and our skilled gardening team will take care of the rest on your behalf. This tree will serve as a beautiful tribute to your beloved mother." Lorenzo tenderly handed Sabrina the spade. Sabrina stood there, adorned in her wedding dress and barefoot, offering a silent prayer. "This is for you Mama," she whispered. The promise etched in her heart forever. Sabrina, overcome with emotion, began to dig, tears streaming down her face. Weeks had passed since Sabrina, Lorenzo and Kira had returned to the UK. Sabrina found herself residing in Lorenzo's four-bedroom house while continuing her studies at university. Lorenzo had strongly emphasised the importance of waiting to consummate the wedding, until after Sabrina's mother's funeral, and their delayed honeymoon. Sabrina felt a deep sense of gratitude towards Lorenzo for being so patient with her. At long last, she had received the date for her mother's funeral, and to her surprise, Lorenzo had generously offered to cover all the expenses. The wait for the autopsy results and the coroner's findings had been painstakingly long. The funeral was scheduled for tomorrow, her mother would be laid to rest beside her father. Meanwhile, in the halls of residence, Kira found herself grappling with the overwhelming events that had transpired. With her closest companion having departed, the university now felt like a desolate and solitary environment. She couldn't help but feel lonely. All she could think about was that one night in Tuscany, she remembered quietly making her way to the kitchen of the grand chateaux, hoping a glass of milk would soothe her restless mind. To her surprise, she discovered Antionette lurking in the shadows, seemingly plagued by the same restlessness. Before Kira could utter a single syllable, Antionette's voice dropped to a whisper. "Sabrina is a remarkable young woman who truly deserves better."

Kira's eyes widened as she asked, "What are you talking about?"

Antionette elegantly sipped her drink, before placing the tumbler with a resounding thud, on the luxurious marble kitchen island. "Lorenzo, of course," she began, her voice filled with a mix of sympathy and concern, "he is not the gallant hero that everyone perceives him to be. He is evil. My heart goes out to poor Sabrina." Before anyone stumbled on their conversation, Antionette left the kitchen and returned to her bedroom, leaving Kira perplexed. Antionette's words had been haunting her thoughts ever since. Why would Lorenzo's sister say he was evil? Kira's heart was heavy with concern, as she struggled to comprehend Antionette's words. She had made a solemn vow to keep her mouth shut. Kira had her own reservations about Lorenzo, even before Antionette had spoken with her. She thought he was possessive and controlling. But evil? That was a whole new level. But she didn't want to lose Sabrina's friendship, so she kept her own council.

CHAPTER 20: Bereft.

On that chilly morning, even the heavens seemed to weep in sympathy as Sabrina's mother was laid to rest. The rain poured down, as if reflecting the sorrow of the bereaved. Several individuals had gathered to express their condolences, as her mother was highly regarded within the community. As the priest concluded his words, the coffin gently descended into the earth. A multitude of umbrellas swayed in unison as each person released a solitary white rose into the solemn depths of the burial vault. Kira, Lorenzo and Sabrina stood closely together beneath the expansive black golfing umbrella. The crowd eventually dispersed, bidding their farewells, whilst Sabrina and Kira were left lingering as the others departed.

Sabrina's heart shattered into countless fragments, as she yearned to throw herself in the depths of the burial vault and reunite with her Mama. However, she was well aware that her mother would have wanted her to embrace life and strive for a bright future. So, she concealed her heartache, whilst battling the temptation to join her Mama in the earth. Sabrina had made the decision to honour tradition, by wearing black as a sign of mourning, for her mother. Today, she donned a sleek black trouser suit. Although, she would have to put her collection of black mourning attire on hold. She didn't want to spoil the honeymoon, as they were scheduled to fly out to the Maldives in just two days. The flight to the Maldives was an extravagant adventure, starting with a flight to New York with a layover and then a connecting flight the following day to the Maldives. Upon their arrival at Bandos Island, the couple were escorted to their exquisite garden villa. The views were absolutely breathtaking, with pristine white sandy beaches and crystal-clear waters nestled amidst lush vegetation. "Do you like it, bella?" Lorenzo inquired, his arm wrapped around Sabrina, as they both admired the serene expanse of the ocean, from their villa. "This place is absolutely stunning Lorenzo. It's hard to fathom that I'm actually here." Lorenzo tenderly cradled her face, pressing a gentle kiss on her lips. "Only the best for my beautiful wife." He uttered, whilst extending a gratuity to the concierge. As Sabrina removed her shoes, she revelled in the sensation of the soft sand caressing her toes. She settled herself on the beach, drawing her knees close to her body, and immersed herself in the beauty of the island. A tranquil silence enveloped her, allowing her to fully appreciate the moment. Meanwhile, Lorenzo had indulged in room service before joining Sabrina on the sandy shore. As the waiter approached, he presented a delightful assortment of champagne, accompanied by a delectable platter of cheese and fruit. With utmost care, he arranged everything on the luxurious cabana bed nestled by the beach, before expertly pouring the bubbly elixir into two exquisite crystal champagne flutes. That night, Lorenzo and Sabrina had a truly enchanting dinner on the beach, mesmerised by the breathtaking sunset over the Indian Ocean. The resort exuded opulence, with a dedicated team of staff including a private butler, attentive waiters, an executive chef, and even a personal wine sommelier. The food was an exquisite culinary experience. Sabrina and Lorenzo were completely absorbed in each other, hardly noticing the staff around them. Lorenzo had made a tremendous effort to bring joy to Sabrina's life despite the challenges she had faced. "Tonight, my love, I wish to simply cuddle up with you."

"You have my permission. After all, we are now husband and wife." Sabrina retorted.

"It's not that I don't want you, bella. It's just I don't want us to make love whilst you're so sad." Sabrina's cheeks turned a rosy hue.

"Lorenzo, it's our honeymoon. I don't understand." Lorenzo gently took her hands, lifting her from the chair where they had shared a delightful dinner. With tenderness, he cradled her in his arms and carried her into the vast embrace of the ocean.

"Lorenzo, what in the world are you up to?" Sabrina asked.

"I am standing here in the ocean with you right here, right now bella, till you agree that you will not sleep with me until you are in a happier place. I want it to be special."

In their elegant attire, they gazed out at the moonlit ocean. Sabrina delicately cupped the water in her hands, running it through her hair with a sense of serenity. "Okay Lorenzo, I promise." As Lorenzo pressed his lips against hers, he mischievously released her into the depths of the ocean, his laughter echoing in the air. "That's my beautiful one," he whispered softly, as they both stood there, drenched in their luxurious attire, playfully splashing each other like carefree children frolicking in a pool. Sabrina and Lorenzo concluded their week at the lavish resort with a thrilling scuba diving adventure. Throughout the week, they diligently honed their diving skills in pursuit of their PADI certification. Today marked the final day of their course. By the end of the day, they would have achieved their open water qualification. Sabrina found herself captivated by the ocean, as if she had stepped into a whole new realm. Lorenzo had made the choice to join her in the course, despite already being a certified diver. He recognised that the ocean would serve as the perfect remedy for her grief, and his intuition proved correct - Sabrina underwent a remarkable transformation. Immersed in the underwater world, her sadness faded away as she marvelled at the exotic and unfamiliar surroundings. Experiencing the exhilaration of mastering the art of breathing underwater, Sabrina found herself completely enthralled. Her heart was ensnared by the ocean, its breathtaking wonders, the mesmerising wildlife, and the sheer beauty that surpassed her wildest dreams. Today, however, marked the final two open water dives, signalling the imminent completion of the course. The boat brimmed with individuals, eagerly embracing the art of diving, engaging in lively conversations with fellow enthusiasts, sharing their palpable sense of exhilaration. Sabrina adored the pristine, azure waters, finding solace in their embrace. She had never encountered anything of this nature before, and the impact of this experience would stay with her for the rest of her days. As they meticulously prepared their equipment, double-checked each other's gear, and formed buddy pairs, her heart yearned for the vastness of the ocean. Lorenzo was delighted by Sabrina's natural affinity for diving, as if she were a graceful mermaid gliding through the water. He felt a sense of joy knowing that diving, one of his beloved hobbies, could now be shared with her. Today, they found themselves immersed in the dynamic currents of the channels, where the majestic pinnacles attract a plethora of marine creatures. Delving into the mysterious depths of the caves and the awe-inspiring overhanging caverns. As Sabrina and Lorenzo descended into the depths with their instructors and the rest of the team, Sabrina couldn't help but be bewitched by the vibrant display of colours emanating from the sponges, gorgonian fans, and various invertebrates. It was clear that these organisms were thriving in the nutrient-rich waters. There were plenty of cleaning stations where one could catch a glimpse of larger marine species. When the dive was nearing its end, a sense of awe washed over the divers, as manta rays and various sharks gracefully glided by. Suddenly, a massive whale shark appeared, leaving the divers speechless at the sheer magnitude of its size. As they returned to the boat, it became the centre of conversation among the group during the journey back. Lorenzo couldn't help but notice a shift in Sabrina's demeanour. It seemed as though she had returned to her usual cheerful self, at least for the time being. Tonight, he would seal their union.

He was confident that she was ready for this moment. He couldn't wait to take her purity, for that was his alone to take. Lorenzo had a penchant for virgins, there was something about them that he found enticing. Sex with women who had already been deflowered held no significance for him. His Bella was pure, and he couldn't wait to be inside of her, breaking her in. The sun set as Lorenzo and Sabrina finished their wine. "This day has truly been the most incredible one, Lorenzo. The whale shark was the most exquisite thing I have ever laid my eyes on." Sabrina's smiled with a sense of peace, as if she were still lost in the depths of her oceanic daydreams. "I feel a sense of belonging in the ocean. The encounter with the whale shark left me in awe.'

"Are you happy, my bella?" Lorenzo inquired, his hand gently reaching out for Sabrina's. "Yes, I am. Surprisingly, the sea and the myriad of experiences I have encountered have played a significant role in shaping my perspective." Her voice faded away as she observed the radiant orange sun vanish beyond the horizon. In that moment, Lorenzo tenderly grasped Sabrina's hand and led her to their villa, where they finally made love. The following morning, Sabrina found herself wide awake, perched by the water's edge, gazing out at the vast expanse of the ocean. Last night was truly a dream come true. Lorenzo proved to be an extraordinary lover. With just two days left on the Island, Sabrina was determined to savour every moment and make the most of her time. Despite her fatigue, she mustered the strength to rise before dawn. She yearned for a moment of solitude, to bask in her own musings while the rhythmic waves caressed the shore, and the harmonious symphony of nature's song rang through the air. It was an absolutely enchanting moment. Lorenzo had gone above and beyond to ensure his bride's happiness, leaving her in awe of her incredible fortune. Each night, she gazed at the stars and poured her heart out to her mama before drifting off to sleep. And every morning, she rose with the sunrise to have a heartfelt conversation with her mama. This ritual helped her navigate the pain of her loss. Although she wondered how she would fare once she returned home and life resumed its usual course, for now, she found some comfort in these moments. The following two days flew by in a blur, full of snorkelling adventures, sunset cruises on a luxurious yacht, and romantic evenings spent together. Sabrina had mentioned to Lorenzo that she wasn't taking any birth control pills, yet Lorenzo appeared indifferent to her concerns. He expressed that she had become his wife and that he would be absolutely delighted if she were to give him an heir. Sabrina had made up her mind to leave university, rendering the possibility of getting pregnant inconsequential. Her focus had shifted away from her studies, as she was unwilling to jeopardise Lorenzo's position at the university. It was too risky for her to carry on. Lorenzo's career had to come first. The decision had already been made. Lorenzo had suggested that she could still pursue her degree through the Open University if she desired. In no time at all, they found themselves back on the plane, heading home. Lorenzo had planned a layover in New York, to give Sabrina a glimpse of the places they would be visiting, including the New York Marriott Marquis. Sabrina was quickly adapting to the lavish lifestyle, despite her initial apprehensions. It was as if she had stepped into the pages of a magical romance novel. Everything was absolutely perfect, she couldn't have possibly asked for a more ideal husband and confidante.

Lorenzo appeared to have thought of everything. Even in New York, he accompanied her on a shopping spree to find a new collection of high-end clothing, specifically for her to wear during the period of mourning for her mother. He declared that if she had to don black attire for her mother, she would do so with utmost style, adorning herself in the most exquisite black ensembles money could buy. Sabrina adored New York City and all of its incredible attractions. Lorenzo whisked her away to the iconic Empire State Building and treated her to a picturesque boat ride to see the majestic Statue of Liberty. The following morning, he indulged her with a delightful shopping spree on the renowned Madison Avenue, where she curated a fabulous new wardrobe. It was a much-needed respite, precisely what they required following their arduous journey. That evening, they boarded a luxurious business class flight back to London. Sabrina was filled with anticipation as she made her way home, eager to share every detail of her trip with her dear friend. It had been a long fourteen days since they last spoke, and she couldn't wait to catch up with Kira.

CHAPTER 21: Different worlds.

At long last, Sabrina and Lorenzo had returned home. Sabrina, exhausted from the journey, couldn't muster the energy to visit Kira right away. The effects of jet lag had taken their toll on her. With Friday approaching, she made the firm decision to visit her closest companion. Aware that her friend was back home for the summer break, she understood Kira's distain for staying at the university. But she wondered, where Kira could possibly be staying. Kira's parents adhered to a strict Jehovah Witness lifestyle, which left her with a sense of being stifled and living under a rigid routine. Was Kira staying with her parents? University had proved to be the perfect escape, she had been yearning for. Sabrina was full of excitement as she looked forward to meeting her friend and sharing every detail of her honeymoon. Anticipation consumed her heart as she longed for the warmth and connection of their cherished friendship. But one shadow loomed, as the daunting task of informing Kira about Sabrina's departure from university weighed heavily on Sabrina's mind. Concerns arose about Kira's reaction and the potential void she might experience with Sabrina's absence. On that Friday, Sabrina caught a bus to her friend's family home. As she rang the doorbell, she waited reluctantly, but there was no answer. Sabrina decided to go to the local Kingdom Hall to see if she could find Kira's parents. They had to be there; it was late Friday teatime, and Kira's parents were always there after work. As Sabrina reached their place of worship, her unease grew, something felt amiss. She knew Kira would refuse to go with her parents to worship, but where was she? Just then, Sabrina bumped into Kira's mom, she was a thin, stone-cold-looking woman with pinched features. "Oh, Sabrina, what are you doing here, dear?" Kira's mom inquired with the New World Translation of the Holy Bible in her hands. "I am trying to find Kira, do you know where she is?" Sabrina enquired.

"Yes, dear, give me one second, would you". With that, Kira's mom dived back into the hall, and returned within minutes. "Here's her address dear, now off you pop, dead quick. Only if my husband catches me." Kira's mom seemed alarmed and worried, and although Sabrina really wanted to understand her predicament, she thought it best to leave Kira's mom, without any further lines of questioning. Sabrina cautiously tapped on the door, finding herself in a less-than-desirable neighbourhood, she wondered why Kira, would be staying in such a place. A figure emerged, his imposing stature filling the doorway.

"Excuse me, but I was wondering if Kira happens to be here?" Sabrina inquired, her breath catching in her excitement. The man swung the door open, urging Sabrina to enter.

Sabrina stood her ground on the pavement, whilst politely requesting, "I would prefer her to come to the door, please."

"Kira, there is a visitor at the door for you." He spoke in a deep voice, clearly showing his irritation. Kira arrived at the door in a revealing outfit, casually holding a cigarette. Sabrina felt a sharp pang in her heart. "Oh, my goodness, Sabrina, it's really you! Why don't you come in and give me a moment to get dressed? Then we can go out for a little while. Don't worry, Jack is harmless. He's letting me sofa surf at his, until I get a place. My father decided to kick me out. I met Jack at the nearby game store, during an intense session of Dungeons and Dragons." Sabrina couldn't help but feel a sense of dismay as she observed the dismal state of the studio flat, yet she chose to keep her thoughts to herself.

As they sat in a coffee shop, the two friends engaged in a lively conversation, covering a range of topics, from Sabrina's recent honeymoon to Kira's new accommodation. As fate would have it, Kira's father stumbled upon her diary and discovered the intimate details of her life at university, including the traumatic incident she had endured. This discovery ignited a massive argument, that ultimately resulted in him throwing her out of the family home. She found herself with no place to go, until Jack graciously offered her a place to crash on his sofa. Although he may not have been the tidiest individual and had a fondness for marijuana, he conducted himself with utmost courtesy and genuinely enjoyed her company. Kira's heart ached over the family feud, a bitter reminder of the longstanding discord between her and her parents. On hearing Sabrina's vivid account of her honeymoon, Kira decided it would be wise to heed Antionette's cautionary advice in silence. Lorenzo appeared to embody all of Sabrina's dreams of an ideal spouse. Kira hesitated to deliver the unfortunate news, witnessing the sheer joy radiating from her friend. A hush fell between the two friends, as if they had both been transported to the depths of their own minds. The comfortable silence was quickly shattered, as the two friends eagerly shared their news simultaneously.

"I have made the decision to leave university." They both blurted out in perfect synchrony.

"I've submitted my application to work as a flight attendant for a prestigious airline based in the Middle East. In three weeks', time I will be flying to Dubai where I will stay for the duration." Kira informed her friend. Sabrina was overwhelmed with a wave of apprehension, her entire being pleading with her friend to reconsider. She realised that her efforts were futile. Kira appeared to be filled with excitement. "I need a change of scenery, a fresh start, I am confident that it will bring immense benefits to my well-being. It's an exciting new adventure, just what the doctor ordered." Kira spoke with a sense of anticipation, as her gaze fixed on Sabrina, brimming with enthusiasm for her upcoming adventure.

"If you're absolutely certain about your decision, Kira, I will support you wholeheartedly. Aren't you worried? They are quite strict over there. There are restrictions on alcohol, and you need to be mindful of the dress code."

"They provide me with a uniform and training. The financial compensation is quite favourable, and they provide you with lodging. I can't wait to leave this place. It is going to be quite the adventure." Sabrina departed that day, feeling a sense of loneliness as her closest companion, her best friend, was bidding her farewell. Their bond had remained unbroken ever since their fateful encounter in school. Life seemed to have divergent paths for the duo. Sabrina was overcome with sadness and a sense of emptiness. She was worried for Kira. She would be the other side of the world, on her own. She also had concerns about the country's rules and laws. Kira had always been one to break the rules. It was clear that Kira had firmly decided on her course of action. Sabrina found herself unable to dissuade her friend from leaving. After all, Kira was an adult and in reality, there was no reason for her to stay here in the United Kingdom. As Sabrina strolled home, a mix of emotions churned in her stomach. She pondered whether it was the fear of the unknown, or her own selfishness that caused this turmoil. The thought of losing her friend to a distant land weighed heavily on her mind. She would miss Kira, they had never really been apart. It felt like the world was once again trying to send them on different paths. Sabrina rarely had the opportunity to see Lorenzo, as he had been consumed with work lately. He could often be found either at the University or in his home office. He had made it clear to Sabrina that she was not to disturb him while he was working. There was a noticeable shift in their dynamic, leaving Sabrina perplexed. Recently, she experienced a sense of confinement, lacking companionship and feeling disconnected from the world beyond her reach. Kira had been absent for half a year, and despite maintaining communication via letters, the correspondence was infrequent and lacking in specifics. Sabrina whiled away her days, eagerly anticipating any morsel of affection, that Lorenzo would show her. She wondered if her recent weight gain was the reason for Lorenzo's increased focus on her breasts, which appeared slightly more voluptuous despite their small size. She had inexplicably gained a dress size, leaving her confused and searching for answers. As she reflected quietly, a realisation struck her. She couldn't believe it, she couldn't be, could she? Her mind racing with disbelief. She grabbed her handbag and made her way to the pharmacy. Sabrina returned to the family house in record time, anxiously pacing the bathroom as she awaited the appearance of the two pink lines on the pregnancy test. Lost in her thoughts, she pondered Lorenzo's potential reaction, hoping it would mend their bond. She longed for Kira's company, wishing for her trusted confidant and childhood friend. Kira would know what to do, she should have been here. Perhaps, this could restore her relationship with Lorenzo. He wanted children, while Sabrina wasn't so sure, she felt she was too young. She still had her whole life ahead of her. She hadn't even considered being a mum at the age of twenty. She hoped a child would alleviate her sadness and uphold the customs of her lineage. Despite her youth, she found herself anxious with fear and a sense of isolation. Without the guidance of her mother, she felt adrift, desperately hoping that this baby would provide the answers she sought. As these thoughts swirled in her mind, she reached for the stick and discovered two pink lines, indicating that she was pregnant. With the arrival of Lorenzo's heir, a glimmer of hope illuminated their lives. Sabrina's empty days would finally be filled with the love she longed for. The unconditional love that only a child could bring. That evening, Lorenzo returned home later than usual. He quickly grabbed some food from the fridge, before heading straight to his office. Sabrina made a valiant effort to arrive at the office on time, only to have Lorenzo abruptly shut the door in her face. Sabrina felt a surge of surprise and hesitation, unsure of her next course of action. She remembered

Lorenzo's strict rule about not disturbing him in his office, but surely this situation had to be an exception to his rule. Sabrina turned away from the door, her body sinking against it. Frustration and shock coursed through her veins as she realised, he no longer bothered to greet her when he returned home. He had stopped joining her for dinner approximately four weeks ago. Confused by his sudden transformation and the deteriorating state of their relationship, she found herself with unanswered questions. Amidst this confusion, one certainty remained: she was carrying their child, while he continued to disregard her. He would only show her any kind of affection when he would slip into bed late at night, gently caressing her breasts before proceeding to have his way with her, without uttering a single word. Afterwards, he would simply roll over and drift off to sleep. Every night followed the same monotonous routine, devoid of meaningful conversation or acts of chivalry. She found herself sinking down the unyielding oak door, tears streaming down her face in silence. Her inner world was consumed by a storm of conflicting emotions. Was he having an affair? What were the reasons behind their marriage? What could have caused such intense animosity that led him to treat her with such disdain? She was completely baffled, sitting in the dimly lit hallway with tears cascading down her cheeks. Brushing away the tears, she made a resolute decision in that moment - she would embark on a relentless pursuit to reclaim his love. Not only for her own sake, but for the sake of their precious little one. Knowing Lorenzo's nightly routine of having a glass of milk before bed, she attached the pregnancy test to the fridge door. Accompanying it was a heartfelt note expressing her love, longing, and the news of her pregnancy.

'I am pregnant. I love you & I miss you. Your Bella.'

Later that night, Sabrina retired to her bed, overcome with sorrow, her tears flowing until she found solace in sleep. As the sun rose, Sabrina was greeted by the delightful aroma of Lorenzo's culinary creations wafting from the kitchen. "My bella, please take a seat. I had planned to serve you breakfast in bed," he beckoned. Sabrina appeared fatigued, her eyes still showing traces of the tears shed in previous nights. Lorenzo appeared oblivious to the situation. Sabrina perched on the breakfast bar, clad in elegant black silk pyjamas.

"You're going to make me a father. That's fantastic news! How far along do you think you are?" Lorenzo gently kissed Sabrina on the head before presenting her with a beautifully arranged plate of poached eggs and avocado on toast. "It's been a few months, I suppose. With my mother's passing and Kira being so far away, it somehow slipped my mind." Sabrina spoke with complete sincerity. "Today, I've decided to take the day off from work, so that we can go shopping for the baby. We should purchase all the necessary items for a nursery, and I've made us an appointment with a Doctor on Harley Street, to ensure everything is in order. You have brought me immense joy. I am going to be a dad. My wife and son deserve nothing but the finest." Sabrina remained quiet, her smile gentle, relishing in Lorenzo's undivided attention. She didn't want to disrupt the moment, yet a multitude of unanswered questions swirled in her mind. Nevertheless, she made the conscious choice to set aside her fears and fully embrace the present. Finally, Lorenzo had returned to his former self, resembling the man she had married. Sabrina's heart overflowed with love for him, wanting nothing more, than what she had finally found. Her greatest fear was losing him, but this pregnancy seemed to have rekindled their connection. "Go ahead and enjoy your meal, my bella, you're eating for two now. We have a chauffeur arriving in thirty minutes to pick us up. Everything has been carefully arranged." Lorenzo's voice was tender. Sabrina devoured her meal hungrily, washing it down with a refreshing cup of sweet tea. Afterwards, she prepared herself for their day out. As she perused her wardrobe, she longed for her mama to take part in her happiness. Lorenzo chattered incessantly in the car, his excitement overshadowing Sabrina's subdued demeanour. The doctor on Harley Street thoroughly examined Sabrina and ensured that everything was in order with her pregnancy. Lorenzo couldn't contain his excitement when he received the confirmation. From that moment on, Lorenzo became completely devoted to taking care of Sabrina. He no longer isolated himself in his office, instead, he eagerly attended to her every need. He lovingly prepared baths for her, cooked delicious meals, and even discovered smoothie recipes that were beneficial for both her and the baby. His gallant demeanour had returned. Sabrina effortlessly sailed through her pregnancy, she had no morning sickness, and maintained her petite figure. Despite her breasts growing larger, her small bump was the only visible sign of her pregnancy. Sabrina thrived during her pregnancy, showing no signs of fatigue. She poured her heart and soul into Lorenzo and creating the perfect nursery for her little one. The doctor confirmed that Lorenzo was correct during her sex scan - she was indeed having a boy. Lorenzo had been a constant support throughout, faithfully sending her flowers every week and accompanying her to appointments with private Harley Street doctors. Sabrina and Lorenzo had chosen a private hospital for the birth of their son. Kira was still on the opposite side of the globe, totally engrossed in her work, communication between the two of them was sporadic at most. They were drifting further and further apart with each passing day. During their previous meeting, Kira was adorned with luxurious gold accessories and had even received a Rolex watch as a gift from her wealthy prince charming in the oil industry. Sabrina couldn't shake the nagging suspicion that Kira was keeping things from her. They had always shared everything, their deepest darkest secrets, but now things had changed. She couldn't help but feel a pang of sadness as she noticed her friend's dwindling trust in her. Kira found herself surrounded by a vibrant circle of companions and immersed in a world of extravagant soirées and opulent dining experiences. Meanwhile, Sabrina was on the brink of embarking on the beautiful journey of motherhood.

CHAPTER 22: Adultery.

As the clock struck 4pm, Lorenzo arrived home from work. With culinary finesse, he embarked on the task of preparing a delectable meal for them both, as he had done every night since he had found out Sabrina was having his child. Engrossed in conversation, they shared the events of their respective days. However, in an unexpected turn of events, Sabrina suddenly experienced a sharp pain, causing her to bend over in discomfort. And then, as if on cue, her waters broke, signalling the imminent arrival of their little one. Lorenzo hurriedly sprang into action, his heart pounding in his chest. Sabrina, consumed by pain, paid little attention as Lorenzo swiftly retrieved the hospital bag and dialled the hospital to inform them of their imminent arrival. After a long wait, their precious baby boy finally arrived, bringing joy and excitement to their lives. Sabrina had declined any pain medication, despite her exhaustion. She was completely besotted by the little boy she cradled in her arms. His appearance was truly captivating, with flawless fingers and toes and a lush mane of jet-black hair. Lorenzo effortlessly played the role of a devoted husband and father. Everything seemed as it should be, perfect. They were finally permitted to return home the following day. Together they had made the decision to name the baby Lorenzo Davide Jnr, a name that held great significance for both parents. Lorenzo, in particular, was adamant about respecting his father by passing on his name. Meanwhile, Sabrina chose to honour her late father by adding Davide to Juniors name. They reached a mutual decision to refer to him as Junior whilst in the family home, ensuring that his name would be distinct from Lorenzo's. Life was wonderful. They appeared to be a perfect family. After Junior's first birthday, a shift occurred in Lorenzo's demeanour, as he gradually let go of the facade of a devoted father and husband. Lorenzo had taken to isolating himself in his office after work once more, and each evening he would arrive home and express his frustration towards Sabrina due to the household not meeting his expectations of cleanliness. Sabrina was constantly sleep-deprived as Junior had never managed to sleep through a single night. The house was immaculate, yet it exuded a sense of being well-lived-in, much to Lorenzo's intense displeasure. Each night, his temper got worse, and the relentless barrage of criticism lasted longer with each passing evening. He would enter the house in a mood, forcefully placing his cup on the kitchen counter, and then proceed to call out loudly for Sabrina's attention. Sabrina felt a sense of apprehension whenever he returned home lately. He no longer shared a bed with Sabrina, opting to sleep in his office instead. He claimed it was necessary for his work, and that Sabrina would wake him when she attended to the baby. Sabrina found herself once again in a state of solitude and seclusion. She was isolated from the world and her self-esteem was at an all-time low. Tonight, Sabrina anxiously observed the ticking clock, having exerted herself to the point of exhaustion, caring for the baby and ensuring the house met Lorenzo's standards. Surveying the family home, she couldn't help but bite her lip. The house was immaculate, every corner meticulously attended to. She was confident that nothing had escaped her attention, leaving no room for him to find fault this evening. Lorenzo's attention to detail extended even to the kitchen cupboards, where every food product had to be meticulously labelled and positioned with the labels facing outwards. Every fold of the tea towels in the kitchen had to be meticulously arranged, while the kitchen kettle had to be positioned with utmost precision with the spout always facing to the South, though he never told Sabrina why. Sabrina could never fathom his relentless pursuit of tidiness and perfection in every corner, except for one glaring exception - Lorenzo's office. Not only was that beyond the acceptable limits, but it was securely sealed, preventing Sabrina from accessing it while he was at work. The clock hands seemed to click audibly, and with each movement, her heart raced. She was transforming into a mere shadow of her former self, with Junior being the sole purpose that kept her going - he was her entire world. As the clock struck 5pm, there was no sign of Lorenzo. Minutes passed by - two, five, ten - and still no trace of him. Sabrina patiently endured the passing time until exhaustion overcame her, rendering her unable to stay awake any longer. The beckoning of sleep grew stronger, knowing that she would only have a few precious hours before Junior would awaken and begin crying. Thus, she had to seize any opportunity to rest. As the hours passed, Sabrina awoke from her slumber. It appeared that her body and mind refused to grant her more than a few hours of sleep these days. She found herself awake, even before Junior. Quietly descending the stairs, she was careful not to disturb the peaceful sleep of her little one. Her top priority was to savour a soothing cup of tea. She could hear peculiar noises emanating from the bottom of the staircase - a curious mix of gargling and grunting. Curiosity piqued, she stealthily made her way through the hallway, determined to uncover the source of the mysterious noise. Her body tensed as she caught sight of Lorenzo's office door, slightly ajar, with mysterious shadows moving inside. Sabrina quietly approached the door, ensuring she had a clear view. The scene before her was a complete shock. Lorenzo was completely naked in his office chair, while the woman with blonde hair was on her knees, she appeared to be sucking his cock, with great enthusiasm. Sabrina's hands flew to her mouth, desperately stifling a scream as tears of betrayal cascaded down her face. She quietly made her way to the kitchen, carefully selecting Lorenzo's beloved whisky tumbler. With determination, she returned to the office, bursting through the door, and unleashing a torrent of obscenities at Lorenzo and the girl. She hurled the tumbler towards Lorenzo's head, his naked form a shocking sight before her. He had forcefully pushed the girl away, causing her to fall to the floor. Sabrina was completely taken aback, her heart shattered into pieces. "You... you said you loved me." Tears streamed down her face. "Well, that was before I discovered that you weren't being truthful about your past, Sabrina. It's disheartening to realise that you deceived me. You are a whore just like this one. You were never pure, you lied to me." With a dramatic gesture, he extended his arms, directing Sabrina's attention to the girl lying on the floor. "She holds no significance in my life, Sabrina. She is merely a person of questionable character, whereas you... You were once the centre of my universe, until I came to the realisation that you had already been de flowered, hadn't you? Well?" Lorenzo's agitation was growing with each passing moment. His hands were running through his hair, he was growing increasingly aggressive.

"So, tell me who fucked you, Sabrina? Don't you think you should have told me you were a whore before I married you?" Sabrina was overcome with shock, her face turning pale as her anger dissipated in an instant. Her knees grew weak, threatening to give way beneath her. As the room buzzed with activity, the young girl with flowing blonde locks hurriedly gathered her things and hastily dressed herself. Before Sabrina could even answer him, she found herself in a harrowing situation. Lorenzo, consumed by rage, forcefully seized her by the throat against the wall, his words spewing out in a frenzy as he lifted her off the ground.

"You're a filthy whore. If I had known, I would have never married you. How dare you lie to me. You're a fucking whore." Sabrina's nails were tightly clenched in Lorenzo's hands as she fought desperately to free herself from his choking hold. As her face turned a deep shade of red, she struggled to breathe while his grip grew tighter. With a forceful blow, he struck her in the face, causing her to collapse onto the floor. But it was then the beating really started as Lorenzo repeatedly kicked her petite form. The room faded into darkness as she lost consciousness.

CHAPTER 23: Abduction.

As the sun rose, Sabrina woke up on the sofa, her eyes tired and blurry, her face throbbing with discomfort. As she gently touched her face, she became aware of the tenderness, the swollen eyes, and the bruised lip. With a timid effort, she attempted to lift herself up, feeling the pain coursing through her entire body. Her eyes scanned the area, desperately seeking any trace of Lorenzo. In an instant, a wave of terror washed over her as she remembered the events of the previous night. With a surge of adrenaline, she swiftly rose from the sofa and sprinted up the stairs towards the nursery. A sense of urgency coursed through her veins, as she dashed towards Junior's crib, calling out his name in a desperate plea. To her horror, he was nowhere to be found. She frantically combed every room in the house, finding it devoid of any trace of Lorenzo or her baby. She hurriedly returned to Junior's room, snatched his blanket, and collapsed onto the floor, tears streaming down her face as she clung to her precious baby boy's comfort blanket. Once more, she found herself shedding tears until she drifted off to sleep, right on the floor of the nursery. With a shattered heart, her once familiar life was slipping away. The cruel act of taking her baby left her questioning Lorenzo's motives and destination. She had barely slept, the freezing floor and her broken ribs ensuring her restlessness. Her heart ached with an urgent longing to locate her precious child, leaving no stone unturned in her relentless quest. After getting herself cleaned up and dressed, she was shocked to catch a glimpse of her reflection in the mirror. How could he claim to love her after what he had done? He accused her of being a liar, simply because she had been raped, without ever bothering to ask her side of the story. He had beaten her mercilessly and now he had taken her baby. The overwhelming nature of it all, and the sheer confusion were simply too much to bear. In that moment, she knew she had to gather her strength and locate Junior, determined to find him no matter what. If Lorenzo were aware of the truth, he would surely find it in his heart to forgive her. She was so determined to hold onto Lorenzo, completely oblivious to the possibility that Lorenzo, was at fault. If only Kira was here, she would know what to do. Sabrina focused intently on concealing the bruises with her make-up, wincing slightly as she worked. With her mother gone and her best friend living far away, Lorenzo had become her sole source of support. With only Lorenzo and Junior remaining in her life, she couldn't bear the thought of losing them. Sabrina examined herself in the mirror before stepping out of the house, her destination being the university. She discovered that Lorenzo had informed them of a family emergency and his need to return to Italy, her heart skipped a beat. The thought of Lorenzo taking Junior out of the country, left her wondering if she would ever see him again. Without hesitation, she made her way to the airport and reached out to the private jet company, that Lorenzo had relied on during their honeymoon. When she arrived at the airport, she promptly made her way to the information desk, only to discover that Lorenzo and Juniors names were not listed on any of the flights. Sabrina's desperation grew as she found herself at a loss for solutions. Suddenly the airport ceiling started spinning and Sabrina passed out right in front of the information desk. When she came round the airport staff were incredibly supportive as they made every effort to soothe her distress. "Excuse me, ma'am, it would be advisable for you to contact the authorities and seek legal counsel." The officer at airport security provided her with reassurance. "Unfortunately, we are unable to assist you at this time. There are no such names recorded on our flight lists." Sabrina hurried out of the airport, her mind set on catching a train back home. She would contact solicitors by phone to schedule an appointment. Her thoughts were in disarray, leaving her feeling utterly lost and overwhelmed by the chaos surrounding her. Curiosity consumed her as she pondered alternative methods of departure from the country. They were not aboard a flight nor affiliated with the private jet company. She wondered how they had managed to leave the United Kingdom. Her life seemed to be spinning out of control. The heart-wrenching reality of having her baby taken away, left her wondering if she would ever be reunited with Junior. She struggled to think clearly. A dull emptiness ache was engulfing her to the core. The pain in her chest was heavy, it hurt so bad. Everything hurt so much. The following weeks passed in a whirlwind, leaving Sabrina feeling completely disoriented, as she navigated through numerous appointments with the solicitors. As she emerged from the darkness, a glimmer of hope appeared. She had successfully reached out to Kira, who was now making her way back to the United Kingdom to support Sabrina. Locating a solicitor for domestic violence proved to be a straightforward task in the United Kingdom. These legal professionals were able to discern the visible marks on Sabrina's face. Despite their heartfelt appeals for Sabrina to report the incident to the police and pursue charges, Sabrina adamantly declined. She remained in denial, desperately clinging to the hope that Lorenzo would return, and their marriage could be salvaged. The solicitors had advised her that pressing charges and obtaining photographic evidence would be necessary for family courts, but Sabrina remained resolute, unwavering in her decision. Despite the circumstances, she refused to tarnish Lorenzo's reputation, because her love for him remained. All she desired was for Lorenzo and Junior to return home. Meanwhile, Sabrina had been wandering aimlessly through their desolate house, desperately yearning for a stroke of luck. Unfamiliar with the intricacies of family court and the laws surrounding it, she clung to the hope that the need to battle for custody would never arise. Sabrina had just concluded yet another meeting with the solicitors, so she meandered along on her journey back home. The house, once full of laughter and joy from her beloved family, now felt like a hollow shell, devoid of life. She felt utterly adrift and bewildered, her days consumed by an endless stream of tears. It had been more than a fortnight since Lorenzo had taken Junior, and Lorenzo's family had adamantly refused to communicate with her. Their sole method of communication was limited to interactions with their respective solicitors. When nearing the family home, Sabrina caught sight of workmen who were in the midst of wrapping up their tasks. With a sense of urgency, she hurriedly approached them, eager to inquire about their activities. "This is my home, what are you doing?" she exclaimed, clearly taken aback and slightly breathless. "We are just doing our job Miss. Mr. Gallo instructed us to change the locks and ensure the security of the house." The workmen appeared visibly embarrassed as they responded to Sabrina, fully grasping the gravity of the situation. Sabrina's head was so confused, she couldn't think straight. Nothing made any sense. 'Did they just say they had locked the house up?' The workmen swiftly stowed their equipment and departed, leaving Sabrina standing alone on the front porch steps. Sabrina's mind was clouded, her thoughts scattered as she attempted to open the door, only to discover that her key had lost its power. In a sudden burst of energy, she swiftly pivoted on her heels and sprinted towards the workmen's van. With determination in her actions, she forcefully pounded on the windows, demanding attention. "But this is my house, all my belongings are in there." Her voice echoed with anguish. The driver callously disregarded her pleas and swiftly drove away, leaving her behind and ignoring her desperate attempts to get his attention. She stood there on the pavement, a fleeting moment frozen in time, her world unravelling before her very eyes. With a heart weighed down by sorrow, she made her way to the steps of her family home, sat down and wept, her tears falling into her cupped hands. Time stretched on endlessly whilst Sabrina waited for Kira to arrive. Kira discovered Sabrina shivering on the steps of her house, overcome with cold and a deep sense of distress. Usually, their meetings were filled with joy and warm embraces, but this time was different. Kira embraced her friend, concern etched on her face as she inquired, "Sabrina, what has happened? Why are you sat in the cold?" Sabrina nestled into Kira's embrace, tears streaming down her face, pouring out the details of her tumultuous tale. "He has taken junior, he has locked me out of the house, he hit me, he cheated on me. I found him in his office with a woman. They were , they were..."

Sabrina's voice drifted into the air, as she couldn't catch her breath.

"Shall we find a cosy place to warm up? Perhaps a pub or a coffee shop?" Kira gently comforted Sabrina. The two friends strolled towards the nearby pub, seeking protection from the cold. Kira was shocked by Sabrina's dramatic transformation. She had shed so much weight, that she appeared alarmingly unwell. The darkness in her eyes, had swallowed the once vibrant sparkle. Witnessing her friend in such a state was truly heart-wrenching.

"I'm staying at the Francis Hotel. Let's get you back there, freshen up, and grab some dinner. We can find a solution tomorrow, alright? A couple of drinks might be just what you need, to ensure a restful night's sleep. Tomorrow we can find somewhere for us to live." Kira uttered. Sabrina gazed at her friend with a sense of desperation, confessing, "But I have no money, no clothes, I have nothing. All my belongings are in the house."

Kira rose from her seat and approached Sabrina, enveloping her in a gentle embrace. She leaned in close and spoke softly into her ear, "But I have money okay," assuring her that everything would be alright. After a gentle peck on the cheek, she returned to her seat, delicately savouring her wine.

CHAPTER 24: Truth.

Whilst the two friends sat in the cosy ambiance, they delved into a detailed conversation about all the events that had unfolded since Kira's departure for the Middle East. Sabrina knew that Kira was hiding something from her, but in her fragile state, she couldn't quite pinpoint what it might be. She just knew that Kira would tell her, in her own time. In the meantime, Kira proved to be an absolute blessing. Without Kira, she doubted her ability to handle the situation. Kira instilled a sense of security in her, assuring her that they would go to great lengths, to bring Junior back to his rightful place with his mama. Sabrina was horrified by the news of the warning, that Kira had received in Italy from Lorenzo's sister. 'What did she mean, by saying he was evil? If his own sister was saying such a thing, maybe , just maybe , it wasn't her fault, after all.' A shiver ran down her spine as she clung to the fragile hope of his return, yearning for a fresh start. Sabrina still wanted Lorenzo. 'He couldn't be evil, could he?' She wanted her baby back. She wanted her life back. Yet deep down, she couldn't deny the childishness of her hope. Little did she imagine that her life would take such a drastic turn, leaving her as a divorced single mother. It went against all of her convictions, yet in her heart, she acknowledged that she had no alternative. Lorenzo had made the decision on her behalf. As they settled into the cosy pub, she and Kira engaged in a deep conversation, attempting to unravel the complexities of family courts. Their knowledge on the subject was limited. Kira had gained some insight during her first year at university, although she didn't complete the year. In fact, one of the reasons she abandoned the idea of becoming a social worker was due to her occasional disagreements with her lecturers. She had never disclosed this to Sabrina, but Kira's perspective on life and relationships underwent a profound transformation after they both experienced assault. Her perspective on the system she once aspired to join had shifted. She had come to the realisation that they were unjust and dishonest. The system was rigged against the poor classes of the world. If you were rich, you pretty much could do anything and get away with it. The poor were left to suffer. Single parent mother's had children removed as they were easy targets. It wasn't about safeguarding, it was about money. The following morning, the girls enjoyed a delightful breakfast at the hotel, before embarking on their house-hunting adventure. On that chilly winter day, the two friends were filled with anticipation. They had the pleasure of exploring five different houses, each boasting lovely gardens and convenient proximity to excellent schools. Kira had planned every detail. "Do you not agree that this is the one?" Kira embraced Sabrina with uncontainable excitement. The house had been beautifully updated, featuring elegant magnolia walls and en-suite bathrooms, attached to the two main bedrooms. The garden was well manicured, providing ample space for Junior to flourish.

"Absolutely! I believe Junior will enjoy a game of football in the garden as he grows older, and his bedroom is simply ideal." Sabrina remarked, whilst gazing out the kitchen window. The estate agent, an elegant woman in her fifties, was eagerly vying for the opportunity to let out the property. "Shall we return to the office then? We can complete the necessary paperwork at that location, and I will gladly provide you with the keys." The estate agent proposed. "I'm curious about your occupations. What do you both do for work?' she inquired.

'Well," Kira interjected, "Sabrina is currently not working due to a complicated divorce. However, I am an air hostess, and I have no doubt that Sabrina will find employment in the near future. Meanwhile, I can provide a deposit equivalent to six month's rent and cover the next six month's rent in advance." The estate agent was quite impressed. With a smile, she responded, "Oh, you poor thing. Divorce is never easy, is it? I'm sure that will suffice for the property owner. It's ultimately up to me, and you both appear to be lovely young ladies."

Before they knew it, the tenancy agreement was signed, and both friends were on the hunt for furniture and electricals for their new home. As the sun began to set, the pair found themselves in a charming local pub. Kira had graciously treated them to a meal, a perfect way to commemorate the occasion. "Kira I must ask, how do you manage to finance all of this?" Sabrina asked. "During my time in the sky, I had the pleasure of meeting a wonderful work colleague, who introduced me to a whole new existence, a fresh perspective on life. When I first arrived in the Middle East, I was assigned a minuscule box room that was incredibly cramped. Life was miserable for a while. It was so tiny that you couldn't swing a cat in it. My friend always flaunted her collection of Rolexes and other expensive jewellery, she happened to introduce me to some incredibly affluent Oil Princes. They showered me with shopping trips, fancy dinners, they went above and beyond, by generously providing me with an apartment. I was treated like royalty throughout. Nearly all the air hostesses engaged in the activity to earn some additional income." Kira responded to Sabrina with a warm smile.

"Essentially, I found myself in a situation where I was financially supported as a courtesan. Without this arrangement, my income would have been meagre, and I would not have been able to afford the luxuries I enjoy now." Kira concluded with a playful giggle.

"You didn't? I can't believe it!" Sabrina exclaimed, with astonishment.

"After the assault, I thought why not make them pay for it. At least then I get something out of it too. It means I can comfortably afford all of this." With a flourish of her hands, she proudly displayed her Rolex watch. "But Kira, do you have sex with them?" Sabrina let out a startled breath. "Please lower your voice. Yes, I do. I was tired of being financially strained, thousands of miles away from home, when my friend introduced me to an entirely different world and a completely different way of life. So, I took the plunge. I didn't have many other options, to be honest." Kira finished with unwavering determination.

"I will continue my work as an air hostess for the time being. The financial benefits are quite appealing, and I thoroughly enjoy the lifestyle it offers. Moreover, it allows me to help you, until your back on your feet."

"There's no need for you to go out of your way for me." Sabrina said sincerely.

"I wouldn't have it any other way. The sense of freedom it brings me is unparalleled, and I wouldn't trade it for anything else. You need to prepare yourself for the upcoming court proceedings, as family court can be quite challenging and demanding. It is important to be financially prepared for this endeavour. It is imperative that we organise the house to meet the requirements set by social services, ensuring that Junior can reside with you. Additionally, it would be beneficial to update your wardrobe and actively pursue employment opportunities. This way, the court can witness your ability to support Junior. I'm happy to assist you. You are my best friend, I understand how important this is to you. Besides having a homebase would be beneficial for me." Kira's lips curled into a gentle smile as she savoured the taste of her wine. "If you're certain it's alright." Sabrina questioned.

"Absolutely, we'll find a way to make this happen together. It'll be you and me, against the world just like we used to be." Kira lifted her glass, silently inviting Sabrina to join her in a toast, their glasses meeting with a delicate clink. After several weeks had gone by, Sabrina was still unable to see her son, or receive any communication from Lorenzo. Meanwhile, Kira was working on a twelve-week rotation and making every effort to come back home to the UK as frequently as possible. On court day, Sabrina studied her reflection in the mirror, whilst smoothing down her outfit. She had accepted a position at her local pub on a part-time basis. It may not have been a substantial job, but it satisfied the legal requirements, as her solicitor had advised. Sabrina's heart raced with anticipation as she prepared to enter the family courts. At last, she would have the chance to lay eyes on Lorenzo. She desperately hoped for a miraculous change of heart, but in her heart of hearts, she knew it was an impossible dream. There was a noticeable shift in Lorenzo's demeanour after their honeymoon. It felt as though he had transformed into a completely different person, gradually altering his behaviour. His demeanour had become callous. By the time of the altercation, he had been neglecting her for quite a while. Sabrina longed to reunite with Junior, her heart filled with anticipation, of witnessing how much he had grown during their time apart. Her heart shattered as a single tear cascaded down her exquisite countenance. She brushed away the tear, and scolded herself in the mirror, repeating the mantra, 'Don't reveal any vulnerability, don't reveal any vulnerability,' echoing in her mind. As she entered the courts, a sense of unease washed over her. The imposing building loomed before her, commanding her attention. She was required to pass through a metal detector and undergo a thorough security check, adding to the gravity of the situation. Sabrina was made to feel like a criminal. Her solicitors greeted her in the lobby and escorted her discreetly up the back stairway to a private room, ensuring that she and Lorenzo remained separated. As she settled into her seat, a sudden knock on the door interrupted their meeting. A portly gentleman poked his head inside, inquiring about her solicitor. He appeared quite agitated and perspiring as he inquired, "May we engage in a brief conversation with the judge?" Sabrina's solicitor apologised, whilst asking Sabrina to stay where she was. Then her solicitor left the room. Sabrina's stomach growled, a result of her neglected breakfast. Her mind was consumed with worry as she pondered the identity of the mysterious gentleman who had snatched her solicitor away. After what felt like an eternity, her solicitor finally made an appearance.

"Alright, we'll be going in soon. Remember, only speak when spoken to. I will handle all the communication on your behalf. Don't get your hopes up for this dispute resolution hearing. It's unlikely that anything significant will occur." Sabrina felt saddened by her solicitors words. An awful sinking feeling enveloped her. "So, I still won't get to see Junior?" she asked, her eyes were starting to betray her with tears. At that moment, the solicitor's demeanour softened, "While there are no guarantees, we will make every effort to facilitate contact until custody is determined. Now, please follow me?" Sabrina cautiously trailed behind her solicitor as they entered the court room. The room exuded a sense of understated elegance, with its beige walls and a distinguished judge presiding over the large commanding table at the front. A diligent lady sat beside him, effortlessly typing away. Meanwhile, Lorenzo and his solicitor occupied another table. She couldn't avert her gaze from Lorenzo, as if compelled by an unseen force. His eyes exuded darkness, and his dishevelled appearance was a stark departure from his usual self. It was peculiar to witness him burdened with exhaustion and anxiety. However, he had brought it upon himself. A myriad of thoughts raced through Sabrina's mind, as the solicitors fiercely debated their case before the judge. Sabrina recognised the portly gentleman who had been occupying her solicitor's time. He was Lorenzo's solicitor. Why was he talking to her solicitor in private? Surely that shouldn't happen. It didn't make sense. He was currently accusing Sabrina of domestic abuse against Lorenzo and arguing that she should not have contact with Junior due to her mental health. Sabrina clenched her hands tightly, her nails digging into her palms with each falsehood he uttered. She hastily jotted down a message for her solicitor.

"IT'S ALL LIES, IT'S NOT TRUE."

She handed it over to her solicitor, but it was all in vain. Sabrina was granted the opportunity to have contact, but it was specified that it must take place in a contact centre. She would have to arrange it all and pay for the privilege.

CHAPTER 25: Lies.

Sabrina departed from the courts with a sense of disappointment, as everything suddenly fell into place. Lorenzo had executed his role masterfully, now she regretted not reporting him to the authorities following their altercation. She had borne the marks of the violent encounter, her eyes bloodshot and her neck adorned with choking bruises. Bruises also marred her ribs and face. But she hadn't reported him, praying that he would change his mind and take her back. But instead, he had used her love for him, as a weapon and gaslighted her in the court room. She was dumfounded and confused, luckily Kira was on her way home today. She needed her friend now more than ever. Sabrina couldn't do this on her own. She experienced a profound sense of heartache. In three weeks', time, the next hearing was scheduled. She would need to locate a contact centre willing to handle her case, allowing her to reunite with her son. 'Three weeks, another three weeks.'

The words swirled in her mind as she made her way home at a slow pace.

But it wasn't three weeks, two months had already passed. She had missed countless milestones - the sweet scent of her baby, his comforting warmth, his contagious laughter, and his thick mane of hair. Every time she remembered him calling her "mama," she felt the weight of all that she had missed. Resentment was starting to overshadow the anguish and sorrow. The whole situation was baffling, how could he accuse her of domestic violence, when she wouldn't even harm a house spider. Lorenzo towered over her, his imposing figure seemingly swaying the courts in his favour. Why would her solicitor suddenly leave her to speak with the opposition? It was all so confusing and unexpected, she felt disoriented. It was turning into a never ending nightmare. In an instant, she found herself unjustly labelled as a wrongdoer, despite the complete absence of any truth to the accusations. The courts worked on finding of facts, but that was just it, there were no facts. The courts believed whomever they favoured on any given day. Sabrina was desperate to be believed and heard, but she quickly realised that family courts didn't care about the truth.

After another useless day in court, she eventually returned to her quiet home, anticipating Kira's imminent arrival. However, in the meantime, she found herself at a loss for how to occupy her time. Lorenzo's gaze pierced right through her, as if she were nothing more than a ghost in the courtroom.

The solicitor offered little consolation, informing her that the situation boiled down to a mere dispute of words, with the other party having the advantage of being the first to present their side of the story. As if that was meant to bring her any comfort. It didn't matter how many times Sabrina went into court, the outcome was always the same. She was the one accused of being abusive. She retreated to her room, shedding her court attire without a second thought, leaving them strewn across the floor. She swiftly donned her cosy fleecy pyjamas, seeking comfort and warmth. When she entered Kira's room, her purpose unclear as she made her way to the bathroom and cautiously opened Kira's medicine cupboard. There were multiple pots of medication, Sabrina carefully examined each one, studying the labels for a moment. Afterwards, she gazed at her reflection in the mirror and criticised herself. "Not today, not ever. Oh no you don't, missy. You are stronger than that."

After carefully returning the pots to their rightful place, she closed the cupboard with a sense of satisfaction. Descending the stairs, she indulged in the comforting ritual of brewing herself a cup of sweet tea. When Kira arrived home at around 8pm, she was immediately struck by Sabrina's distressed state. Her eyes were swollen and red, and streaks of mascara stained her face, evidence of the hours she had spent crying.

"So, what went down in court?" Kira asked. Sabrina proceeded to recount the entire story to Kira, leaving no detail unmentioned. "Well, I absolutely refuse to accept that." She casually strolled over to the fridge, a mischievous smile playing on her lips, as she reached for a bottle of chilled white wine. "I know what you need." Kira informed Sabrina, whilst holding up the wine. "Let's have a few strong drinks, blast some tunes, and get the party started! We can collaborate to minimise the potential harm tomorrow. But tonight, you're mine, okay?" Kira was adamant. "I'm not sure I should Kira, I don't feel like socializing at the moment." Sabrina interrupted. "Sabrina, you're a vibrant young woman, it should be well within your capabilities to summon the energy for a night out. I think we need a blow-out. Let's go out and enjoy ourselves, it will take your mind off things. I promise it will lift your spirits." Kira insisted. Sabrina stood up, swiftly snatched Kira's wine glass, and effortlessly finished its contents in a single gulp. "That's my girl." Kira said with a proud smile. The following day, the duo began their task of contacting the list of contact centres, assiduously making phone calls to inquire about availability. Sabrina was burdened with exorbitant prices, for a contact supervisor. She would have to endure constant surveillance while caring for her child. Sabrina and Kira were worn out from the countless rules and regulations, but they finally managed to find a place that was willing to accommodate supervised contact. The entire process left Sabrina with a chilling sensation, as if she were immersed in the mind of a notorious criminal. The fees she had to pay exceeded her weekly wages, she would have to rely on Kira's kindness once again. She hated feeling like such a burden. She had no means to cover her own meals, let alone contribute to the bills during the weeks she had contact. Kira had graciously offered to cover the expenses, but Sabrina had no desire to depend on Kira. She believed it would be unfair to her friend. Furthermore, she and Kira had reached the conclusion that Sabrina's solicitor was not advocating for her. They suspected that the solicitor, who was funded by the government, was colluding with Lorenzo's legal team, and that the outcome of the case had already been predetermined. Lorenzo hailed from a privileged background, with the means to acquire the finest things money can offer. In contrast, Sabrina found herself dependent on government assistance to cover her legal expenses. Without any money, they had quickly come to the realisation that her chances were slim. Sabrina had vehemently declined Kira's offer to cover the expenses of a legal team. "I must find a solution. My son's well-being is at stake, and I am determined to secure the services of a skilled solicitor." Sabrina stated.

"There is a way. Would you be happy to do it though, I'm not so sure. I know someone who happens to be the owner of a lap dancing club, in Bristol. If your happy to take a train, there and back. You have the body and the looks. I can't dance for toffee, but I've seen the way you move, you can dance. And don't forget you were really good at gymnastics at school. I've heard that his girls make a substantial amount of money. It's not in close proximity to where we live, so it's unlikely anyone would find out about it." Kira said.

"I'm flat chested though, Lorenzo would often comment and call them two fried eggs. I'm not sure if I would have the courage to do it." Sabrina said bitterly.

"Don't listen to him, he just liked putting you down. Your drop dead gorgeous and you can dance. I believe you have great potential, and once everything is resolved, you could always get a boob job. You are incredibly attractive, and I believe you would quickly gain a large clientele base." Kira exclaimed with enthusiasm.

"Do you honestly believe I can do it?" Sabrina couldn't help but interject, her laughter betraying her nerves. "I think you would greatly benefit from this opportunity, as it would enable you to cover your legal expenses and upgrade your legal representation. Have a think about it? I will be flying out again on Friday. Take your time to consider it, and in the meantime, let's explore other solicitors that may be more suitable. Then on Thursday, if you're interested, I can set up an audition for you." Kira stated with a smile. Thursday arrived swiftly, and the pair boarded the train to Bristol. Sabrina's nerves were palpable, yet she mustered the courage to face the daunting task ahead. Together with Kira, she had discovered a reputable solicitor's firm to handle her family court case, instilling a sense of optimism in Sabrina for what lay ahead. The new law firm came with a hefty price tag, but it enticed her with a multitude of promises, as long as she could cover the expenses. Kira offered to cover the initial substantial deposit, while Sabrina assured her that she would reimburse her in due time. Upon arriving in Bristol, they made their way to the taxi rank. "Are you ready for this, Sabrina? We can always return home if you've changed your mind." Kira chuckled, a smile playing on her lips, as she addressed her friend. "I am determined to bring Junior back home with me, no matter what it takes." Sabrina replied. Despite her inner turmoil, a newfound sense of purpose washed over her, filling her with hope that their plans would lead to a positive outcome. Kira had already been incredibly generous. Sabrina had to find a way to pay her back. She could never have imagined that she would find herself working as a lap dancer and pole dancer. However, desperate times called for desperate measures. She had to find a way to support her finances and cover her family court fees. Kira and Sabrina made their way to the clubs front door, nestled on the outskirts of town, concealed along a secluded back road, far from the curious gazes of the shoppers on the main streets. Kira pressed the bell, and was greeted by a slender, fair-haired girl who led her inside. Kira introduced Sabrina to Raz, the club owner. She recounted their chance encounter, during his visit to Dubai to spend time with his family. With his commanding presence and undeniable charisma, he effortlessly charmed those around him. Standing tall and possessing a sturdy build, he emanated an aura of power that was impossible to ignore.

"Welcome, ladies, to my humble club. Would you both care for a drink?" He inquired, his gaze sweeping over Sabrina. "Sure, I'm feeling a bit anxious," Sabrina confessed. Raz snapped his fingers, beckoning the tall blonde over. She promptly arrived, balancing a tray of drinks for the trio. "So, if you wouldn't mind, I'd love to hear a bit about yourself, Sabrina. I like to know everything about the girls I decide to employ. We function as a tight-knit community, so it's crucial to ensure that you align well with our values and dynamics. You definitely possess the qualities we need." He added with a smirk.

Kira interjected "She's my best friend, and I can wholeheartedly vouch for her. She really needs this job. And she is a really good dancer. She requires funds to cover the expenses of family court." Sabrina gazed at Kira with a deep sense of gratitude, her mind swirling with uncertainty over how to express her emotions. "Marcella, could you please do me a favour and give Sabrina a tour of the club. Then, guide her to the dressing room so she can select an outfit, then she can audition, so we can see if she has what it takes." The tall blonde girl obediently carried out his request, and Sabrina trailed behind her throughout the club, resembling a bewildered stray. The club exuded an air of elegance, with its abundance of mirrors and mesmerising neon lights. Within its walls, there were multiple podiums, each leading to a discreet corridor. Marcella revealed these were where the private lap dances took place. Music filled the club, enveloping the atmosphere as Sabrina gracefully took the stage. With fluid movements, she skillfully manoeuvred around the pole, showcasing her strength and flexibility. With arms extended and a body that glided effortlessly to the rhythm. With her flowing ebony hair cascading in the air, she twirled and contorted around the pole, exuding an aura of natural grace, and captivating the audience. Kira was fascinated by her every action, just as Raz was. Their eyes met, exchanging a knowing glance that spoke volumes of their shared victory. Sabrina seemed to be born for this, moving to the rhythm of the music. As she gracefully concluded her performance, she surprised everyone with a backflip off the pole, leaving the onlookers in awe. Even Marcella couldn't help but be quietly impressed. "Typically, I would request a lap dance from potential dancers, but I must admit, your moves are exceptional and more. You're hired.

Is it possible for you to start tomorrow evening?" Raz inquired, rising to enfold Sabrina in his arms.

"Yes, I can start tomorrow." Sabrina let out a joyful shriek, clearly pleased with herself.

"It seems that my dedication to gymnastic lessons during my younger years has finally paid off." Sabrina made a witty remark whilst a whistling Kira embraced her warmly.

"Well, I always had faith in your abilities." Kira said in a straightforward manner.

Before long, the pair embarked on their journey back to their residence in Bath. Sabrina was filled with a sense of optimism. She had taken to dancing on the stage like she had been born for it. Now she hoped that being a lap dancer was as lucrative as Kira said it would be. But she had no reason not to believe her friend, Kira had always been there for her.

CHAPTER 26: The club.

Sabrina's heart raced as she stepped into the club, her nerves tingling with a mix of fear and determination. She knew that this was a moment she couldn't back down from. With the burden of legal fees and the need to repay Kira looming over her, she found herself compelled to choose this, as her only viable solution for the time being. Marcella warmly greeted her, ensuring she felt at ease as she introduced her to the rest of the girls who were part of the club. The dressing room exuded a sense of belonging, as the girls prepared themselves for the eventful night that lay ahead. Sabrina embraced the warm camaraderie of the group, a tight-knit sisterhood eager to unravel the tapestry of her life. As they meticulously applied their makeup and styled their hair, each of them bombarded Sabrina with a flurry of questions. "Girls... girls, please leave Sabrina alone. Frankly, dealing with all of you feels like being interrogated by the Spanish Inquisition." Marcella projected her voice, ensuring that her words reached the ears of everyone present, and playfully winked at Sabrina. "I don't mind." Sabrina insisted. "It will take my mind off my nerves." A tall, mysterious woman, set a perfectly poured glass of Brandy on Sabrina's elegant dressing table.

"Bottoms Up." She nodded to Sabrina. "This will calm your nerves, considering the glowing reviews Marcella has given about your ability to impress the customers, you really don't have anything to worry about." Sabrina's first night was truly remarkable. She had managed to earn a little over a hundred pounds, and although one might expect her to be exhausted, she was instead filled with a thrilling surge of adrenaline and boundless hope. She was making such rapid progress that she could easily settle all her debts in a matter of months. It was a rare occurrence for her to finally experience the feeling of relief. The heavy burden that had been haunting her, was now dissipating. Her mind was no longer consumed by darkness, instead, she had found a glimmer of hope at the end of the tunnel. At last, she discovered a sense of direction, filling her with newfound hope, after a prolonged period of uncertainty. She gathered her belongings while Ginny, one of the other girls, stood beside her.

"We're heading to the New Yorker. It's a place where a friend of ours, opens up just for us in the morning. Would you like to join us? It's become our regular haunt, after a long night." Ginny inquired. "Dancing is hungry work. I'm famished. A full English would go down a treat right now." Sabrina replied.

'Oh, we all need sustenance, my darling, every morning after we've finished. It's all the calories we've burned off during the night," Ginny exclaimed, her laughter bubbling up. As Marcella and the group approached the door of the New Yorker, they were met by a robust gentleman, who had a friendly expression and an unconventional way of welcoming them all. He took a bow as if greeting royalty. Then he kissed each of the women's hands, as each stepped over the threshold, like a true gentleman. He then invited the women inside and guided them to their usual table. "Who is this new girl?" he asked, gently taking hold of Sabrina's hand and bestowing on it a kiss, reminiscent of a chivalrous gentleman greeting a lady. Sabrina introduced herself with a warm smile, to the owner. Seated at the table, Ginny, always the curious one, inquired, "So, what's your story? We all have our own reasons for doing the job we do." Sabrina fell into a momentary silence before responding, weaving her tale from her university days to the present. The girls were captivated, hanging on every word. Zara, the most reserved member of the group, whispered softly after Sabrina had concluded her heartfelt account of her life and the challenges she faced.

"It seems we're in the same boat. I'm also dealing with family court proceedings. My former partner is currently serving time for assaulting me. He's attempting to force me to bring our four children to prison, so they can visit him." Zara spoke with sincerity, her voice tinged with a hint of nervousness. Sabrina's horror was palpable as she questioned, "How can it be justified if he's in prison for hurting you? Why are the courts allowing this?"

Ginny interjected, "Oh, my dear, you have so much to learn about life. I experienced a deeply traumatic event when I was raped by a stranger, resulting in the birth of my child. Unfortunately, the British court system has forced me to allow visitation between my son and his rapist father."

"But you were sexually assaulted, by a complete stranger," Sabrina echoed Ginny's words, her voice filled with utter disbelief. "That's the British justice system for you. There is no justice!"

Marcella interrupted. "When I was a child, I endured the unimaginable pain of being exploited by men. My father, a vicar, callously sold me to the highest bidder. I shared my concerns with the school and a social worker, my words fell on deaf ears. Nobody believed me, nobody listened. At the tender age of fourteen, I ran away, I was a street kid. For many years the streets became my home, it was cold miserable and dangerous. Once I became old enough to work in a club, dance emerged as my saviour, rescuing me from the depths of despair." As breakfast was served, one by one, each girl began to reveal the events that had brought them to the club. Among the group of women, there was a notable exception. Kara, hailing from a privileged background, stood apart from the others with her absence of a tragic past. However, her father had entered into a new marriage with a woman significantly younger than him, and Kara found herself unable to tolerate her. As a result, she presented her father with a difficult choice, either his new partner or his own daughter. Regrettably, Kara was defeated. Her father abruptly severed all ties with her, leaving her in a state of silence and without a trust fund. He had totally cut her out of his life and his will. Rumour had it that he had relocated to Spain, accompanied by his new spouse, but beyond that, she remained in the dark about his life.

Sabrina found herself aboard the train, heading home after breakfast with her work colleagues. Engrossed in her own musings, she gazed out of the window, pondering the sad situations she had been told about in the morning. She was terrified by the stories she had heard. A faint whisper echoed within her, hinting at the futility of trying to reclaim Junior. However, she quickly dismissed it, pushing it deep into the corners of her mind. The eerie stories she heard over breakfast had consumed her once optimistic perspective, with uncertainty. With no power to influence the situation, she could only cling to the hope that justice would prevail. She fixated on the bright spots in her life. Kira had been a life saver. And now her recent employment would enable her to cover the expenses of her legal team. In that very instant, it became the only thing that captured her undivided focus. Given the limited resources available to her, she could only maintain a glimmer of hope that the family courts were not as plagued by corruption as they were rumoured to be. Today she needed to be bright and optimistic in front of her solicitors. The meeting was set for the afternoon, giving her the opportunity to savour a precious few hours of rest beforehand. Following the appointment, she would need to head back to the club. Kira found herself back at home during her break, feeling a sense of relief now that Sabrina was also contributing financially. She had even accompanied the girls at Sabrina's workplace for breakfast on a few occasions. Kira remained unfazed by their stories, unlike Sabrina. Kira had chosen not to disclose the true motive behind her decision to leave university to Sabrina. After experiencing the assault, she had come to a profound realisation about the inherent corruption in the system, prompting her to distance herself from it entirely. The handbook she received at University for Social Work was riddled with inconsistencies, leaving Kira with a sense that the entire system was unfairly manipulated. She had initially envisioned herself as a social worker, driven by her desire to make a difference in the lives of vulnerable children. As she delved deeper into her research, a sense of dread washed over her. The knowledge she acquired revealed a disturbing truth - it was clear that the intentions behind these actions were far from benevolent, especially when it came to the well-being of humanity and, most importantly, the children. It appeared that splitting families apart was deemed more financially efficient than keeping them together, and Kira strongly disliked the establishment, of the Neuro Linguistics Programming hub by the University. Kira possessed a unique ability to perceive beyond the surface of conventional teachings. It didn't take long for her to discern that this path was not aligned with her true aspirations in life. Kira had been captured by her own naivety, her heart yearning to become a social worker. She thought she would be making a difference in the world. But once she came to the realisation that pursuing her chosen career would require compromising her morals and values, she made the difficult decision to not continue with her degree. Though this led to a state of confusion, with no alternative course of action. She had never dreamed of doing anything else. Kira had kept it all concealed from Sabrina, not intentionally, but because during that period Sabrina was so engrossed with Lorenzo that Kira never found the right moment to confide in her friend. Now though, listening to Sabrina and her morning with the girls, she felt a pang of guilt. Maybe she should have warned her, but seeing the glimmer of hope in

Sabrina's eyes, she didn't want to darken it with the undeniable truths she had learned.

CHAPTER 27: Systems and Bias.

Sabrina had attended court on multiple occasions before she was finally granted a date to visit Junior at the Contact Centre. She felt a deep sense of frustration and couldn't comprehend why the legal process was dragging its feet in granting her the contact she desired. Sabrina and Kira had been diligent in sorting out a centre, but then the dates and schedule had to be agreed in court. Despite the necessary time slots in place at the contact centres, her desperation to see her child was palpable. At long last, the day she had been waiting for, had arrived. The Contact centre had made a special request for her to enter through a side door, ensuring that she and Lorenzo would not cross paths at the centre. She had purchased a teddy bear and an alphabet bus for Junior. Her nerves were on edge, as she anxiously awaited Junior's arrival in their allocated private room. The contact support worker sat poised in the room, notepad, and pen at the ready, diligently jotting down notes, despite Junior's absence. Finally, the much-anticipated moment had arrived when a staff member brought Junior in to see her. Tears welled up in Sabrina's eyes, overwhelming her with emotion. "Oh My God, you're so big now Junior," she said with a smile, amidst her tears of happiness. In a heartbeat the tears of happiness turned to tears of heartbreak. Junior, failed to recognise her. He let out piercing screams that echoed throughout the building, and despite Sabrina's best efforts to comfort him, her attempts proved futile. Junior's screams reached a crescendo, getting higher pitched and uncontrollable, causing Sabrina to break down in heart-wrenching sobs. He pushed her away, refusing to let her come near him. The child was clearly traumatised, and Junior seemed to have no memory of Sabrina being his mother. The support worker in the corner continued to jot down her observations, meticulously documenting every aspect of the room. Sabrina grew increasingly agitated, and her son followed suit, unleashing a torrent of screams that forced the contact session to be abruptly halted by the contact support worker. Sabrina's face was drenched with tears and her eyes were swollen with frustration and the injustice of it all as the member of staff led

Junior away. Sabrina hurriedly placed the presents for Junior in her arms, before dashing out to catch up with him. However, her path was blocked by the contact worker, who had previously been taking notes. Sabrina collapsed onto the floor, overcome with emotion. Shortly thereafter, she was guided out of the establishment by another staff member, who refused to pass the gifts on. She strolled home in a daze, utterly baffled by Junior's unexplained behaviour. Her heart shattered into a million pieces. She was overwhelmed with a sense of despair, as if all hope had been extinguished. Her baby no longer recognised her. It was a shocking turn of events, one that she never could have anticipated, not even in her worst nightmares. Her mind was in a state of disarray, overwhelmed by a torrent of emotions she couldn't find solace in. Kira swung open the door to their shared house, to greet Sabrina. In that moment, the weight of Sabrina's vulnerability washed over her, as she collapsed into Kira's arms. "Oh, my goodness, what happened?" Kira inquired while embracing her cherished companion, as though she were there to support her in case she stumbled.

"Junior, it's Junior. He didn't recognise me, all he did was scream the place down," Sabrina said, as her heart felt like it had been stabbed a thousand times. "He was so scared of me, he was terrified. I should never have left him. If only I had chosen to remain by Lorenzo's side, this whole situation would have been avoided. I should never have left. I am a complete stranger to my own baby, he didn't know me. He wouldn't let me near him." Sabrina muttered, her words tumbling out in a rush, as she struggled to catch her breath. Kira led Sabrina to the sofa in the lounge, gently helping her settle down. She then went to prepare a comforting cup of sweet tea for both of them, to help ease the shock. Kira couldn't shake the uneasy feeling that settled in her gut. Sabrina might not have the strength to get through this. She was all too familiar with Sabrina's emotional state, so she knew it was time to reach out to Raz. Sabrina definitely needed a few days off. Fortunately, Raz proved to be a loyal friend, from the moment he crossed paths with Kira. Their connection was truly special, and Raz had always held a deep affection for her. Kira knew Raz would understand, he actually cared about the women that worked for him, which was unusual in their line of work. It was one of the reasons Kira liked him so much.

"I'm not sure if I can subject Junior to this again. I can't believe this," Sabrina said, her voice trembling as tears welled up in her eyes. "My boy was so scared of me, his mother. I don't understand. Why on earth would he be like this?" Kira gazed at her friend and spoke with a soothing tone, "He's just a baby, in an unfamiliar place, and it's been almost four months since he last saw you. He just doesn't understand. But you can't give up on him, Sabrina."

"I know, I'm just thinking out loud, he was so scared and confused. It broke me. It shattered my soul. As for that woman jotting down the notes, she was absolutely horrible. She just watched it all unfold. She didn't help, she didn't care that Junior was screaming. It was like she was just there to be juror and judge. The lack of encouragement was palpable, making the notion of a supportive worker seem like a cruel joke." Sabrina delicately blew over the surface of her tea, a gentle breeze meant to cool the steaming liquid. Meanwhile, a subtle shake of her head conveyed her disapproval. "I never told you, but now I must be honest with you. The system is against parents and keeping the family unit together. I quickly realised during my time at university, that many of these so called professionals were biased and they would do anything to reach the quotas set by their departments. They would remove children with fraudulent reports to feed the system. Councils get quota bonuses from central government. It's an industry, working within the system, that is supposed to protect and look after the vulnerable. Frequently, their notes are brimming with prejudice." Kira spoke with complete honesty. "Is that the reason you decided to leave university? Is it because everything seems to be stacked against the parents?" The words slipped from Sabrina's lips, yet she found herself dreading the forthcoming answers. "Yes, that and other reasons." Kira mused as she looked out the window hoping the subject would shift slightly. The last thing Sabrina needed to hear right now, was that the whole system was stacked against her. A number of months had passed, and the matter that was being heard in family court had been going on for what seemed like an eternity. With the intention of portraying Sabrina as a careless mother, Lorenzo had hurled as much dirt as he could at her. Additionally, the contact support worker had written down complete and utter lies, regarding the contact sessions that Sabrina had attended. In spite of the fact that Sabrina had spent a significant amount of money on her legal team, the situation was deplorable, the odds seemed stacked against her. There had been an increase of contact over the course of time, and Junior had taken some time, but gradually he remembered her. The moment he called Sabrina mama, at the contact centre for the very first time, her heart had exploded. Sabrina dared to hope that everything would turn out in her favour, and that she would be able to take Junior home, one day soon. Whilst she was waiting to be summoned into court, she was sitting in a private room, and Kira was sitting right next to her, holding her hand. This was supposed to be decision time, the last court hearing, where the Judge would decide where Junior would live and how to proceed with custody and contact. Kira was not permitted to enter the courtroom, she would have to wait outside for the verdict to be announced. She was sitting in the waiting room when Sabrina was brought into the Court room, by her legal team. She was holding both hands up in the air with her fingers crossed, as Sabrina disappeared through the court room doors. 'Please God, please give Sabrina her baby back,' was all she could think silently.

As the minutes went into hours, Kira sat outside the door to the courtroom and watched the clock tick over and over with each passing second. In spite of her anxieties, she managed to maintain her cool and squeezed her hands together. With regard to their residence, the Cafcass officer had penned a report that was favourable to Sabrina and was of some quality. The social worker, on the other hand, had an entirely different report in favour of Lorenzo. Despite knowing that the social worker had bias towards Lorenzo, Sabrina and Kira had tried to win him over, but he continued to find fault in their accommodation and lifestyles where there was none. At precisely the moment that Kira's thoughts were racing through her head, she became aware of the most dreadful scream coming from beyond the door of the court room. After that, there was a swarm of individuals who emerged from the courtroom, and Sabrina's attorney was helping to hold her up. The mascara on Sabrina's face had run, she looked dishevelled with her hair plastered to her face. She appeared to have aged ten years in a couple of hours. Sabrina was inconsolable. In order for Kira to accompany Sabrina's solicitor to their private room, she had to be invited to do so. She sat Sabrina down, and as she did so, Sabrina let out a series of gut-wrenching howls that would make even the most resolute of hearts melt. The barrister glanced at Kira and proceeded to convey the sad situation in its entirety. Sabrina's activities at night, at the lap dance club were documented by a private investigator that Lorenzo had hired. And because Sabrina had connections with the club owner, who was a well-known face to the police, as well as the fact that she had lied to the courts and social services about her money and job. The fact that she was a lap dancer, all of these things worked against her in court. She had lost custody of Junior, she was never permitted to see him again. Junior was to be taken back to Italy, to be raised at the family vineyard, and Lorenzo had been given complete freedom to do so. " Sabrina found herself reluctantly resorting to lap dancing as a means to cover her mounting legal expenses." Kira let out in a high-pitched exasperation. "I regret to inform you that there is nothing more I can do. I would have appreciated it if you had informed us of your activities. But you lied. I must take my leave." The solicitor declared, gathering her belongings, and departing, leaving the two women alone in the room. Shortly after, a security guard swiftly appeared to escort the two women out of the court building. Treating them as if they were seasoned criminals. He possessed a robust physique, with a scar adorning one side of his face, yet his words exuded a gentle demeanour. "I apologise ladies, but I must insist that you vacate the premises as per instructions." He spoke with a hint of timidity, his eyes betraying a touch of melancholy.

"Can't this wait, until we are ready?" Kira inquired, her impatience evident in her tone.

'I'm sorry, but I'm afraid not miss, orders are orders." The security guard said, whilst appearing shamefaced. "Just doing my job! Right? Now where have I heard that one before?" Kira responded with venom. Guided by Kira's gentle touch, Sabrina was consumed by the grief that only a mother bereft of her child could feel. They were led out of the private room. As they passed through the waiting room, it was filled with sympathetic gazes. They descended the stairs and emerged through the main doors into the cold unforgiving crisp air. Without hesitation, Sabrina succumbed to nausea and vomited uncontrollably.

She was rendered speechless, her breath caught in her throat, overwhelmed by the unbearable pain. At that very instant, she sensed the end of her existence. She longed to be reunited with her mama in heaven, more than anything she had ever desired before. In death, the pain would cease, and peaceful nothingness would embrace her. She couldn't bear to continue, for how could she go on, without her beautiful boy, that once illuminated her world.

Her heart fragmented into thousands of tiny pieces, as her precious baby boy was cruelly torn from her embrace, leaving a void that seemed unbearable to endure. She felt her life was over, all she wanted to do was die, how on earth could she go on. Life was so cruel, she had carried him, spoken to him when he was in her tummy, she had sung to him every night. He was her world, her life. How could it all go so horribly wrong, what had she done to deserve losing her baby, her light, her life. It was all such a mess, such a blur, every inch of her being wanted to scream at the injustice of it all.

CHAPTER 28: Family.

Days had passed since Sabrina was brought home by Kira, and she had not ventured beyond the confines of her bedroom. She found herself unable to confront the outside world, yearning for the earth to devour her. If Kira hadn't been home, she would have gone without food or a drink. The pain became unbearable for Sabrina. Kira, with her caring nature, insisted that Sabrina eat soup, and drink water to stay hydrated. Sabrina's heart longed to be reunited with her mama in heaven. She had lost all desire to continue living. Kira's growing concern stemmed from her upcoming flight, as she had already taken a few days off on compassionate leave. Kira doubted she would be granted any extra time off. She was unsure of how to proceed. Sabrina couldn't be left alone, not in this state. Kira had provided Raz with daily updates on Sabrina, ensuring he was informed of her continued absence from the club. Raz was as understanding as ever, and reassured Kira that Sabrina's job at the club would still be waiting for her whenever she was ready. On a Friday morning, Kira was in the midst of brewing a pot of tea when the sound of the doorbell interrupted her erratic thoughts. She opened the door, and to her astonishment, she found herself face to face with all the girls from the strip club. After their nightshift, they had all decided to head to their house in Bath for a visit. They were all concerned about Sabrina. Kira's heart swelled with joy and gratitude as she welcomed them into her home. A single tear of relief escaped her, with the immense emotions that flooded her, at their arrival. Every member of the Gentleman's club's staff made an appearance, including the dedicated bar staff and Raz. Kira pressed her lips against Raz's, expressing her gratitude with a tender kiss.

"I am so glad you are all here, Sabrina won't leave her bedroom. She barely eats, she won't talk, she just spends most of her time sleeping or crying. I'm at a loss as to what to do." Kira Informed them. Marcella and the girls excitedly raised their bottles of Champagne, eagerly requesting for glasses to be brought upstairs. Whilst Raz and the doormen settled into the plush lounge chairs. Kira gestured towards the kettle and the bar, inviting the men to serve themselves. With a graceful stride, she gathered a multitude of glasses, carefully cradling them in her hands. As she ascended the staircase to follow the other women, her elegant white dressing gown flowed behind her like a trail of silk. Kira's heart raced as she hurried to Sabrina's bedroom, her breath catching in her throat. To her utter surprise, the sound of laughter filled the air - was that Sabrina laughing? The girls gathered around her bed, some perched on the bed itself while others settled on the floor. Sabrina was accompanied by Ginny and Marcella, she was sat upright in bed. It was the perfect remedy for her, as she smiled weakly. Kira distributed glasses to everyone in the room, while one of the other girls skillfully opened the Champagne and poured it into the elegant retrospective glasses. Marcella was regaling the room with her tale of last night's adventure, where a group of office women had entered the club. Then they had proceeded to pay all the girls for private dances. The behaviour of the office women was truly appalling, surpassing even that of the men. They would rudely grab the dancers and viciously dig their nails into them. One of the girls, Katie, bravely revealed the scars she had acquired from this ongoing battle. "Look," she exclaimed, revealing the three perfectly aligned scratches on her buttock. "Those women were absolutely scandalous. We were left with no choice but to have them forcibly escorted out of the club, due to their blatant disregard for the rules." Katie remarked as she adjusted her trousers back up to her waistline. "The security staff, Sabrina, honestly you should have seen their faces. One of the ladies even playfully grabbed Nige's ass, as he escorted them out of the club. Now he has matching scratches just like Katie's. Do you want me to ask him to come upstairs to show you?" Marcella inquired, with a mischievous chuckle.

"Oh, my goodness, absolutely not! I have no desire to see anyone's hairy ass in my bedroom at this early hour." Sabrina quipped, her voice carrying a touch of elevation. Laughter bounced through the entire room, echoing off the walls. Ginny abruptly halted their mirth, "Seriously girl, you can't let these bastards grind you down. Once the courts are involved there is literally nothing you can do. They have the law on their side. As disgusting as it is, we have no control over our lives once they are involved." The room sobered up pretty quickly. Then Kira spoke. "You need a completely new life. You need to lock all this away and do everything in your power to stop this ever happening to you again."

A hush descended on the room once again. "Oh, that's a piece of cake." Sabrina murmured. "I have decided not to have another child, and to never depend on a man again. I will never trust another man again, not after this." All the women in the room raised their glasses and gently tapped them together. "Never again," they all exclaimed in unison, their glasses clinking together. All the members of the club lingered until dusk, bidding farewell to the day before embarking on their return to Bristol. A few of the women chose to remain with Sabrina, since they were not scheduled to work that evening. They had unanimously decided that those who were able, would remain with Sabrina for the next two weeks until Kira returned from her travels. Raz's incredible efforts resulted in a seamless rearrangement of the girls' shifts to accommodate the necessary changes. As the sun began to set on Sunday evening, Kira reluctantly prepared to depart for work, while Ginny made plans to spend the following day and evening with Sabrina. Two weeks had passed since the group of women from the gent's club had gathered together to assist Sabrina in her journey out of the depths of despair. Sabrina felt an overwhelming sense of gratitude. These women had become like family, and they had even managed to bring laughter back into her life, a joy she believed was lost forever. Within her, a lingering emptiness persisted, yet she found solace in the company of the women who had rescued her from the edge. Through their patient guidance, she gradually rediscovered the art of embracing life once more. Every action was deliberate and purposeful. She began with a refreshing shower, taking her time to cleanse and rejuvenate. Next, she carefully selected her outfit, ensuring that every detail was just right. Finally, she savoured a satisfying meal, savouring each bite and appreciating the nourishment it provided. One step at a time, one action at a time, she gradually emerged from the depths of her profound state of despair. Today, she headed to the club, eager to immerse herself in the vibrant atmosphere of the dressing room, where she would be surrounded by the diverse group of women, she now called family. As she gazed at her reflection in the mirror, a profound realisation washed over her. The passage of time had left its mark, transforming her from a youthful girl into a mature woman. Her eyes bore faint traces of fatigue, yet skillfully concealed beneath a layer of makeup. Despite the weight of her past hardships, the reflection staring back at her possessed an undeniable allure. Ginny and Marcella were the primary duo, who had brought her back to life by engaging in endless conversations with her.

Their discussions would stretch on for hours, occasionally lasting well into the night.

The reflection of the woman who now stood before her, exuded an aura of resilience, her anger towards the world evident, and her demeanour as tough as nails. She was determined to protect what was rightfully hers, and no man would ever be able to take it away from her. Never again would she allow herself to be deceived by false promises. Now, a deep and intense loathing consumed her whenever she thought of Lorenzo and those of his kind. If men dared to treat her as Lorenzo had, she would ensure they paid dearly for the audacity. From now on, she would dictate the terms, and the terms would be hers alone. The woman in the mirror exuded an undeniable strength, radiating from within. She exuded an air of mystery, no longer the innocent girl she once was. Reality had stripped away her idealistic illusions, revealing the true nature of the world. It was a ruthless world, and she was determined to never be a victim again.

CHAPTER 29: The Business.

Ginny and Sabrina arrived at the bustling club in Bristol. The music filled the air, drowning out all other sounds, while the diligent staff busied themselves with preparations for the upcoming evening. Raz warmly welcomed the two women who were employed under him, as they arrived at the entrance. He graciously escorted Sabrina to his table, where they settled in, as the attentive bar staff promptly uncorked a bottle of fine Scotch for them. Raz was resolute in his mission to guide Sabrina back on the right path. Back to his ranks, back to the family fold. She was invaluable to his club, and he urgently sought to have her back on the dance floor. He had a genuine fondness for Sabrina, recognising her as a remarkable individual who stood out from the rest of his employees. One of the reasons he was drawn to her friend Kira was her innocence, which stood in stark contrast to the women he usually surrounded himself with. He encountered Kira during one of his business trips to the Middle East. Her red curls and green eyes stood out among his circles, capturing his attention. During his time there, they developed a close bond. Although she was new to her profession as a flight attendant, Kira had a charming personality that captivated men. Sabrina remained oblivious to the true extent of Kira's extracurricular pursuits, while Raz pondered the possibility of enlisting Sabrina into their ranks. The conversation was filled with laughter as Sabrina and Raz enjoyed a quarter of the bottle of Raz's exquisite twenty-five-year-old scotch. Sabrina was slightly intoxicated, and Raz saw this as the perfect opportunity to make a move.

"So, Sabrina, what is it that you desire in life?"

"Well, what I want and what I can have are two different things. My life as I knew it is over, so now I must find a different path." Sabrina replied, venturing deeper into her thoughts. After savouring the last drop of her scotch, a fiery sensation coursed through her throat, while she valiantly fought against the tears welling up in her eyes.

"Do you have an interest in exploring new places and experiences, perhaps escaping from your current surroundings? Perhaps a new beginning?"

Sabrina gazed at Raz with a look of awe, as if he had just come up with the most brilliant idea imaginable. "But how, how could I do that ?" Sabrina asked. Raz casually swirled his drink in his tumbler, contemplating the most tactful approach to bring up the topic. "Have you ever considered joining Kira in her career as an airline hostess?" Raz reclined in his seat, a mischievous smile playing on his lips, as Sabrina responded. "I'm not quite sure where to begin, but it's definitely an intriguing concept. Why are you attempting to get rid of me?" Sabrina responded with a hint of confusion. "Oh no my dear, Kira actually does business for me when she's over there. I thought it would be wonderful if you joined her. Think about it, okay." Razz beamed with satisfaction, confident that Kira would handle the rest of the explanation. In the darkness of the club, Sabrina made her way to the changing rooms, where she joined the company of the other women for the evening. Each of them had the opportunity to sit and enjoy a drink with her. At approximately 2am, Sabrina made a firm decision to act, realising that waiting any longer was futile. She was here, she was finally here, back where she belonged, back where she was with family, so why not make some money. The combination of the vibrant ambiance of the club, and the potent beverage she had indulged in, had completely engulfed her senses. With a sense of urgency, she realised the time had come to escape from her troubles. Determined to return to her former self, she gracefully adorned herself at her dressing table and ventured into the vibrant club scene. There, she unleashed her passion for dance, not only as an emotional outlet, but also as a means to earn a living. Her life had been completely transformed, but this place and the people in it, had been her unwavering support, guiding her through every step of the way. She had this, this place, these people, it was like a second home to her if nothing else. When Kira came back, she discovered a house that was completely silent. Her worry vanished as she caught sight of Katie lounging on the couch. In spite of her initial hesitation, she found herself able to leave Sabrina in her fragile condition, thanks to Razz and the girls at the club. She would be forever grateful. The reassuring notion that the club girls would be there for Sabrina, in her absence eased her worries. Katie awoke with a gentle stirring, stretching her limbs out like a cat that had just stirred from its slumber, as she slowly blinked open her eyes.

"Hey stranger." She lazily purred.

"Hey Katie, how's Sabrina doing?" Kira asked as she placed the kettle on the stove.

"Her progress is amazing. Last night, she went to the club, and she danced her socks off. She spoke with Raz beforehand, I am not sure what he said, but whatever it was, it worked." Katie released a weary yawn. "Wow, that is absolutely incredible!" Kira declared.

'It appears that Razz has managed to persuade her to join you on your exciting escapades." Katie nonchalantly commented as she lifted herself off the couch. Kira seemed surprised, as she finished the task of making three cups of tea, her movements accompanied by a peaceful silence. Her mind was consumed by a whirlwind of thoughts. 'But Sabrina doesn't really know that much about my other job, I've never really gone into great detail with her.' Kira thought to herself. Her expression tightened as she carefully placed a cup of tea in front of Katie on the coffee table. With a fluid motion, she gently lifted the last two cups of tea from the kitchen counter and made her way up the stairs towards Sabrina's room. With a wave of thoughts running through her mind, 'Has Raz told her, Oh God I hope he hasn't. Not the whole truth surely?' Kira knew they had discussed her job briefly before, but due to the state of mind Sabrina was in, she didn't think that Sabrina had heard a word of it. Kira softly tapped on Sabrina's bedroom door before entering with a poised demeanour, carrying two cups of tea, emitting steam. Sabrina stretched and sat up in bed, eagerly reaching out to grab her mug. "Thank you. I'm glad you're back home." Sabrina murmured, her eyes fixed on Kira with a tired gaze. "I heard you had quite the eventful evening." Kira said, as she gestured towards the door. Sabrina nodded her head in agreement. "Last night, I went to the club and experienced a sudden moment of clarity. I decided to dance and well, the rest is history." Sabrina boldly pressed on. "Razz mentioned to me that he believes I should accompany you in the mile high club." Sabrina let out a playful giggle.

"If you're insisting on it, I believe it would be prudent to have a proper chat about it first."

Sabrina expressed her agreement with a nod. "I'll freshen up and get ready to meet you downstairs in a little while," she said with a smile on her face, although it didn't quite reach her eyes, as she spoke. "Alright, I'll catch you down there." Kira said in passing, as she exited the bedroom and proceeded down the hall towards her own room, eager to change out of her uniform. Kira had descended the stairs ahead of Sabrina, poised to brew another cup of tea for everyone. However, before she could begin, Katie nonchalantly deposited her cup in the washbasin and declared "No need to fuss over me. Now that you're here, I'll be heading home." Kira expressed her gratitude to Katie for her companionship with Sabrina, wearing a warm smile on her face the friends hugged their farewells. Katie quietly exited the lounge, and Kira could hear the sound of the front door closing behind her. Kira busied herself in the kitchen, skillfully whipping up a batch of mouthwatering pancakes. Hunger gnawed at her insides, reminding her that she couldn't engage in conversation with Sabrina until her own stomach was satisfied. She felt a sense of trepidation as she prepared to reveal the truth to Sabrina. Despite knowing that Sabrina was non-judgmental, her nerves still got the best of her. With a sip of tea, she gracefully moved to the rhythm of the music, effortlessly pouring the pancake mix into the pan. As she sliced the fruit, Sabrina suddenly entered the room.

"What's the occasion?" Sabrina inquired, playfully snatching a chopped strawberry from the cutting board. "Sabrina, we must have a conversation. I'm delighted to hear that you're feeling better, but there's something I need to discuss with you. How about we discuss it over breakfast?" Kira gestured towards the table, inviting Sabrina to sit down. With care, she carried the plates of pancakes and fruit that she had prepared and settled herself across from Sabrina. Kira squirmed in her chair while she spoke. "The thing is all this time I haven't just been working as an air hostess. How do you think I can afford all this?" There fell a hush, and then Kira pressed on. "I... I..." she stammered, grappling for the right words. "I engage in escort work catering to the affluent and influential clientele in the Middle East. It's the means by which I can cover my expenses and acquire my precious jewellery collection. I receive compensation in the form of luxurious gifts, high-end clothing, designer shoes, designer handbags, and exquisite jewellery."

Sabrina couldn't help but burst into laughter. "Is that all it is? Honestly, for a moment, I thought you were about to confess to being a drug smuggler. You had already told me briefly, the day I got kicked out of Lorenzo's house. I know what you do. The thing is I need this. My life's been a train wreck for so long now and seeing how this has helped you become the independent woman you are. Is it wrong of me to want a slice of it too?" Sabrina queried.

Of all the reactions Kira had anticipated, this was the most unexpected. "You're serious, aren't you?" I was under the impression that you would despise me for it. I even thought you would no longer want to know me." Kira expressed a profound sense of relief on her face. Sabrina eagerly devoured a mouthful of pancake, unable to contain her amusement as she covered her mouth and let out another delightful giggle. "To be honest, I had a feeling that you were involved in something more substantial than just being a flight attendant. The pay isn't exactly lucrative. And you're well aware of the gossip that circulates among the girls at the club. I wasn't explicitly informed by Razz, but one tends to pick up on things. When you first told me, I thought it was a cover story, but then after hearing all the gossip at the club. I knew you were telling the truth." Sabrina concluded the discussion while savouring a delectable combination of blueberries and pancakes. Kira was taken aback, genuinely believing that Sabrina had no idea. "So, you've been aware of this all along?" she inquired, her eyebrow elegantly raised. "I heard from Katie that you might be considering joining me on my adventures. Is that true? You don't have to do the escorting. I can assist you in obtaining an application to become an air stewardess with my company. I can speak to my supervisor to see if we can be scheduled to work together. You really don't have to sell your body, like I do. It can be quite dangerous, it is illegal, out there. And the men over there have the upper hand. It's a country where women are classed as third rate citizens, and they hate the West. Sometimes I've had to do things that I don't want to, just to prevent a client from having me arrested. The money may be good, but it's really dangerous at times." Kira's worry for her friend was evident. Sabrina was bewildered, "Listen, Lorenzo had an abundance of wealth, far surpassing anything I have ever possessed, and he consistently outperformed me in every aspect. I've come to realise that without financial resources, one's ability to accomplish anything is severely limited. If I had money and he hadn't, I think I would have won custody. If I had money, perhaps I would have seen the red flags. If I were financially secure, I could liberate myself from the need to depend on others." She spoke with a hint of resentment. "You can always count on me, you know." Kira interjected seeing the sadness and the determination on her friends' face. "I just don't want you to go through some of the things, I have." Kira stated honestly.

"I know, but nothing can be as bad as I have already been through, and if I have to rent my body out to all and sundry to get some semblance of stability in my life, then that is what I will do." Sabrina insisted.

CHAPTER 30: A brave new world.

Sabrina found the training to be an air stewardess, surprisingly straightforward, although it was quite intensive. She had to wait a whole six long lonely weeks before she was finally given permission to take flight. She looked stunning in the uniform, and it was a whole new world for her to dive into. It was an odd sensation, being in uniform, people looked at her differently. Her previous life was now a distant memory. The uniform commanded respect from strangers and passengers alike. Occasionally, a wave of sadness would wash over her, but she found solace in Junior's blanket, which still carried his scent. She would cradle it close to her heart every night, finding it comforting, as tears streamed down her face. However, for the past six weeks, she had been unable to do so, as she had been sharing training quarters with other aspiring air stewardesses. It seemed the longer she was made to go without Juniors comforter, the less she had needed it. Sabrina and Kira strolled through the airport lounge on her inaugural day, she sensed numerous gazes as they fixated on her. The uniform she donned exuded an air of authority, instantly earning the respect of all the travellers. It filled her with a deep sense of pride. Her anticipation for her first journey to the Middle East was a delightful blend of excitement and nerves. Kira had strongly emphasised the importance of Sabrina familiarising herself with the Middle East, before embarking on her career in the escort industry. The cultural differences were as much of a shock to Sabrina as the customs and lifestyles. She found herself in a world that was unfamiliar, unlike anything she had ever known. Even though life was destined to improve from this point forward, the differences between the UK and the Middle East would take some getting used to. Despite their collaboration in the skies, Sabrina couldn't help but feel a sense of displacement as Kira frequently indulged in luxurious hotels and high-end shopping, leaving her behind. Sabrina longed for Kira, whenever she was absent. The Middle East was a profound cultural adjustment, as Kira had accurately predicted. Women were a rare sight on the streets, and Sabrina was instructed to remain within the confines of her resort during her lay-over. The food left much to be desired, and life felt quite solitary. While the other new girls provided a temporary escape from the sweltering, oppressive days spent confined in the compound, none of them compared to Kira. Sabrina experienced a profound sense of solitude and disorientation during her time in the Middle East. She was bored, she was lonely, and she was still fighting the sadness that had once engulfed her. The laws seemed unfamiliar and overly constricting to her, reinforcing the notion that without money, one was treated as a second-rate individual. After several months of traversing the globe, she couldn't help but yearn for the opportunity to accompany Kira on her thrilling adventures as an escort. It all seemed so glamorous to her. Each time she returned to England, her anticipation grew. Sabrina despised being confined to her cramped lodging during layovers. The accommodation was far from what she had envisioned. She experienced a sense of confinement, with guards stationed at the gates. She was informed that if she needed to leave, she would be required to wear a provided hijab. Sabrina's excursions beyond the compound were limited to essential errands, always under the watchful eye of her personal escort. Everything seemed surreal and incredibly restrictive. Kira had provided an explanation for the delay in allowing Sabrina to join her, she didn't want to put Sabrina in danger, emphasising the importance of her security and safety. But life seemed to be slipping away from her. Sabrina's only comfort was found in Junior's cherished blanket. She was desperate to persuade Kira, that she was ready for the escorting business. She couldn't face this loneliness and isolation a moment longer, she feared it would drive her insane. Sabrina missed the club and her friends, she had gone from one extreme to the other, and although the lay overs were only a day or two at a time, she felt like a prisoner. They were scheduled to fly home on Friday, she couldn't wait to go home and see her friends and sleep in her own bed once more. Sabrina had a sinking feeling that Kira was purposefully prolonging the unavoidable, leaving her perplexed and uncertain. She wasn't sure why, but Kira made excuses every time they went home, this time though Sabrina wouldn't hear of it. She'd had enough. The two friends returned home after yet another exhausting flight. Completely drained, they each took a refreshing shower before retiring to bed for a few hours of much-needed sleep. As Kira opened her eyes, she was greeted by a bustling kitchen, filled with the aroma of freshly brewed coffee. The enticing scent roused her from her sleep, leaving her feeling ravenous and craving a strong cup of black coffee. As she entered the kitchen, a wave of surprise washed over her when she saw Sabrina, fully dressed and skillfully preparing a hearty English breakfast. "Why are you spoiling me?" Kira said, her smile lazy and relaxed.

'I know how hard you work so I thought you deserved a treat. I was also kind of hoping we could discuss the possibility of me joining you in the business. It's so lonely over there, I hate it, I truly do. I feel like a prisoner when I'm there, and to top it off, I miss you." Sabrina finished serving up the breakfast, as she casually took a bite of her toast. Kira gazed at her with curiosity, "I had a feeling, that might be the case. Are you ready do you think, honestly Sabrina?"

"Initially, you will collaborate with me, but once you become accustomed to the process, you may be required to work independently with a client. Do you think you can do that?" Kira inquired, her eyebrow raised. "I am more than ready. Anything would be an improvement, compared to the cramped living quarters they provide us with during our time there. I can't bear the monotony of staring at the same four walls every single day." Sabrina spoke with complete sincerity. "Well, it seems like our next step is to pay a visit to Raz, he takes care of organising the lists for us ladies. He will coordinate our schedules so that we can spend the first few weeks together. How does that sound?" Kira inquired.

"It sounds amazing, although I'll admit I might feel a bit anxious. However, my experience with Lorenzo has taught me the power of financial influence. Men possess it, and I yearn for it." Sabrina let out a nervous giggle.

"Honestly, I'm curious to know how you're managing Sabrina. I understand that we don't have the opportunity to have conversations while we're at work. I miss our chats and I do worry about you." Kira expressed her worry for her friend.

"I long to hold my boy again. Every time I see a child it breaks my heart all over again. I still have his comforter blanket, and its scent remains a poignant reminder of him. Truth be told, when I find myself alone in that place, I cry myself to sleep. I must admit, it has been a rather solitary existence. Being confined within the same four walls has proven to be quite challenging. Now my sole opportunity lies in securing a prosperous future and ensuring that no individual can ever shatter the fabric of my existence ever again." Sabrina's lips curved into a bittersweet smile, and in that moment, her appetite vanished.

She absentmindedly toyed with the food on her plate, lost in her thoughts. "I apologise if I unintentionally caused you distress, I just really didn't want you tainted, by doing this business. You're my best friend, I was being selfish. I see that now. But a certain stigma comes with this work, and I guess I was hoping you would change your mind. It's a vicious cycle, once you start there's no going back." Kira murmured softly, rising from her seat and gently enveloping Sabrina in a comforting hug. The same day, the two friends ventured to the club where Sabrina had previously been employed, eager to have a meeting with Raz. They received a warm welcome from the entire staff, as Razz escorted them to his office. Where the three of them engaged in lively conversation and enjoyed a few drinks. "So, ladies, what brings you here? Not that I have any objections to a delightful visit from two of my most favourite ladies." Razz remarked, with his torso extending upwards whilst sinking comfortably into the plush leather armchair. "Sabrina believes she is ready to take on clients, but I believe it would be best for us to be like a tag team, work the clients together." Kira informed him, while Sabrina remained silent, fixated on her drink. Raz observed each girl intently before producing a file. As he sifted through the papers, he assured them, "I believe I can make the necessary arrangements for both of you. Please return tomorrow, and I will have your appointments organised. Is that agreeable?" Kira and Sabrina expressed their gratitude with a nod.

"I will say one thing though, girls, please exercise caution. Some of these clients are new, and I cannot speak for their moral character."

Kira gazed at Razz with a curious expression, "I am always cautious, as you are well aware." After savouring their drinks, the two girls headed towards the club's changing rooms to meet up with their friends. On the following day, the friends collected their schedules from the club. They were set to depart on Monday and had rigorously planned their layovers to meet clients as a team. Sabrina felt a mixture of nerves and determination. She had a debt to repay to Kira, and she was dead set on not wishing to disappoint her. Kira, on the other hand, had made numerous attempts to dissuade her from pursuing the escort business, fully aware of the immense risks involved. Her affection for Sabrina was undeniable. But try as she might, Sabrina had pleaded with her to emulate Kira's path. No matter what Kira said, Sabrina remained resolute. She wasn't going to change her mind. Sabrina had been stripped of everything she held dear, thanks to the family courts. With nothing left to lose, would engaging in the world's oldest profession make any difference? She had already been denied any involvement in her son's life. So, what did it matter, nothing really mattered anymore. So, why should it matter what she did with her own body? Sabrina understood the power of wealth and the generous compensation she would receive for providing companionship to men during their travels. She was well aware that her payment would come in the form of valuable goods, which would later be sold on to make a profit. It was an opportunity to start building up her savings for a comfortable future. Money became a pressing matter, with an urgency she couldn't ignore. Should she ever have another child, she would take every precaution to ensure that no one could rip them away from her ever again. It was way in the future, so meanwhile she should refrain from entertaining such thoughts. It felt like the pain was unbearable, it hurt so much. Grieving for a child that was still alive somewhere in the world, had a weird effect on one's psyche. Accustomed to a life of luxury, acquiring nice things became her temporary means of satisfaction. Sabrina was determined to reclaim her independence, willing to go to any lengths necessary. It was that simple really.

Sabrina and Kira found themselves on a layover, Sabrina decided to accompany Kira to her apartment in the Middle East. It was a completely different world compared to the compound where Sabrina and the other new air hostesses were required to stay. There were no armed guards, although Kira had her own personal chauffeur, Kira's apartment was luxury in comparison. The apartment exuded a sense of brightness and airiness, with Kira enjoying the luxury of her own private pool. The gated complex was home to a number of other air hostesses as well. The clients generously covered the expenses for their apartments and security. Sabrina found herself in a world that was unlike anything she had ever experienced before. Tonight, they were going to a lavish party in the basement of a prestigious hotel, the two friends were to accompany members of affluent families that had booked them. There was always an abundance of alcohol, and drugs, even though it was illegal in the Middle East. Sabrina was a little concerned as she had seen the religious police walking the streets, the Mutawa, she had been warned about, they posed a significant threat to individuals from the Western world. Kira managed to soothe her anxiety and provided reassurance that as long as one maintained the satisfaction of the local dignitaries, there would be no issues to contend with. "Just make sure you keep the clients happy, and I promise you the police won't be a problem."

"I'm a bit confused. Do they give you gifts before you engage in any intimate activities?" Sabrina inquired.

"No, typically they come prepared with gifts or they arrange for them to be delivered to my apartment the next morning. Rest assured, everything is meticulously planned. This is the way it has to be, as you are not permitted to transfer money out of the country. But gifts are considered acceptable. Now, let's see what we should wear this evening." Kira said as she walked into her bedroom and opened her wardrobe. "Are you sure you want to do this? Only, if you choose to accompany me tonight, you must understand that there is no room for hesitation. Once you commit, there is no turning back. It's important to avoid making enemies of these individuals, as I mentioned before. They hold all the authority, and as long as you maintain a good relationship with them, they will treat you well. You can't make enemies with these people, which means you can't say no to anything they ask of you. Do you understand what you are getting yourself into?" Kira's voice was full of concern whilst she was diligently arranging a collection of exquisite designer dresses on the bed before them. "I understand completely. I am ready. I won't let you down." Sabrina stated with a broad smile. The next morning after breakfast, the two companions were chauffeured back to Kira's apartment in the upmarket complex. Their chauffer carried all of their high-end bags into the hallway. As they eagerly opened the bags, a treasure trove of luxury awaited them. Exquisite Channel handbags, stunning designer dresses, and in each bag, a dazzling array of jewellery. A Rolex watch to grace their wrists, accompanied by two elegant gold Tiffany bracelets and a radiant solitaire diamond ring. Sabrina was overwhelmed with awe, as she gazed on an abundance of exquisite wonders. Kira couldn't help but chuckle at Sabrina's expression - she resembled a child in a candy store. "It's truly astonishing how much we acquired in just a single evening.' Sabrina gently slipped the solitaire diamond ring onto her finger, admiring its brilliant sparkle as the sunlight seemingly danced off the diamond.

"It's absolutely mind-boggling, isn't it?" Kira let out a playful giggle. "And when we return home, Razz takes care of selling everything for us and voila, bills paid and bank accounts looking healthy. I need a shower. We'll be flying back to the UK this evening, personally, I am quite exhausted. We'll wear or stow our gifts in our carry-ons, and once we're in London, Razz will arrange for a collector to retrieve the items." Sabrina stretched and yawned, expressing her fatigue, acknowledging the need for some sleep before their upcoming flight that evening. "I hope the person you were with, was considerate and treated you well." Kira inquired. "He was really kind, we were both a bit anxious, I decided to pretend he was my boyfriend, it made things a lot easier to deal with that way." Sabrina let out a playful giggle.

"That's the way to do it. Just be aware that they're not always as pleasant as the two last night. However, they all pay the same way, usually in abundance. So, as long as you maintain that mindset, you'll be just fine. I'm going to take a shower and get some sleep. I'll see you later."

The next few months felt like a surreal experience for Sabrina, as she became accustomed to the lavish lifestyle that came with her work as an escort in the Middle East. She and Kira had enjoyed several luncheons with potential clients. They were granted the opportunity to freely explore high-end designer stores, with their expenses already taken care of. Sabrina had become accustomed to men using her body. Kira had expertly guided her through the intricacies, and in an instant, the once daunting Middle East appeared far less intimidating. If you were wealthy, it became your personal playground. She and Kira were merely objects of desire for the wealthy. Life brimmed with extravagant soirées, exquisite dining experiences, and indulgent shopping sprees, all while jetting back and forth between the UK.

Life was truly blissful, as long as they kept the clients happy, they were showered with expensive gifts. After another long weekend at home in the UK, the best friends were savouring the blissful home comforts. It was great being back in the comfort of their own home and country, with no obligations or tasks to occupy their time. They were engaged in lively conversation in the kitchen, discussing their upcoming adventure. The day before their departure, they opted to embrace relaxation by staying in their cosy pyjamas, indulging in movie marathons, and treating themselves to delicious junk food. The following day, they rose with the sun, having meticulously packed their belongings, to resume their professional duties. The journey mirrored their previous experiences - a gruelling long-haul flight that left them both with excruciatingly sore feet, upon their arrival in the Middle East. They were driven to their luxurious complex, where they would enjoy another two day lay over. Exhausted from a long day, they eagerly anticipated the fresh start that awaited them tomorrow. With lunch plans already set in motion with their new clients, they would reconnect with them in the evening.

CHAPTER 31: Go with your gut.

The next day they arrived for their luncheon dates, but instead of the usual hotel setting, they were escorted to a grand residence. The area was secured with perimeter fencing and a gate. The friends exchanged uneasy glances, it was a situation they had never encountered before. In the past, they had always met clients at hotels. Sabrina felt a growing unease as they approached the grandiose mansion. Their chauffeur emerged from the vehicle, graciously opening the car doors for their arrival. Standing before them were a group of distinguished gentlemen, positioned by the grand ornate doors. Every person was dressed in the traditional Jubba attire, complete with the keffiyeh draped over their heads. A group of six men stood in the doorway, patiently awaiting the arrival of the two women. Kira and Sabrina exchanged worried glances. It was unusual, and there were more men than had been agreed. Kira and Sabrina were just meeting the clients for lunch. There had never been more than three men before. It felt unnerving and out of the ordinary. Maybe the clients wanted a more private setting. The two friends reasoned with themselves, thinking, ' Maybe they were higher up the royalty list, so needed to be more discreet.' It was common practice for older relatives to provide financial support for their younger family members. Although it was quite uncommon, to have more than three gentlemen present at the luncheon.

Usually, the clients were at the lunch with an older relative who agreed to the terms and conditions of the date. Thankfully the lunch meet and greet with the clients and the elders, went off without a hitch. Everything seemed in order and the two friends fears were laid to rest. On returning to the apartment complex, Sabrina and Kira engaged in a thoughtful conversation about their lunch. "That whole situation struck me as rather peculiar. It felt uncomfortable, I felt like we were pieces of meat at a meat market, I have never felt like that before. They seemed to undress us at lunch with their eyes. Normally I love the lunches but this time, it just didn't feel right." Kira confessed.

"I'm glad that we'll be rendezvousing with them at a hotel we know, this evening. At least I know the staff and my way around it. I don't think I have ever seen so many security guard's in one place before." Sabrina murmured.

"I wasn't particularly fond of Abdulla either. He was creepy with an unfriendly demeanour."

"It seems that he specifically desired a redhead, so you won't have to handle him. I on the other hand, will." Kira remarked.

Sabrina made a grimace, "Are you alright with that? He made me feel incredibly disturbed."

Kira arched an eyebrow and replied candidly, "Beggars can't be choosers, some of these men have rather peculiar customs. It's the way they are raised, they don't know any different."

"I guess you're right, but compared to the other guys who were laid-back and friendly, Abdulla gave off a slightly unsettling vibe…" Sabrina's voice faded away as she recalled that it was Kira, not her, who would be sharing a bed with him. "Let's not think about it for now. What should we wear tonight, a red dress?" Kira inquired, admiringly holding a breathtaking Louis Vuitton dress against her figure. Sabrina beamed with delight as she responded, "I love that dress on you." They both began preparing themselves for the evening ahead, meticulously styling their hair and applying makeup for the upcoming evening. As they worked in silence a sense of unease fell over them both, neither were comfortable with the men they had met earlier, but neither would admit it. Sabrina and Kira found themselves in the penthouse of a luxurious five-star hotel. The opulence of the surroundings was undeniable, yet an air of foreboding settled on them, due to the unusually heightened security presence. Kira speculated that the clients might have connections to the royal family. She thought it was perfectly normal for royalty to have a sizable security team. As Sabrina entered the opulent dining room of the penthouse, a hint of confusion appeared evident on her face. The six men were there from earlier, they were seated around the table, they all stood up to welcome the two women. "Don't worry. We should have said that the elders would be present for dinner before leaving us to our own devices." Abdulla gave Kira his assurance. Right before settling down at the table, Sabrina requested to use the toilet, subtly encouraging Kira to join her. The two friends politely excused themselves as they were escorted by security to the toilet. Stepping into the grand bathroom, adorned with gold accents and exquisite decorations, the door closed behind them, and the women breathed a heavy sigh simultaneously. Sabrina was the first to speak, expressing her concerns, "This situation doesn't sit well with me. I have a bad feeling about this." Kira gently caressed her friend's arm, a gesture that was trying to assure her friend that everything would be okay. "Occasionally, situations like this happen, we have to spend time with individuals who may not be our cup of tea. It's just a part of the job, unfortunately."

Sabrina pretended to put two fingers down her throat, prompting laughter from both of them. "We had best get back to them, before they send out a search party for us." Kira insisted. Sabrina reluctantly followed Kira's lead, recognising her experience in this world, compared to her own novice status. Throughout the extravagant dinner, consisting of seven delectable courses, the two companions shared an intimate proximity, occasionally exchanging subtle taps beneath the table. They always made it a point to accompany each other to the toilet whenever one of them needed to use it. The event seemed to stretch on endlessly, and despite Kira's naturally sociable nature, she found it challenging to engage in meaningful dialogue with the gentlemen present. The culinary affair was filled with numerous uncomfortable silent pauses. The elders would raise their hands to the women's faces to signal them to stop speaking. Kira found herself facing a new challenge, as these individuals clearly held a deep-seated prejudice against women. These men seemed to belong to a bygone era, where women were expected to remain silent and invisible. Their trips to the toilet became their sanctuary, it felt invigorating, as if a gust of fresh air swept through. These men had Sabrina on the edge of her seat, her nerves tingling with worry. They appeared to have a strong aversion towards the women, often displaying a look of contempt on their faces. Kira had stressed to Sabrina the need of perseverance in meeting their clients' requests, despite of the obstacles they may encounter. Sabrina's gut churned as she sensed these men's deep hostility against women, particularly ones like her. The entire evening appeared doomed to be as painful as the dinner had been. These individuals were distinct; they appeared hateful, domineering, and frigid. There was something very wrong with this situation. Kira and Sabrina, both knew it. They thought they had no choice but to go ahead with the night because it had already been planned. In this country, everything revolved around men.

The friends couldn't risk upsetting the delicate balance, for fear of the Mutawa religious police, being summoned to arrest them. That would be a fate worse than death. It just wasn't worth the risk. They couldn't escape these men now. They were trapped, trapped like wild animals in a gilded cage. They were now at the mercy of these men.

CHAPTER 32 : FREEDOM over fear.

KIRA AWOKE TO THE GENTLE touch of water cascading over her face and body, rousing her from her slumber. Her concentration wavered as an obstruction obscured her vision, leaving her unable to perceive the events unfolding before her. Her hand extended to touch a bare figure beside her. She attempted to turn her face away, from the liquid pouring into her mouth, causing her to gasp for breath. As she reached for the muslin cloth that was covering her face, a putrid odour filled the air, assaulting her senses. She was filled with horror as she saw a uniformed guard standing over her, his actions unspeakable, as he urinated on her and the motionless naked body beside her. Her eyes strained to find clarity as she let out a piercing scream, desperately pleading for him to stop. The guard sneered, he continued urinating on her exposed form while she struggled to avoid his strong-smelling liquid. He swiftly leapt off the bed and forcefully seized her by the hair, while she struggled to regain her composure, she desperately thrashed her arms in resistance. 'Oh no, this cannot be happening.' Her mind was filled with a whirlwind of thoughts. In an instant, the guard forcefully hurled her across the room, causing her to emit a high pitched scream, as an intense wave of agony surged through her body. Out of nowhere, another guard appeared, and together they aggressively seized her arms, hoisting her off the ground and dragging her down the hallway.

She suddenly experienced a sinking sensation, as if she was being engulfed by an unknown force. With her gaze sharpening and her determination to regain balance, she came to the realisation that the two guards were violently submerging her head into the fish tank. She briefly recalled seeing the fish tank the night before, as it had been a new addition to the hotel's penthouse. Gasping for air, she was struck with sheer terror, as she remembered the tank contained a swarm of ravenous piranhas. Her heart pounded as the men mercilessly submerged her head into the water once again. She shook her head violently in the water, in an effort to scare the piranhas away. Kira exerted every ounce of her strength to fend off the two men. In a moment of sheer determination, she unleashed a powerful kick, reminiscent of a wild stallion throwing off its rider. The force of her kick caused one of her assailants to loosen his grip. Granting her a momentary reprieve from the unexpected onslaught of aggression. Her voice echoed through the room, piercing the silence. "Sabrina! Sabrina!" she cried out, gasping for air after her harrowing ordeal in the depths of the fish tank. Despite the guard's grip on her, she could sense the other regaining his composure, as he unleashed a barrage of obscenities into her ear. Without warning, he delivered a forceful blow to her kidneys, leaving her in excruciating pain. As if that wasn't enough, he then proceeded to submerge her head underwater in the tank once again. Kira cautiously turned her head in the water, mindful of the lurking piranhas ready to attack. She struggled to accept the unfolding events, desperately fighting to stay afloat. Sabrina awoke, gently stirring from her slumber, and tenderly rubbed her eyes to dispel the lingering haze. Upon awakening, she found herself on the unforgiving marble floor, surrounded by a pool of liquid. The air was tainted with a repugnant odour, and she could have sworn she heard her name being shrieked.

Sabrina's view was briefly blocked by the Muslin cloth, but she quickly removed it from her face. With her eyes squinting against the blinding sunlight, the scene unravelled right in front of her. Two men in uniform firmly held onto Kira's vulnerable form, seemingly restraining her in a headlock with her head submerged in the fish tank. Amidst the chaos, Sabrina found herself standing in a pool of vibrant yellow liquid, her thoughts racing. With a surge of adrenaline, she darted across the hallway, snatching a heavy exquisitely crafted table lamp. With a swift motion, she swung the lamp, striking the head of one of the guards. The wound on his body released a torrent of red, staining the floor as he crumbled to the ground. Sabrina resolutely charged at the second guard, who callously persisted in holding Kira's head underwater in the murky depths of the fish tank. The floor shimmered with a glacier sheen of water, remanence of their failed attempt to drown Kira. Sabrina found herself in a sudden clash with the guard, their bodies meeting the ground with a forceful impact. His hands tightened around her throat, constricting her breath, as if he aimed to erase her from existence. She desperately dodged the guard's saliva as he unleashed a barrage of vulgarities, his breath reeking of decay. There was no hope, he towered over her, his weight pressing down as Sabrina lost her grip on the lamp in her fall. In an instant, Kira seized the fallen lamp, wielding it as a weapon, striking the unsuspecting guard with a forceful blow to the back of his head. The guard collapsed to the floor as Kira loomed over him, tears of fury streaming down her face. In her hands, she tightly gripped the blood-stained lamp, whilst repeating the following words like a mantra over and over again with shock.

"Oh fuck, what have I done, what have I done."

Sabrina lifted herself from the floor, "We must find a way to escape."

She tightly grasped Kira's arms and shook her. "Kira, I need you. We must find our clothes, and leave this place, before the guards are discovered." The two girls hurriedly tried to orient themselves, their garments and underwear were scattered across the furniture. With no time to spare, their very survival hinged on their desperate bid for freedom. They hastily got dressed and located their shoes, Kira was just about to slip on her Christian Dior high heels when Sabrina intervened. "We must go barefoot, to avoid making any noise."

The friends felt a mix of anxiety and dread as they approached the grand marble doors that led to the lifts. Sabrina cautiously peeked around the doors, ensuring that no one was in sight. "Hurry, we'll need to take the stairs instead of the lifts. We need to make our way through the emergency exit to the service corridors, through the kitchen to the back service yard.' Kira spoke with a deep understanding and knowledge of the building.

As they ascended the emergency stairwell, they had only reached the fourth floor when chaos erupted. The sound of footsteps echoed through the hallways, causing Sabrina to cautiously peer around the door to the fourth-floor stairway. She swiftly retreated back behind the door, concealing herself from view. Armed guards with machine guns were moving through the corridors, searching for them. "They have machine guns," Sabrina said with a trembling voice. "We must escape immediately." The guards proceeded around the bend in the corridor. Kira and Sabrina stealthily made their way through the service corridors, their hearts thundering in their chest. They found themselves trapped, overwhelmed by fear, in an unfamiliar land. "We have to escape, we have to get out of here." Kira murmured.

Sabrina and Kira were filled with panic as they cautiously made their way through the staff corridors. Sabrina stumbled on a fire alarm call point, and, with a sudden burst of clarity, she shattered the glass and firmly pressed the button. "Great idea." Kira exclaimed, perspiration trickling down her spine. The Friends stumbled on the staff changing rooms, where they noticed the staff diligently following their fire alarm protocols. Seizing the opportunity, the two women discovered a pair of identical black Burqas and speedily donned them, effectively concealing their identities. They had escaped armed guard's with machine guns, drowning and being battered. Now though as they stepped out of the hotel building, a world of unknowns lay before them. But for now, they had escaped their tormentors' clutches. They made their way to the local market, seeking refuge from anyone who might be on their trail. As they briskly walked away from the hotel, they observed the security teams frantically searching for them amidst the crowd of departing guests. "Starting the fire alarm was a stroke of genius." Kira spoke softly from beneath the Burqa.

"But what do we do now? We must find a way to leave the country. We can't get our passports. We can't risk going to the apartment to retrieve our belongings. They will be looking for us." Sabrina responded.

"I believe I have a contact who can assist us. They come highly recommended through a mutual acquaintance. He's a bootlegger. He makes his own spirits. He caters to the elites and the royal families. He is familiar with the roads, and I have complete confidence that he will help us." Kira declared. "It's quite a trek to get to his place though. He has a military pass due to his employment at the American base, where he serves as a chef in the kitchens."

"Do you know his actual place of residence? Some of these compounds house up to twenty people at a time." Sabrina inquired.

"There's this person I know who happens to live in the same complex. We'll need to make our way there and patiently wait for them to finish their shift. It's risky though."

"More danger, really? I'm already scared to death. How in the world are we going to get out of this Godforsaken country?" Sabrina asked, her desperation evident, but she wasn't sure she wanted to hear the answer. "I've heard of an underground network designed to aid Westerners facing dire circumstances here. I'm sure it's real, I've heard the stories." Kira declared. "Oh great, so we are putting our lives in the hands of myths and legends, could this get any worse?" Sabrina uttered in dismay.

"You're aware that we were drugged and raped by god knows how many men, right?" Kira exclaimed.

"Yes, I am well aware that our lives were in grave danger, and we might have faced the horrifying fate of being sold into sex trafficking or murdered, had we not fought with the guards."

"It was a do or die situation, talk about history repeating itself and biting you in the arse. I still feel like I'm drowning, but it's imperative that we find a way to escape from this place." Kira declared. A disconcerting quietness descended on the friends, their minds consumed by the journey that lay before them. Their lives would never be the same again. On their return to England, assuming they made it back safely, both of them would require testing for STIs, as they were unaware of the number of men who had violated them while they were under the influence of drugs. They were both aware of their discomfort, feeling a burning sensation in their thighs and bottoms. The number of perpetrators was unknown to them. But it was evident that they had endured a relentless sexual assault that more than likely had lasted hours. They were sore, they were hurting. But they couldn't think about that for now. Now the only thing they needed to concentrate on was their escape. Getting out of the country was all that mattered. It was a life and death situation.

CHAPTER 33 : The escape.

The day was absolutely stunning, with the sun relentlessly beating down on the two friends. The stench emanating from them due to the heat was overpowering. Even though it was beautiful, the arid and isolated surroundings failed to alleviate their worries. Every passing car sent a shiver down their spines. Kira displayed remarkable foresight by purchasing bags of fruit and vegetables from the markets, creating the illusion of two ordinary housewives on their routine shopping excursion. The bags, burdened by their weight, proved invaluable in concealing their true identities. As they strolled away from the bustling market town, a sense of relief washed over them. The once crowded streets now seemed more peaceful, with fewer cars and people in sight. The shopping bags they carried, along with the Burqas they wore, had proven to be their saving grace thus far. They were ignored by everyone, as if they were invisible. Even the passing police car didn't give them a second glance. The heat was stifling beneath their Burqas, but they had no other choice but to keep them on.

"How much longer until we reach our destination?" Sabrina inquired, breaking the silence, that had lasted for almost thirty minutes. "It's not far now. Take a left at the next road and we'll come across a gated community. This is where the workers from the base reside." Kira responded with a hint of enthusiasm. "There is a lovely green area just across the road from the complex. We can find a nice spot under a tree and patiently wait for Aaron or Ben to arrive. Hopefully the wait won't be too lengthy. They don't allow locals in the complex so it may be necessary to consider removing the Burqas before we enter the compound. Keep the Burqas though. Remove a few items from the shopping bags to make some space for them."

After what felt like an eternity, Ben finally arrived, strolling casually through the lush greenery. Kira skillfully managed to capture his attention. His height was impressive, complemented by his sandy blonde hair and captivating piercing blue eyes. Kira had encountered him while escorting clients at parties. The two of them instantly took a liking to each other.

"Ben, Ben," she called out, hesitantly.

Initially, Ben's expression shifted to one of confusion as he observed the two women in Burqas making their way towards him. His perplexity quickly dissipated when Kira unveiled her face, revealing her identity to him. "We are in deep trouble. We desperately need your help. We are being hunted." Kira stated, nervously. Ben's rich Southern accent provided a sense of comfort. "In order to gain access to the compound, you'll need to remove the Burqas. But once you're there, I promise that you'll be safe. You can fill me in on the details then." Sabrina and Kira exchanged knowing glances, before removing their disguises and carefully stowing them away in the shopping bags. "Allow me to assist you with those bags, I don't think they go with your designer evening dresses. People might ask questions. Besides, I'm an old fashioned kind of guy." As they stepped into the military gated community, Sabrina and Kira let out a collective sigh of relief. Seated in Ben's lounge, Kira massaged her tired feet while Sabrina gazed out the window at the well maintained gardens. Ben entered the room, carrying a tray filled with steaming cups of tea and sandwiches. As he passed them their mugs, he inquired about the girls' reasons for seeking his assistance, eager to hear their story. Ben let out a low whistle as Kira and Sabrina recounted every sordid detail to him.

"I believe it would be best for you to stay here for the night. Unfortunately, we won't be able to retrieve your passports or belongings from your place. It will be closely monitored, so we need to be realistic about the situation," he said with a sigh.

"It will make things difficult but not impossible. We have a vast network, who assist individuals in leaving the country when they get into trouble. I will have to go make some arrangements for you. So, I recommend that both of you get some rest, and get some food down you. Tomorrow is going to be a long day. I will warn you now, it won't be easy to get you out of the country, to safety."

Kira mustered a faint smile and asked, "Could we both possibly take a shower?"

"I thought you would never ask. To be honest you both stink. I think you've been shit on, quite literally. Some of the men in this country are into that sort of thing. I have already put combat trousers and t-shirts on the bed for both of you. I'll need your shoe sizes, because we can't have you running around in Christian Dior high heels, can we?" The words were delivered with an air of certainty, leaving no room for doubt. "Make yourselves at home, I will be gone a few hours." Ben departed, leaving the two friends to their own devices, slipping out to make arrangements for them. Over the next few hours, they remained vigilant, having freshened up and dressed in the clothes that Ben had provided. They settled into the lounge, their eyes fixated on the door, anticipating Ben's arrival. The hours slipped by, as they took turns peeking through the voile curtains. They talked about their injuries and made a conscious choice to focus on the future instead of dwelling on the past. All they desired was to escape the country and return to the safety of their home in England. They anxiously awaited Ben's return for three long hours, their anticipation palpable. As he entered the apartment, he discovered that both women were hiding in his wardrobe.

"You can come out now, it's only me." Ben insisted. Slowly, the two women cautiously revealed themselves from behind the wardrobe doors. Sabrina couldn't contain her words any longer and confessed, "We didn't know what to do, so we hid in the wardrobes."

"I noticed," Ben remarked, his eyebrow raised. "You're safe here. Only I, have the keys. I've been busy, please have a seat whilst I pour you a glass of my homemade Scotch. Then we can discuss the plans I have made for tomorrow." Kira and Sabrina exchanged a knowing glance before settling into their chairs, captivated by the sight of Ben discreetly entering his bedroom and emerging with a bottle of homemade Scotch. He then made his way to the kitchen, to collect three tumblers. He carefully filled each glass to the brim before graciously passing them to the two women, reserving one for himself. Sabrina eagerly took a sip, her taste buds delighted by the unexpectedly velvety flavour. "This is truly exceptional." She commented." The statement was followed by Kira also deciding to take a sip.

"Indeed, it is quite remarkable, crafted with the utmost care using only the finest ingredients. It proves to be a lucrative venture, but a dangerous business to be in, especially in this dry country." Ben responded after taking a sip of the richly hued liquid himself.

"Allow me to paint a vivid picture of what lies ahead, I have successfully acquired a military vehicle for our use. I have US soldier uniforms that you must wear on the journey, that will take us to the Suez Canal. It'll be a long arduous journey and very dangerous. I've secured Military passes for you, complete with different names on the badges. However, approximately twenty miles from the canal, a vehicle switch will be necessary, you will be accompanied by your British escorts who will then blindfold you, ensuring the secrecy of the S.B.S base's location. This is a matter of utmost importance and national security. They will then escort you to a ship that will transport you along the Suez Canal and into the Mediterranean." Ben informed the friends whilst pouring himself another glass of Scotch.

"You've certainly been keeping busy. I'm curious, what does S.B.S stand for? I've never come across it before." Kira yearned for the answer, the mention of blindfolds had her worried. "They go by the name Special Boat Service, a formidable group of British Elite Forces. Their mission? Safeguarding boats navigating the treacherous waters of the Suez Canal, shielding them from the clutches of pirates. They are very secretive, not the sort of people you want to get on the bad side off. Being British, they frequently lend a hand. I once knew a dear friend who arrived here to pursue a nursing career. Unfortunately, he faced some challenges due to his sexual orientation and engaging in intimate relationships with the locals. He was facing the death sentence. This place is absolutely unforgiving. The S.B.S successfully facilitated his departure from the country prior to his sentencing. He has returned to the USA, completely safe and sound." Ben shrugged. "It's crucial to have these underground systems in place, as no Westerner would want to end up imprisoned in this country. Prisoners are tortured and mistreated, few make it home and our governments can't, or won't help them."

Sabrina sighed heavily before posing another question. "Can these S.B.S be trusted?' Her eyes beseeched Ben, the fear becoming even more tangible in that moment. The situation they found themselves in was more dangerous than either she or Kira ever thought possible. Ben ran his fingers through his sandy hair, his frustration evident in his voice.

"Well, they have experience in assisting many expats in the past, I'd say their British background, makes them trustworthy. You're quite fortunate that they aren't charging you. Typically, they request donations to facilitate the transportation of individuals out of the country. Listen, I understand that you're feeling anxious, but no one ever claimed that this would be a walk in the park. These individuals possess a strong background in the military, specifically in special forces, and adhere to a strict code of honour. They will keep you safe. You must have faith. I imagine that your blindfolds will remain in place until you are safely aboard the containment ship, where I assume they will conceal you in the hold. The captain has a strong bond with the team and will ensure your safe return to Europe. Afterwards, you'll need to visit the British consulate to obtain an emergency passport for your journey back home. Europe will provide a safe haven for you."

"Thank you, Ben. We are indebted to you. We owe you, our lives." Kira exclaimed, leaping from her chair, and making her way towards Ben to plant a gentle kiss on his cheek. Ben's cheeks turned a shade of red as he replied, "I'll do anything to assist two lovely maidens in distress.' Accompanied by a mischievous grin and a playful wink directed towards Sabrina.

"Alright ladies, time for bed, we need to be on the road by 5am. It would be wise for all of us to get to bed early. I need my beauty sleep." Ben casually mentioned as he rose to his feet and began to tidy-up, his surroundings. Sabrina smiled, then joined him in the kitchen to wash the dishes. She needed to be preoccupied, consumed by the fear of an uncertain tomorrow. Her existence had been marred by relentless upheaval in recent years, and now she found herself in a battle for survival. She was certain that sleep would evade her. Her anxiety was overwhelming, her fear all consuming, she felt like she was on the verge of collapse. Would life ever show her kindness once more, or was she destined to relive painful experiences endlessly? Only a higher power understood, she yearned for God to go easy on her. Life seemed so much simpler back at the club. She couldn't help but wish she had stayed there, instead of coming to this dreadful country. She scolded herself for entertaining such thoughts, and suppressed all her concerns and anxieties, burying them deep within, alongside the other distressing experiences she had endured. Out of sight out of mind she reasoned, and tomorrow she would need every ounce of strength she could muster. They were going to get out of this, one way or another. Sabrina rose before the break of day, the world still cloaked in darkness as the minutes passed by. As the sun rose, she was already up and dressed in her US military uniform, waiting for Ben and Kira to join her. With a warm smile, she poured each of them a steaming mug of coffee. Her anxiety was palpable, and she quivered as she handed Kira and Ben their mugs. "Cheers to our little escapade," she exclaimed, lifting her cup with a sense of uneasy excitement. Ben savoured a sip of the rich black coffee, then lifted his cup with a sense of purpose. 'Cheers to avoiding, getting our asses handed to us." He chuckled softly. Kira eagerly raised her mug in the air, not wanting to be the odd one out. At the same time, she anxiously crossed all her fingers and toes. The night had been filled with restlessness, but she was grateful that Sabrina had the wisdom to brew a potent cup of black coffee. After finishing their coffees, Ben dramatically gestured towards the door with a bow.

"After you, my fair ladies." Once they stepped outside the complex and hit the road, their safety became uncertain. Ben had carefully planned their route to steer clear of any checkpoints, but there were no assurances. The atmosphere inside the Jeep was suffocating, with an oppressive sun casting its relentless heat on the occupants. The land possessed a breathtaking beauty, yet it exuded an arid and barren nature. Roadsides were scattered with abandoned buildings as they embarked on their journey. Beads of perspiration formed on Ben's shirt, tracing a path down the centre of his back. The gruelling three-hour journey had taken its toll, leaving them a mere thirty miles away from their designated rendezvous. Their paranoia grew with every car that passed. They were on the brink of safety, yet peril still loomed. Ben fearlessly transported them through various towns and cities, putting his life on the line. The two friends were constantly glancing at the back window of the jeep, ensuring they weren't being pursued. "There's a small market town up ahead that we'll pass through, and then we'll be on our way without any obstacles." Ben relayed the information to them.

"Can we go around it?" Kira asked, her nerves getting the better of her.

"It's actually a sixty-mile round trip if we take the longer route, which would undoubtedly cause us to be late for our rendezvous with the S.B.S team. We can't risk it." Ben said with a finality. As the jeep approached the town, Ben slowed down, there were so many people dawdling and mulling around. "Dammit, its market day." Ben groaned. "We are out of options ladies, I'm afraid we have got to go through the crowd."

Kira and Sabrina looked at each other with dread, people were everywhere, and up ahead they could see a Sheppard herding goats. All they could do was maybe hide in the back seats until they had got through the chaos. "Get down in your seats." Ben ordered, as the jeep struggled to find the right gears.

People were banging on the sides of the car, banging with fury because the car shouldn't be there on market day. The sounds from the market sellers wafted through the air. Dust was being kicked up from the dry barren road from the herd of goats. It was all so surreal, but then Sabrina's short life had been chaotic and full of surreal life experiences. After what seemed like an age, they finally got to the end of the market stalls and passed the traders and shoppers alike. Were they now on the home stretch?

The two friends breathed a sigh of relief as Ben told them they could sit up straight once more in the back of the jeep. They were barely out of the towns boundaries when Bens heart sank. "There's a checkpoint up ahead, lets pray your military passes work, ladies. Keep your cool, do as they ask and hopefully, we can get through without any trouble. Once we are through this, we should be okay. Remember to keep calm. Eyes straight ahead." There was a makeshift cabin and a barbed wire fence barrier. Two guards were stood at the barrier, checking locals papers and stopping cars. The two soldiers beckoned for Ben to pull over. Ben lowered his window to speak with them. Kira and Sabrina didn't understand what was being said as Ben was speaking with the soldiers in Arabic. Both Kira and Sabrina pulled their caps down slightly and held their breath. They were terrified, the soldiers looked bad tempered and miserable. Ben asked them to hand their military passes to him , then he passed them to the soldiers. It seemed like hours slipped by, but in reality, it was only minutes.

The soldier nodded to Ben, then handed the passes back through the window of the Jeep. He then waved them through as they then opened the barrier to let them pass through. Ben slipped the gear into place and made a steady getaway, they were finally on the last part of their trip. They all breathed a sigh of relief. "That was a close one, I thought we were going to get arrested then." He stated honestly. "Another fifteen minutes and you meet the S.B.S guys. You will be safely on your way home then." Ten minutes later the two friends were escorted out the Jeep by Ben, as he introduced Kira and Sabrina to the S.B.S team. The men were all in military uniform with machine guns holstered to their shoulders. "Nice to meet you ladies." The commander said. "Time to blindfold you and get a move on, we've got a container ship to catch." He smiled and nodded to his men to blindfold the women, but just before they could get to Sabrina, she ran up to ben and planted a kiss on him.

"Thank you, Ben, you have literally saved our lives." Sabrina said as she kissed him. Kira shouted thank you too, as she was already blindfolded.

"Your welcome ladies." Ben stated with a curt nod of his head and then he swiftly pivoted on his heels, got into his jeep and drove away. The car journey to the boat was short. Sabrina and Kira were both escorted onto the S.B.S boat, then taken to their rendezvous with the container ship, that would take them to the Mediterranean Sea and to their freedom.

To be continued.

ABOUT THE AUTHOR.
ROXY RICH

I am an author with a disability who lives in Somerset with my two children and my husband. My unusual experience, which includes having worked in the sex industry over 17 years ago, serves as a source of inspiration for my writing. I feel it is my duty to bring light on the tales of working girls, the social injustices they suffer. This experience has provided me with unique insights into the life of working girls. I am currently working on my second novel, as I intend to write a whole series that will be devoted to investigating the lives of women who work in the sex industry. Each new installment will focus on a different aspect of their life, thereby delivering a holistic and compassionate perspective of the world in which they live. By combining my years of lived experience with a more mature view on the complexities of the human condition, I believe that now is the ideal time in my life to offer these stories to a broader audience.

Don't miss out!

Visit the website below and you can sign up to receive emails whenever Roxy Rich publishes a new book. There's no charge and no obligation.

https://books2read.com/r/B-A-URRMB-LAFWD

BOOKS 2 READ

Connecting independent readers to independent writers.

Did you love *WORKING GIRL 'Afflicted' Book One*? Then you should read *WORKING GIRL 'Fractured' Book One*[1] by Roxy Rich!

Psychological Thriller.

    Working Girl Fractured follows the harrowing journey of Jolene, a young girl grappling with the tragic loss of her mother and the ensuing torment inflicted upon her by her stepfather. As circumstances spiral out of control, Jolene and her sister find themselves ensnared in the horrifying world of human trafficking.

---

1. https://books2read.com/u/b5RRl7
2. https://books2read.com/u/b5RRl7